a Gale Hightower mystery

FOULED OUT

Laura S. Jones

tidal
PRESS

WWW.TIDALPRESS.COM

When getting the story can get you killed.

DEDICATION

This book is for my husband, Rob, without whom nothing would be any fun at all. I am also grateful to my parents for showing me a life with newspapers and sports. Finally, I will always be in awe of Phil Ford for executing the Four Corners offense with such panache.

A BIT ABOUT RACE

My protagonist and sleuth, Gale, is black. I am white. What does a white woman know about being a black woman? Nothing. But Gale appeared in my imagination fully formed about 12 years ago and wouldn't leave. She looked like she looked.

Gale's friend Leo is a white, gay, male dancer with rheumatoid arthritis. Aside from being white, I have nothing in common with Leo either.

In general, I write (and read) to spend time with people I like. To get to know them. I really like Gale. Do I know what it is like to be her? Only to the extent that she can tell me, and I am curious enough to ask. And she can't tell me very much because she isn't real. These are the limitations of fiction. But I try and put myself in her shoes by using my imagination and the bits and pieces I have experienced in the world.

I walked into this minefield and wrote this story because I thought it was worth writing. I also thought people might like to read it, and that in the act of writing and reading we might all share something worthwhile.

This is not a book about race. It is a book about the abuse of power and how people fight or succumb.

I hope I got something right about Gale. That is all I really hope about anyone.

ONE

Last spring

They needed to talk.

He knew that if he could just talk to her, he could fix everything. So, Connor grabbed his keys and drove to Gina's apartment even though it was two in the morning. Even though he was probably too drunk to drive.

But there were no cops, every light was green, and the trip took less than ten minutes. That was a good sign, he thought. He parked and took the stairs two at a time, excited and hopeful.

He would remind Gina that in a week, they'd both be college graduates. Basketball would be behind them. He would give up the NBA dream; deep down he knew he never really had a real shot at the pros anyway. The rest of their lives could start. They would be together. Just the two of them.

When he got to her door, though, it wasn't just the two of them. Marcus was there. Marucs was his teammate. Friend even. He shouldn't have been there, goddammit, not with Connor's girlfriend. But Marcus answered the door like it was his home, like he was king of the castle. Connor's hope snapped into a white-hot anger.

It would never have happened if Marcus hadn't been there.

When it was over, Connor couldn't even tell whether he was sorry. He knew he should be, but he was confused instead. And still angry. How long had it been? Five minutes? An hour? He couldn't tell; time made no sense anymore.

He watched the blood spread across the yellow linoleum and started to feel the anger drain away. Suddenly he was so tired, like there was nothing solid left in his body to hold him up. He sank down to the kitchen floor. Connor wished he had saved some of the anger, at least enough to get out. Away. But the anger wasn't something he could ration. It wasn't something he could summon up when he wanted and push away when he didn't.

The blood moved more slowly now, in no hurry to get anywhere. As if it were tired too.

With the point of the knife, Connor played with a piece of Gina's long black hair, swirling it into a little pile.

His mind was getting fuzzier. It always happened this way. Sleep was the only thing that would help.

As soon as he shut his eyes, he heard the sirens.

TWO

Friday, July 1, 2016

"Gale, can you come to my office right away? Or maybe yesterday? God, yesterday would be so much better...." Alex paused on the phone, clearly contemplating whether her editorial powers extended to time travel. "Anyway, Jerry is AWOL, and I need you to go to Waynesville to cover Connor Braxton's murder trial. He killed – sorry – *allegedly killed* his girlfriend and a teammate last May. The trial starts on Monday. No, wait. It starts on Tuesday. Damn holidays. Okay? See you in a shake."

She hung up. I sighed into the empty receiver. Alex loves military lingo even though she never would have lasted two seconds in any army. She has problems with authority – other than her own – and with guns. Jerry wasn't absent without leave anyway; he was just late. Undoubtedly hungover as well. He is counting the weeks until retirement with beer bottles.

I was happy to fill in. Okay, to be honest, I was not *happy* to cover a double murder trial in a backwoods Virginia mountain town where I would stand out like a sore thumb and there would be no decent scotch. I was *relieved*. For the past two months, I'd been pulled off the Metro beat and stuck writing obituaries in the basement – standard probation at the newspaper – and I was ready to come up for air. I was getting rusty.

Before obits, my job as a Metro reporter was to cover whatever happened in the city or that affected the city. It was a beat defined more by geography than subject, although since crime is always a top subject, I covered a lot of crime. Metro reporters are generalists, and we can be asked to fill in on other stories at a moment's notice. I liked the variety. With my back-

5

ground, I was pulled in on sports whenever they were short of bodies. Connor Braxton's murder trial was sports plus crime. It had my name all over it. It just wasn't in the city. But I had little room to argue the fine points of job descriptions.

My probation was for misquoting a source, which wouldn't have been such a big deal if the source wasn't the mayor's wife, Louise Mattison. "Call me Louie," she had said, "all my friends do." Stupid, gullible me.

I took my lumps after it all shook out, even though I knew charming "Louie" was lying. I didn't misquote her – she just chickened out. Of course, calling the former first lady a thief was a bold move even for the confident Louie, and maybe I should have softened her language, or called to make sure before we ran it. Jenny Turnbill, the former first lady in question, was a thief, though. She gave taxpayer money to her friend's design firm for a renovation of the mayor's mansion that turned out to be little more than a rearrangement of the furniture. I hate that stuff.

While it wasn't like me to let a lie slide, I sensed I might be owed a favor in the future if I did. Plus, having tossed my notes of our conversation during my annual fit of cubicle cleaning, it's not like I was going to mount an effective defense anyway. Maybe I did accidentally put a few extra words in Louie's mouth, too.

I fumbled under my desk for my shoes and regretted my ultra-casual Friday attire of ratty gray Converse sneakers and a sleeveless black jumpsuit. The jumpsuit was "athleisure" explained the saleswoman in a store I should never have gone into. Maybe it was athleisure when it was new three years ago. Now it was just ratty. But comfortable, even though it didn't fit very well. No one makes athleisure for six-foot-tall women. The banded cuffs hit me at mid-calf, not at the ankle like they were designed. I looked "leggy" according to the saleswoman. That sounded okay.

"So, I'm out on time served? Back in your good graces?" I asked as I walked into my boss's office.

Although "office" doesn't really describe the space very well. "Museum" is more like it. Twenty years ago, Alexandra Fall – Alex to both her friends and her enemies – had inherited the office and all its contents from the previous Metro Editor, and she never updated or even moved anything that didn't plug into a socket. The leftover furnishings were showing their age. But she did upgrade the electronics, mostly so she could watch sports. Televised sports are a constant in Alex's life, a fact that confounds me because she is completely, happily sedentary. She has two televisions, and there is always a game on at least one screen, sometimes a different one on each. Today it is baseball. I can't tell who is playing.

Alex looked me dead in the eye. "Maybe. For now, at least. No expensive hotels, and twenty column inches a day plus a photo. Take one of my cameras. And some better clothes." She waved me toward her bookcase where there were three cameras and four lenses to choose from, then went back to staring at her computer screen.

I took my time selecting a camera and lens pairing, although I knew I would mostly use my phone. For some reason I wanted to linger. I hadn't talked to Alex much since I was sent down to the basement, and I missed her. Not that I could tell her that straight up. That wasn't our relationship, or my relationship with anyone, really.

"First, I don't think there are any expensive hotels in or near Waynesville and second, even if there were, I'm out of there as soon as it's over. Trials are dull as church."

Alex snorted. "Fair enough." Then she looked up with

a sudden expression of radiant joy. She always looked like that when she thought of something important. Like a Madonna in a Renaissance painting. Which made sense when you realized that for her, work was a religion. For me, too, sometimes. But I operate in boom and bust cycles. Zeal, then burnout. Alex only has zeal. I don't know how she keeps her energy up.

"Your swimming background should come in handy," she said.

That was not the thought I expected.

"How?" I asked.

"You were an athlete! Which Olympics did you swim in – 1992? I know, I know, but you still look like one, all 18 feet of you with your long muscles and short hair and hungry walk. The defendant is an athlete. Or was an athlete. Maybe someone will spill their guts to you. If there is anything to spill about. You're kindred spirits!"

Having never played sports, Alex has a misguided view of athletes and their similarities. I wasn't quite sure how I felt about the way she saw me, either. Hungry walk?

"It has been a long time since I considered myself an athlete, and I was never a college athlete," I said. "Basketball players and swimmers didn't spend much time together, either."

Alex made a noise that may or may not have been on purpose. "Don't you athletes have some Spidey sense for character in other athletes?" She wiggled her fingers.

"Sure. Character comes through in how you practice, how you race, how you play a game. But I'm not watching Connor or his teammates play. I'm only covering a trial." I did not want to go down this particular memory lane. Not today. Not ever.

Alex took a different tack. "Well, you're from North Carolina. Doesn't basketball run in your people's blood?"

I raised my eyebrows.

"By 'your people' I mean North Carolina people. Tarheels. Not black people. Jesus Christ. This probation thing has made you sensitive." Alex rolled her eyes. "Look, something just seems off about the way the pre-trial jousting is playing out. It's more the fact that there is no jousting. The defense seems to be playing possum." She acted that out, too, closing her eyes and tilting her head to the ceiling. "For a rich, white kid to have a do-nothing lawyer, that is weird. So, just see what you can dig up, if you're not too rusty."

Alex spent a year in law school before realizing she hated playing games that involved lying, and she learned a lot in that year. Still, I had to argue with her. Mostly because she expected it, and partly because I was bored.

"What is there to dig up about an entitled white, male athlete getting drunk and killing his girlfriend and a teammate who probably was a rival in every sense? Sounds like a near everyday occurrence to me," I said.

"It isn't, and you know that."

I shrugged. "It's still not a mystery. People kill each other all the time without anyone taking notice. Seriously, the kid played at a public Division III school that no powerful people around here went to or care about. There are no scholarships, no television contracts, no money. Nothing. And the dead girl wasn't even blonde."

Alex glared at me, and I ignored her. We all know that blonde girls get the most ink when they die; we just aren't supposed to say it. But by not admitting it, we—the "media"—are part of the problem.

"You cannot have gotten that cynical," was all she said.

I shrugged, and then I pushed because I was curious. "But

really, how does the trial deserve this many resources?"

"I'd rather overreact and be wrong than underreact and get scooped," Alex said with finality. "Plus, I'm feeling flush, although you're not that expensive. And look at the picture of the kid.... he looks so lost. Come on," Alex turned her computer screen to me, "aren't you curious about *why* he did it, even if he is guilty?"

I looked and shrugged again. "If I remember correctly from scanning the headlines over the past months, Connor has a history of out-of-control behavior and a father more concerned with money and golf. Oh, and he played a violent sport. The story is why nobody stopped him before two people died," I argued, before I realized I was playing into her hand. Damnit.

"Then write that story. I don't care. There is something here; we just have to find it. Where there is smoke, there is fire."

I groaned.

"Okay, sorry about the cliché. But I need column inches, and I need them to be good. You need to shake the rust off too. You've been in the basement too long. And basketball is not a violent sport."

"Hah! The way they throw their bodies around under the net? The refs are allowing more and more contact each year."

"Aha! You do follow basketball."

"I pay attention," I admitted. "It is the birthright of 'my people,' after all."

"There is no better state for basketball than North Carolina, historically speaking. I mean the 1982 and 1983 championships alone, two different schools just down the road—" Alex said, warming up for her lecture.

"You're getting soft-hearted," I said to ward her off.

"I just have a feeling. A nose for news," she made a production worthy of community theatre out of pointing at her nose, and I had to shake my head in defeat.

Alex took my silence as unhappiness, which it wasn't, really.

"Look Gale, you've got to know by now that this big game that we all play is just a life-size version of Whack-A-Mole. Sometimes you're the whack and sometimes you're the mole."

"What does that even mean?" I asked in mock confusion.

"Just try not to be the mole on my dime." Alex smiled and waved me out. I saluted and turned to leave. "Oh," she called to my back, "I can get you some film of Connor's games, if that helps."

"Maybe," I said, not meaning it. This assignment is about a trial, not basketball. Why would I need to waste my time watching old games?

I arrived back at my desk just as Olivia was returning from lunch. Olivia is my best friend in the office and also my complete opposite —small and demure in her sweater sets and pearls. She is quiet and kind, but whip smart. I try to be kind, although it doesn't always come naturally. My smarts are getting duller each year, too.

"What's new?" Olivia asked as she sat down across from me. The newsroom desks are arranged in pairs that face a shared partition. We have all learned to talk without looking at each other. It was weird at first, then freeing in a way, like being in a church confessional. Although everything I know about that is from movies.

"I've got to go to Waynesville and cover Connor Braxton's murder trial," I said.

"Ugh. Better you than me. I don't think I could stand

11

listening to all that evidence. You know they say the scene was more Charles Manson than humiliated boyfriend. Not one and done, in other words."

"Lovely. You know, you should stop reading that stuff."

Olivia covers the education beat but likes to spend her spare time poking around the sleazier "news" sites for leaked tidbits whenever there is a grisly murder.

"I know. It's a horrible habit. I have bad dreams."

"Try drinking yourself to sleep. It has always worked for me!" I mimed throwing back a shot, an action I could do in my sleep back in college. But I have slowed down a good bit lately, which sometimes feels like all I have left to be proud of.

"Jerry's from Waynesville, you know," Olivia said. "Maybe when he gets back he can give you some tips."

"I'll take all the help I can get. Yeah, if you remember, tell him to call me. Wait—never mind. I'll just leave a note on his desk."

Jerry developed his personal communication system pre-voice-mail. He would grab whatever note was left for him, stuff it in his wallet, and then call you the next time he pulled his wallet out to buy something. His system would work until he lost his wallet. Which he did once a year. I was always happy to get his name in the office holiday gift exchange, and he was always happy to get a new wallet.

"When are you leaving?" Olivia asked.

"Monday, I guess. The trial starts Tuesday."

"Okay. Have fun and bring me something."

I laughed. Olivia gets out of town more than I do. "A bottle opener from some backroads truck stop?"

"Sounds perfect." Olivia smiled and went back to work.

Having made peace with my fate, I figured I better get prepared. I clicked on the icon for the newspaper's intranet and started looking into Conner Braxton, former star forward for the Blue Ridge University Knights and current accused double murderer. All I had to do was type his name in the search box, and for that modicum of effort, I received in return a beautiful list of 16 articles we had written about him. Most were about the murders, one covered a streak of great games he had two years ago, and one was about a vandalism incident when Connor was in high school. Another 37 mentioned the Braxton family name. A quick scan of those headlines revealed stories mostly about his father's charity golf tournaments and business deals. Mr. Arthur Braxton hobnobbed with the rich and powerful.

Research is so easy now. Back in Seattle, in my early days as a cub reporter, we had to traipse down the back stairs to the morgue—our profession's word for library—to look at actual clippings that the librarian had torn out of the actual paper, using a ruler to keep the edges neat. (At least we didn't call the librarian the coroner.) Those clippings were then filed in manila envelopes that ended up in swinging metal bins that sat in rows in giant revolving motorized files the size of small Ferris wheels. There were four of them, one just for photos, and they took up an entire wall. You could hide an average sized human body in one of those rows of files.

The librarian, Martha, was a hoot. She was barely five feet, counting her high heels and hair, and she wore jewelry that weighed more than my arm. When the files jammed, Martha would take off her leather pumps, climb a ladder and thrust a broomstick handle into whatever row was out of place, stabbing the bin back into line. She always looked like she enjoyed the process. Even back then, newspaper budgets didn't stretch to include repairmen.

I miss Martha and the morgue. I miss a lot of things from my past, come to think of it. Fat lot of good it does me to dwell on it, though.

I leaned back in my chair as far as it would go and started reading the twelve articles about the murder in the order they originally appeared. I learned that Olivia was right. The murders of Gina and Marcus were gruesome crimes. Both victims were stabbed to death and suffered multiple wounds. Connor was sitting in their blood when the police arrived. Gross.

The second story covered the events leading up to the killings. Fourteen months ago, on the Thursday before final exams in May 2015, all the Blue Ridge basketball players went out on the town. "It's a tradition," explained one of the players interviewed. I groaned. Traditions always bring trouble of one sort or another, in my experience. The team rented a bus, and just after noon started visiting all the bars within a twenty-mile radius of the campus. There were rules for what to drink where and prizes for completing the "goals," as well as penalties for failing to keep up. The cheerleaders met them at the last bar as the icing on the cake. All good clean fun and not sexist at all.

Supposedly, Connor was far from the life of the party that night, which was out of character for him. People said he kept to himself and acted like something was eating him instead of taking his usual place right in the thick of everything. He went through the motions, they said, but without his customary zeal. Now, I tend to be suspicious of people's descriptions of criminals or their victims after the fact. Their memories are tainted with what think they are *supposed to* have noticed or thought. Still, I filed that tidbit away to think about later. What made him feel or act out of sorts?

The school's public relations office immediately labelled it an "alcohol fueled tragedy." The administration promised to tighten regulations on student drinking. The coach – the legendary Haywood Ford - mourned publicly over losing two star players in such "an awful way." Ugh. I hated the way he lumped killer and victim together, but I guess from his perspective, there were his players before they became killer and victim.

A couple of the photos accompanying the later stories said even more to me, though. Not about the crime, but about the killer. Or the accused as I would be calling him in writing. When I compared his mug shot and an old basketball team photo with a picture taken recently at a pre-trial hearing, it looked like Connor had lost something like sixty pounds in his fourteen months in jail. He looked diminished.

I filed that away too and went back to reading. I learned that the case was going to trial, despite the overwhelming evidence of Connor's guilt because the prosecutor never took plea deals. She said her policy was that "the community should always have a say, that it shouldn't be up to her." Huh. Madison Kupchak, Esq. must either be an idealist or a publicity hound. Or not very busy. At the least, extremely unorthodox. But Waynesville was a strange place to be unorthodox, I thought.

Connor's lawyer, Isaac Sutton, was another unorthodox piece of the puzzle. I could not find a single comment from him. Most defense lawyers would play the press, but not this one.

I was starting to see why Alex wanted boots on the ground. I still wished they didn't have to be my boots.

I pushed the keyboard away and put my head on the desk. My traditional thinking pose. If the thinking got really heavy, I put a jacket or sweater over my head to block out the world. I have been known to use a box, too, in a pinch.

I tried to digest what I had read. The more I chewed over the situation, the more a lot of things didn't make sense. Why did this rich kid have such a limp lawyer? Why had he lost so much weight? I rubbed my eyes and stretched and pulled up the next to last article. It was on courtroom renovations. Boring.

I grabbed my mug and took the last sip of the tepid brown liquid that was still trying to be coffee and forced my eyes back to the screen when my phone buzzed. Internal calls buzzed, external calls rang. It could only be Alex.

"Did you find Jerry?" I asked.

"Nope –"

"Hey," I said, interrupting. "I think I will take you up on the offer of looking at film of some of Connor's games. It will at least give me something to do in my boring evenings." I was getting sucked in, like I always do. It's why I never have a life outside of work. Or it's part of the reason.

"Roger that. I will have it sent up. We don't have much, but some magic interns scrounged some last summer. I called because I need that piece on the Bay Bridge repair timetable before you go." I was still working a little for Metro on the sly. No by-line, but I didn't care. Alex did take care of me. She said she didn't want me to get stale.

"Sure. Anything else?"

"Drive carefully," Alex said and hung up.

THREE

Saturday – Sunday, July 2- 3

I finished the Bay Bridge repair story on Saturday morning. I already had all the research and interviews and photos, I just hadn't put the pieces together. Basically, the bridge will take forever to fix. And then it will need to be fixed again. I gussied that conclusion up a bit, but it was clear enough to probably make those in charge of the project not so happy. The truth is the truth, though, and my job is to find it and write it without regard to anyone's happiness.

After I sent the story on to Alex, I went to the kitchen and snacked on the food everyone brings in to ease the pain of having to work on a holiday weekend. Newspapers run on a skeleton staff on holidays, but they do run. Nobody is happy about it. Except me. I hate holidays, so I like an excuse to avoid them.

No luminaries died, so obits was quiet. I took the time to organize the past two months of my work so I could hand it off, assuming (hoping) I would be back at Metro full time after the trial.

I left the building around 4 pm and walked home. The paper is about three miles from my neighborhood, and I usually take the Metro, but I didn't feel like waiting. I also wanted to pick up some wine, and my favorite shop is halfway between home and work. I needed dinner, too, but mostly wine. It took forever to get home, and I was drenched with sweat when I arrived. But I had two bottles of Pinot Gris and a chicken kebab platter for the evening's sustenance. which I set on the kitchen counter.

My apartment occupies the middle floor of an old

rowhouse, which is gorgeous but definitely not made for tall people; I hit my head at least once a week. It's also long and narrow – I think of it as a ranch-style apartment. The kitchen is at the back and my bedroom and tiny bath are in the front. The living room is in the middle.

The third floor is vacant and has been since I moved in three years ago. It is wonderful not to have to listen to anyone banging around up there. Part of the first floor is an art gallery. The front door of the building door opens to a tiny lobby. From there you can choose to take the staircase up to my apartment, go straight and end up in our shared laundry and storage space, or turn right and pop into the gallery. Kathleen Price owns the gallery and the building, as well as the one next door where my favorite neighbor Leo lives. Leo is on the top floor of that one – in the winter he can look down from his balcony onto mine. Nice young professional couples move in and out of the other two apartments.

Kathleen is a fantastic landlord. She hasn't raised the rent in three years, she's quick to call a repairman if something needs fixing, and I like the art in her gallery. All in all, it is a pretty good living situation. The icing on the cake is that I get to park my Corvette snug and dry and safe in her garage around the back because she doesn't drive.

The lemon-yellow machine is my prized possession, a gift from my mother to entice me to move back east. Okay, so it was a bribe, but I didn't care. Everyone can be bought, and the car reminded me of my father—wild and free and beautiful.

I was looking forward to a quiet evening. I had been on a streak of bleak Scandinavian movies that I thought I would try and continue if I could find a good one. Sounds of avian rustling interrupted my search.

"Hey, you," Hawk seemed to say, "I'm still here. I know I'm just a bird, but I'm your bird, your responsibility. Feed me. Love me!"

"Okay, okay, I am coming," I said.

One rustle from Hawk can say a lot. I got his food from the Tupperware on the counter, walked back into my wreck of a bedroom and gave him a scoop. He acknowledged the arrival of dinner with a spasm of feather cleaning which is his regular pre-meal ritual. I keep his cage where he can look out the window. Sometimes I wonder if that is mean. I hope it isn't.

Hawk is not a hawk. He is a cockatiel. The irony amuses me and, I assume, him. While he tolerates the commercial cockatiel pellets, he prefers the homemade meals my ex-husband, Brian, used to make for him. Brian got Hawk for me as an anniversary present, back when we gave each other presents. I think Hawk was for our fifth. God only knows why he got me a cockatiel. Our disconnect went far deeper than misguided gifts. When I left Seattle and Brian, it just seemed easier to take the little guy than argue about it. Hawk and I have our good and bad days; but I'm used to him now, and except for missing his personal chef, I think he is used to me, too.

With Hawk fed, I did the same for myself and turned my attention more fully to the television and the wine. Wallowing in misery, my mother would call it. My mother was a big believer in staying busy. All my life, I never saw any white space on her calendars. Even on the weekends. But I knew better. Wallowing in misery was much, much different. This was surviving, my way.

After drinking the entire bottle of wine, I got what I deserved when I woke up on Sunday. My head was killing me, and my mouth felt like it was stuffed with half a dozen used cotton balls. I couldn't remember when I went to bed, and I was still wearing yesterday's shirt. The more the fog lifted, the worse I felt. I did not intend to drink so much. I opened and closed my eyes.

Sensing the activity, Hawk flapped his wings and scratched at the newspaper, eager for his breakfast. I looked at the clock: 9:15 a.m. Ugh. Turning my head made me nauseous. That did not bode well for anyone's breakfast.

Five minutes later, I scrunched up the courage, untangled myself from the sheets, placed my feet on the floor, willed the room not to spin, and stood up. Hooray for me. Then I lurched to the bathroom, lifted the toilet seat and threw up. It took three tries to get rid of all of whatever was in my stomach. But as I rinsed my mouth and brushed my teeth, I felt much better. I splashed some water on my face and neck, stripped and pulled on an extra-large Seattle Mariners T-shirt and a pair of running shorts. Not that I planned on running for a while, but running shorts have built-in underwear which save a step in the dressing process, a big point in their favor right now.

With my eyes shut against the overeager morning light, I padded into the kitchen as quickly and as gently as I could, touching my fingers against the walls for guidance. The kitchen is my favorite room in the apartment. A few months ago I painted the walls a deep turquoise in my first ever home improvement project. Kathleen says it is a Caribbean blue. Just standing in it makes me feel better.

Squinting, I ground the coffee beans and poured water in the reservoir. Coffee started, I opened the refrigerator and glanced at the vodka bottle before grabbing a yogurt to soften the landing of the aspirin I desperately needed.

"I hope it's a long time before I have to resort to the hair of the dog," I said out loud to no one.

I fed Hawk, and when the coffee was ready, I poured a cup and moved to the back window of the kitchen. It overlooked a garden no one really took care of but that still looked beautiful despite the neglect. It looked like it was going to be a perfect day. There were a few puffy clouds and no sign of the usual summer haze. I leaned against the cabinet and sipped my coffee. First cup down, I drank two cups of water out of the same mug, choked down the aspirin and then poured more coffee. The headache was slowly surrendering, so I went into my living room, which pulled double duty as my office, and turned on the computer to read the *Star*. Nothing earth shattering happened overnight. Then I showered and changed. Exhausted by that effort, I took a nap after which I felt strong enough to do some chores.

Coming back to a dirty apartment after a work trip is unpleasant even for me and my low standards, so I cleaned the bedroom and bathroom. Then I puttered around on the computer again. For a person whose work day is intimately tied to a computer, I am always stunned by how much time I can spend surfing the Internet. There is always something to read, something to look at, something to get upset about, something to think about buying. When it finally got tiresome, I let Hawk out to fly around the apartment. After a quick trip to the market, I fixed our dinners using actual fresh vegetables and had the first drink of the day at 7:30, which seemed quite reasonable. It was Saturday night after all, everyone's favorite time to forget the world for a while.

An hour later, I was curled up on the couch watching a re-run of *The Mary Tyler Moore Show*, contemplating packing for my trip and enjoying a second glass of wine. My last for the evening, I promised. And it was only a half glass.

The crack of a gunshot made me nearly jump out of my

skin.

"What the hell?!" I yelled. Hawk screamed in his cage. Was he hit?

Then more gunshots—pop, pop, pop, pop, pop. I needed to hide, and now, I thought. Fueled by adrenaline and staying low to avoid the bullets, I sprint-crawled across the living room and down the short hall to the safety of my windowless closet. I squatted in the back behind piles of shoes and dirty laundry, chest heaving and hoping Hawk was okay. Then, just as I was bracing for the attack, I heard laughter. With a painful turning of gears in my head, I realized it was almost July 4th. My gunshots were fireworks. Early celebrants.

"Goddammit," I said aloud, grabbing my head with my hands to hold it together. I tried to take a few deep breaths. I hated fireworks. July 4th wasn't until tomorrow. These were just neighborhood idiots. Assholes. I went back to the living room in a fit of anger and opened the front window.

"Could you please not light firecrackers in the street? It's not safe or legal, you know," I said to the man and girl standing about twenty feet from my window. I had expected a group of teenagers when I poked my head out. The man held his lighter to the fuse of the next one.

"These are bottle rockets, ma'am, and they are legal." He waved it at me. "So, what are you going to do about it now?" He looked like he had spent most of his 40 odd years driving a truck during the day and doing a lot of serious drinking at night.

Can they really be legal, and if so, why do those guys always know more about the law than I do? "Nice attitude in front of the girl." I responded.

"You started it. We're just having fun. What's your problem? It's the Fourth of July! You hate America or something?"

"Look, just go somewhere else, please. You scared the shit out of me and my bird." Why did I open the damn window in the first place?

"Don't cuss in front of my daughter. Hey, come back here squirt," he called to the girl who had wandered off. He grabbed her hand, bent down and said something in her ear, and they left, making a path for the park. I closed the window and raised both my middle fingers at his retreating back, unable, or more accurately unwilling, to do anything else. I have turned into a physical coward, which might just be for the best.

Then I went back in the closet to change my shirt. It reeked of fear sweat. I turned on the radio in the kitchen, and a Miles Davis track was playing. It is hard to stay upset while listening to Miles, I thought, as I could feel my blood pressure dropping. I checked on Hawk and let him out of his cage. He immediately flew under the bed. I lay down and shimmied under the bed to comfort him. I can't stand to see an animal afraid. Or a person for that matter. Unless they deserved it.

"It will be okay, baby. It's all over."

His bird eye said: "Yeah, I believe you, but I still need a few minutes. I'm thinking this is somehow your fault, and I want some time to decide if I need to punish you."

I wasn't about to force him. Hawk can leave a mark when he wants to. I reverse-shimmied out, picking off the dust bunnies that had velcroed themselves to my micro-afro, as Brian used to call it. I keep my hair very short partly because I refuse to waste time styling it and mostly because anything else is intolerable in the summer. When I let it grow the year I turned thirteen it felt like a family of feverish, honey-coated muskrats crawled up and died on my head. Never again.

I walked back to my kitchen, ate a handful of almonds

and got more wine, then went to the living room. So much for the half glass. Now I was wide awake, but also a little drunk. It was not a bad combination, I thought, all things considered. And just then, someone buzzed at the front door.

I held my breath, afraid the fireworks guy had figured out which apartment was mine. No, he wouldn't bother coming back, would he?

I opened my door, walked downstairs and looked through the peephole of the front door.

"Hey, check out my outfit for tomorrow!" Leo yelled through the door.

Leo is my neighbor, and the best one in the world. I opened the front door with relief. The sight made me pause. And blink. "What are you wearing?" I asked.

Leo's impish blue eyes sparkled as he flashed his movie star smile. "A hat." He kissed me on both cheeks, then took the hat off, shook out his shoulder length blonde hair with a natural theatricality developed from a lifetime on stage, and bowed with a flourish. I almost applauded.

"That's more than a hat," I laughed. "It's an entire costume. Come on up."

Leo was wearing a stovepipe hat, clown shoes and a long coat that was made of the American flag. The clown shoes gave him a little trouble on the stairs, but his dancer's grace made up for it. Leo is the best dancer in the world, in my opinion. Or was. He could do it all: jazz, ballet, modern. Most of my outings in the first few years I lived here were to see him perform. But he'd been having a lot of joint pain, so about a month ago he finally went to the doctor. The doctor sent Leo to a specialist that day, and we found out within the week that he had rheumatoid arthritis.

"You know, some environmental group tried to stop the fireworks this year. They said it was adding to the Bay pollution," he said.

"It does," I said. "It's really awful. And the noise doesn't help the wildlife either. Can you imagine what they are thinking? The fish and birds and deer and rabbits must all believe the world is ending." Like I did a few minutes ago. "I don't know why we hang on to the stupid tradition."

"Fireworks are festive," Leo argued. "And pretty."

I grunted. It was hard to disagree with Leo. Leo, the one person I could tell anything to who wouldn't keep bringing it up. When I told him about getting demoted and why, he didn't say I should have stood up for myself; he didn't say much of anything. He didn't judge. It sounds uncaring, but Leo is the opposite of uncaring. He is perfect, and I love him. Without him, my heart probably would have shriveled up like a raisin from disuse.

Upstairs, Leo sat down on the couch and I folded myself into the only chair. I was glad to see him with such energy. The diagnosis rocked his world at first. Only 27, he would have had years as a dancer ahead of him if he stayed healthy.

"So," I said, raising my eyebrows again at his get up.

"It was a very good shopping trip." Leo said. He loves dressing up and loves holidays. He says he was born that way. Since his last name is Holiday, I had to give him that. There is no escaping what you're born into. I hate holidays, but I love Leo. It is not the only contradiction in my life.

"Where's Hawk? Is he okay?"

"He's under the bed. Go say hi, but don't expect much. He's really frightened. Or pissed off. I can't tell."

"Thanks for the warning." Leo had been on the receiving end of one of Hawk's nips, or whatever you call it when a bird bites, and still had a small scar on his left thumb to show for it.

"You know, those shoes might actually fit me," I said as he walked down the hall.

Turning around, he said: "I got them at the costume store on Seventeenth. But it's going out of business. I'll miss Edith, she is always so much fun."

Leo makes friends with everyone. He brightens up a room just by walking in.

"You know," he said, looking me up and down like a disapproving aunt, "we could stand to find you a good place to shop for something other than shoes. You are so gorgeous it is a crime to hide it like you do."

"I'm not gorgeous, and I don't dress that badly."

"Hmph. Yes to both," Leo called as he sashayed to the bedroom.

His way of winning arguments is to leave, but he was right about the clothes. As for the looks, I have the good genes of a true mutt. I am half brown Louisiana Cajun thanks to Mom and one-quarter each Jamaican and Native American thanks to Dad. The copper eyes came from Mom and the height from Dad. My black skin from his mother. Back when they were close, they used to joke this is how they knew I was really theirs. They saw all their ancestors in me. Yes, I was lucky in the looks department, although it has never done me any good as far as I could tell.

Leo came back smiling with a much calmer Hawk on his shoulder.

"So, I've got to go to Waynesville for the next couple of weeks to cover a trial," I said.

"Ugh. Better you than me."

Just what Olivia said. "Why?"

"One, I'm gay in all senses of the word. You're just a tall black woman. Two, the way you hold a grudge, I figure you have some Hatfield or McCoy blood in you from some great grandfather somewhere. You'll fit right in."

I had to laugh. It's true, I am not terribly forgiving. It's in the running to be crowned my biggest flaw.

"And three, Cara at the juice bar would miss me."

"She'd miss your wallet."

"True. Want me to watch Hawk?" he asked.

"Do you mind? That would be great."

Leo never minded, but I always asked.

"Not at all. He's actually really good at my house."

"Go figure."

"What's the trial about? Coal mining or something?" Leo's knowledge of the wider world was slim. I loved that about him, too.

"A college kid at Blue Ridge University killed his teammate and his girlfriend. He's facing the death penalty."

"Does he have some slick lawyer?"

"No, that's the funny thing. The kid is from a really rich family—money going back generations—and the lawyer is a local guy with no reputation to speak of."

"You'd think they'd bring in someone from DC, if not New York. A big gun."

"I know, right? And the other funny thing is that the murder scene was supposedly really grisly."

"That's not funny."

"Not funny ha-ha, funny weird," I said.

"Were there drugs involved? I've read there are a lot of meth labs in the valley."

"I haven't found any mention of drugs so far."

"Who did he kill first?" Leo asked.

"The teammate, Marcus."

"Huh. So, what was a rich kid doing going to Blue Ridge University? Couldn't his dad buy his way into Georgetown or Yale?"

"You would think," I said. "But no amount of money would get you on the basketball team. Blue Ridge recruited him. That's flattering." I know. I remembered. "And the other weird thing is that he's lost a ton of weight in jail.

"Was he fat before?" Leo asked.

"Not really. In the photos, he looks muscular with a layer of baby fat. Or probably beer fat. He was a forward on the basketball team. Some size is helpful in that position. I was going to see if he is sick, but I would think his lawyer would be making a big deal out of that."

"Try to build sympathy," Leo offered.

"Exactly," I said.

"Maybe Daddy's buying the jury on the side, or the judge, and he's told the lawyer he has everything under control. You know, to keep his bill down?"

"Okay, this isn't a movie," I said laughing.

"Yes, my darling, but if it were, could we get George Clooney to play the lawyer? Please? He'd be great," Leo said.

I just shook my head.

"It does sound like you have your work cut out for you."

"I am just the reporter, not a private detective. Saving the world is not in my job description. I'm more concerned that it will be boring. I haven't covered a trial in ages, but I remember that nothing happens quickly. So, wish me luck."

"Good luck, my dear. It is all about life and death after all, so I'm sure you'll stumble across something interesting. Hey, isn't your mom a lawyer? Maybe she could give you some inside tips."

My mom. "Yeah," was all I said.

Leo left it alone. "Well, are you coming back on weekends?"

"Absolutely."

"Goody. We'll do something fun."

"Deal. Want a drink?" I said, nodding at my glass. It was part of our routine. Leo always said no, or ignored the question, but I always asked. It made us seem normal.

"No, thanks." Leo flipped around the channels before stopping at *Breakfast at Tiffany's*.

"So, tell me, how come even gay guys grab the remote?" I asked.

"It's just the way it is, my dear."

To my great amusement, Leo recited nearly all the lines in the movie making it sound like a poorly dubbed foreign film. Hawk eventually fell asleep on the back of the couch. When the movie was over, I scooped him up and put him back in his cage with a few peas in case he wanted a midnight snack. It was a good evening.

FOUR

Monday, July 4

To celebrate my last day in DC for a while, Leo and I went out to lunch at the new Mexican place on 18th Street. (I may hate holidays, but celebrations are good.) My huevos rancheros were spectacular and came with a basket of homemade corn tortillas and a fresh avocado and melon salad. A Bloody Mary tried calling my name, but I tuned her out. Instead, I ordered a watermelon agua fresca, which I learned after asking our server, Ana, was essentially watermelon and water, but "really good." She was right.

I hoped the taste memory would help me survive a week of TGI Fridays and Cracker Barrels. I'm not a snob or a foodie, I just like real food free of excess chemicals and factory cheese. The body and mind operate best on good fuel. I told Leo my fears and he reminded me about the fancy new inn not far from Waynesville that received a glowing review from the *Star's* food editor, but then I reminded him back about my expense account limits.

"Maybe if you like it there, we can try the inn for a weekend getaway in the fall. You know, take in the colors and pretend to be a couple. We could shock the locals." He wiggled his eyebrows.

I laughed so hard, I almost spilled my drink. "That's a tempting offer, but it's highly unlikely I'll want to go back. I'm more of a beach girl than a mountain girl."

"Really? I've never known you to go to the beach."

"Yeah, but if I had to pick, I'd take the ocean over a poison ivy infested rocky hill any day."

"You insult our Appalachian Mountains?" Leo asked in mock horror.

"They lack a bit of the majesty of the peaks out west."

"Point for you. But I bet there is some good music in Waynesville."

"If I hear banjos, I am taking off faster than a —"

"No, not *Deliverance* banjos. Americana, roots stuff. Like the Avett Brothers, or June Carter."

"Huh? I have no idea what you are talking about. I like jazz, remember?"

"You'll like roots music. I'll get you some CDs for the trip."

"A gay man likes country? How could I not know this? You may be the first. Should we alert the media?" I rummaged in my purse for my phone.

Leo shook his head. "Roots music is not country, although country came from it. So did blues, kind of. Plus there is as much improvisation in a fiddle jam as in any jazz trio."

"Bite your tongue, but hey, I guess I should be willing to let you expand my musical horizons. You have never steered me wrong."

Leo threw his arms into the air to celebrate his victory. I loved the way he wore his happiness on his sleeve. By not trying to be cool, he was cooler than anyone else I knew. With the soundtrack of my drive decided, we paid the bill and walked back home in companionable silence.

I spent the rest of the day packing and doing errands and then tidying up my life: paying bills, watering the only house-plant that I haven't killed, and emptying the garbage.

As I loaded the car that evening, I told myself to be grateful for missing the real fireworks and the two-week reprieve from the heat and humidity of DC. Just walking up and down the stairs with my luggage made me sweat through my underwear. I didn't think I was bringing that much, but the two duffel bags, one computer bag, and a box with snacks and tape recorder and paper and pens—the tools of the trade—necessitated four trips and left me dripping. My old Corvette was stuffed to the gills. Upstairs I changed into fresh clothes, said goodbye to Hawk, and locked the door just after 8 p.m. I should have left earlier, but it was too easy to put it off. I didn't want a long, boring evening in the motel room. I'd have enough of those ahead of me.

Forty miles outside of DC, it started raining. The trees hugging the road were so thick and heavy with wet leaves that their branches nearly brushed the top of my car. It must have been raining for days out here. I hate driving in the rain at night; I can't see anything. No one can - we're all driving on faith. Luckily, I only passed a few other cars, and no one was on my tail, so I could drive as slowly as I wanted. I checked the GPS and the clock and saw that at this pace, I wouldn't get in until close to 11 p.m. That was not the plan. I needed to be in the courtroom tomorrow by 8 a.m. Ish. Ugh.

I put in one of Leo's CDs and loved the first song. The second was a little twangy, but the third was magical. The melody was simple, but sad and happy at the same time. The tone of the guitar was so clear. I couldn't help tapping my free foot. Clearly, with the exception of Miles Davis, I am ignorant about music. I would have to text Leo when I got to the motel.

When the CD was over, I clicked on the radio. My DC preset apparently shared space with a station from God knows where that was apparently airing a sports call-in show. I usually avoided these like the plague, but the first words I heard were…

"Connor Braxton may have had a shot at the pros before the murders."

"May have? He was a sure thing! And he was white!"

"What does being white have to do with it?" the host asked the caller, who sounded drunk to me.

The caller backpedaled. Was the host black? It was hard to tell by his voice, but I would have said yes.

"Sorry, I just meant that some teams—and I am not saying it is right—look to balance the racial mix for the fans' sake."

"Really? And you know this how?

Click.

"Well, it looks like we lost the connection with Dave from West Virginia. After a short break, we will be back with more about whether Division II and III schools can attract and produce top athletes without the big money. Whether there is a secret sauce someone can concoct...."

No, we won't, I thought, and turned the radio off. I wondered for a minute whether more time was spent—in the aggregate—on talking about sports than watching or, god forbid, playing them. I figured it was by a factor of ten.

I switched the windshield wipers to high just in time to see the animal in the middle of the road before I plowed into it. The impact forced a scream from its soul - a horrible, unearthly sound of pain and fear. I slammed on my brakes and skidded into a spin, which sent everything in the car flying. It all happened too fast for me to be scared.

When the car finally stopped, adrenaline flooded into my body and my heart tried to beat its way out of my chest. I couldn't breathe. Was it a dog? God, I hoped it wasn't a dog. If I killed somebody's dog... I almost started to cry but stopped myself. This is just shock, I told myself. I am fine. I am in the middle of nowhere, but I am fine. Get a grip. I closed my eyes and tried to listen for any more noise from the animal, but I was too far away. I got out of the car and walked to where I thought it would be, taking the baseball bat my father always told me to keep in the car in case it was something vicious.

Damnit. I could tell it was a dog even though my head-lights didn't quite reach it. Why don't I keep a damn flashlight in my car? It didn't seem to be moving, but after a few second my eyes adjusted, and I could see its chest heaving with the effort of panting. Plus I could hear it. So much effort. I stood there next to the dog, trying to come to terms with what had just happened. I carry a lot of anger around in my life, arguably for good reason, but it hasn't made me tough. I have never hit an animal. I have never seen anything die. I was going to cry again, I could feel it. I tried to breathe through my nose until I got a hold of myself.

Just then, another car came around the bend in the road and blinded me with its headlights. The driver braked. "What the hell are you doing in the middle of the road?" he called out of his open window.

I didn't answer. He could figure it out.

"Is that your fucking car?" He pointed.

"I hit this dog."

He got out and walked crookedly over to look at the dog.

"Is that your car?" he asked again. He was wearing a Confederate flag hat. He was the reason I did not want this assignment. Not the processed food or the poison ivy. Him and people like him. They scared me deep in my DNA. The country scares me. But I needed his help.

I nodded.

"Can you drive it?"

"I think so."

"Well drive it back over here and run over that dog again and put it out of its misery, unless you want me to shoot it."

"No!"

"Huh. Fine. You must not be from around here. It's the kindest thing to do, shooting a hurt animal. You're on your own now, sweetie."

I was relieved when he got back in his truck. I went back to my car and slid my bat back under the seat and drove gingerly back toward the dog. A brown medium sized lump. I switched my lights to low beams and pointed them at her. I decided she was a she. I got out and walked back. I could hear her catch and hold her breath when I got close, or so I thought. I looked for what was injured and saw quickly it was her back legs. I could also see now that she was definitely a girl, an extremely skinny girl with very short fur. Every rib was visible. She was bleeding pretty badly, and the rain was making the blood run in rivers away from her. There couldn't be much chance she would live.

I had to try.

I went back to the car and opened my passenger door and tilted the seat back as far as I could, and I got some clothes out of my bag to try and wrap her legs and stop the blood. Then I thought better of it and just piled them on the seat to try and make it more level. She was big, but so thin, I figured I could lift her into the seat easily. I knew it would hurt her, but what else could I do?

Back at her side I bent over her and sucked in my stomach. "Ready girl? One, two three," I said and grabbed her. I lifted. She screamed, and I felt bones move in my right hand.

I froze, holding her. "Shit, shit, shit! I'm sorry." She made no other sound, so I shuffled back to the car and tried to lay her as gently as possible on the seat. I had to fold her a bit to get her in the car. She whimpered once and then stopped. I closed the door and walked around to my side of the car, got in and pushed the car into gear and called Leo. I hoped I was driving in the right direction.

He picked up on the first ring.

"Can you. Find me a vet that's open. Now. In Waynesville?" The words came out in ragged leaps.

"Whoa, hold on. What happened?"

"I hit a dog, and she needs to go to a vet."

"Oh crap. I am so sorry. Okay. Give me a minute. Wait. Are you okay?"

"I'm fine. I just…"

"You don't sound fine. But okay, hold on."

I heard Leo put the phone down and assumed he went to his computer to search the web. I put on my interior light and looked at my passenger. Her eyes were closed, and her lips were pulled back in a grimace of pain. I could even see the outlines of her hipbones. Her coat was short and light reddish-brown, the color of a new basketball, with subtle striped markings or streaks of dirt. I couldn't tell. There was a swatch of white on the right side of her snout, like someone had taken a paintbrush, reached out and playfully tagged her. She had a wide head and big ears shaped like sails that seemed out of proportion to her skinny body. But she was strangely beautiful, even lying there bleeding and broken.

"There is an emergency vet on Airport Road before you get into town. It's open 24 hours. I will text you the address."

I had forgotten Leo was there. I snapped back.

"Thanks. Will you call them and tell them I am coming?"

"Yeah. Are you sure you are okay to drive? You should call the police."

"No. I'm fine. I'm shaken, but fine. She just darted out…"

"It's not your fault. She was probably chasing something."

"Maybe. I gotta go."

"Call me when you get there. Don't forget."

"I will. Thanks."

Leo's text beeped its arrival and I opened it and tapped the address. I followed the GPS voice and ignored the rain, driving as fast as I could. I kept a hand on her chest so I knew she was still breathing, and she knew I cared. Within twenty minutes, I saw the vet's building. It was lit up like an airport runway, impossible to miss. I pulled up parallel to the sidewalk even though it meant taking three parking spaces. A tiny woman dressed in pink Hello Kitty surgical scrubs came out before I even got out of the car.

"What happened?" the little pixie demanded as she pulled open the passenger door and looked at the dog with a flashlight.

"I think I ran over her back end. She just appeared in the road..."

Another person in scrubs—an older man this time—came out with a stretcher. He crawled in through the driver's side and with the little pixie reaching from the passenger side, they pushed and pulled my dog onto the stretcher. He then crawled through my car over the stick shift and they got her out. She didn't make a sound, and I could see her eyes were shut. I told myself that they wouldn't be going to so much trouble if there was no chance.

"Move your car," the pixie shouted over her shoulder.

I did as I was told, and then tried to find the courage to go inside. I could just leave. My feelings for this dog couldn't be real. She wasn't *my* dog. It was shock. What could I really do? After a minute, I made my choice, got out and locked the car. The automatic doors to the clinic opened with a whooshing

37

vacuum sound. There was a curved reception desk to the left and a waiting area to the right. Gray and orange chairs alternated around three sides of the room.

"May I help you?" the receptionist asked.

She had to have known who I was – I had blood all over my shirt - but I figured that was her polite way of asking me to fill out some papers.

"I brought the dog…"

"Would you mind filling these out?" she handed me a clipboard with three sheets of paper and a blue plastic pen.

"Sure," I said, taking them to an orange chair.

"I'm sorry. I know this must be traumatic."

I nodded, grateful for the kindness. Most of the questions on the papers I couldn't answer, but I did fill in my name, address and cell phone number. I returned the clipboard and pen and the receptionist nodded. Then I sat and waited. I realized I should call the motel and make sure they would hold my room, but I really didn't care. I did call Leo and told him that we made it and thanks, but that I didn't know anything yet.

"Hang in there. I'm so sorry this happened."

"It's okay," I said, even though it wasn't. "Bye."

"Bye yourself. I love you."

"I love you too."

I sat there remembering my childhood dog, Oscar, who I hadn't thought about in ages. Oscar was a roamer, but he always came home to sleep at the foot of my bed. He had curly hair like a poodle but a hound's tri-color markings. He was as odd looking a dog as I had ever seen, and we made a good pair. He was my dog and he followed me everywhere, but he loved my father more than life itself. It was like I was his job, but dad was his joy.

Somehow, I fell asleep, and when I woke up, a woman in bloody green scrubs was sitting to my right with her eyes closed. She started talking but kept her eyes closed.

"She's a strong girl. Not young, but not old. Maybe five or six. Usually a dog her age is too smart to get hit. She's as close to a purebred Am Staf as I have seen in a while. I know Pete breeds red nosed pits, and I'll call him in the morning. Although, maybe not, because she is awfully skinny. Must have been roaming for some time. God damn backyard breeders...Sorry. I'm off on a tangent."

The vet took a deep breath and opened her eyes. She was pretty, probably about my age, with long light brown hair pulled back in a ponytail. Not thin and not fat - solid. She was flushed, probably exhausted and not just from tonight. I could spot chronic exhaustion a mile away.

"We'll have to wait and see. She's pretty mangled up, but I think there's hope. And don't worry about the fee," she said anticipating a question I hadn't thought to ask. "I discount heavily for good Samaritans."

She patted my leg and then used it to push herself up. "Go home, get some sleep. I'll call you if anything changes."

"Thank you."

"I'm Sam by the way," the vet said sticking out her hand. "How long have you lived here?"

"I don't. I'm just here to cover the Connor Braxton trial for the *Washington Star*. I was driving into town when I hit..."

"Such a tragic mess. Anyway, she doesn't have a collar. No tags, so we don't know her name. Want to give her one?"

"I don't know..."

"It's okay. Think about it." She stood up. "And good luck with the trial. What a mess. I..."

Just then the pixie nurse came out.

"Mr. McManus' cat is seizing again."

"Gotta run. Why in God's name anyone leaves anti-freeze out in July is beyond me. That stuff is poison. There should be criminal charges for leaving it out, accessible to animals. We'll call you, okay?"

She was gone before I could answer,

My old Corvette still drove just fine, and I was grateful for that. It seemed to have sustained only cosmetic damage, which I could fix later. I got to the motel well after midnight. I checked in with a sleepy woman who looked about 90 and didn't seem to notice or mind the blood on my clothes, got my key and drove around to my room on the back side of the property, farthest from the road. It was quiet, thank goodness. I got my luggage into the room in two trips, stripped down and crawled between the sheets. I fell asleep immediately and had horrible nightmares, but that was nothing new.

FIVE

Tuesday, July 5

The next morning, I was relieved to discover that while my room was sparsely furnished, what was there looked clean. Best of all, the green flowered bedspread felt like cotton and smelled freshly laundered. I'd probably be safe from bed bugs. I'm no clean freak at home, but your own dirt is different from a stranger's. The television worked, too.

I had a hard time believing that last night was real until I saw my blood streaked clothes in a pile on the floor. I looked out the window. The daylight showed that my right front headlight was crunched and that there was a dent in the fender, but that was all the damage. I shuddered. I didn't want the clothes in my room, I didn't want any reminder of the accident right now, so I took them to the car and stuffed them under my seat. I'd try and wash them when I got home.

When I came back in, I noticed on the laminated list of "amenities" that the motel promised free coffee in the lobby. I almost ran over to get some. Happily, it was fresh and strong enough to make up for the tiny Styrofoam cup. Really, who— besides a child—can do anything on six ounces of coffee? And kids shouldn't drink coffee anyway. I got two cups and headed back to my room.

In my foray outside, I realized it was pleasantly cool for July, so I decided to walk to the courthouse, both to get some exercise and to see more of where I was. I needed to orient myself both physically and mentally. I showered and dressed, put on my sunglasses and pulled my backpack over one shoulder. One of the perks of being a newspaper reporter on assignment was that

I could still carry a backpack at the age of 41. The disheveled look is almost *de rigueur* for the men. The rules, of course, were different for women, and even more different for black women. But rules are made to be broken, at least the ones I don't like. I never wear heels. At six- foot-two there is no need. So, the mile distance, even with the rather aggressive hills, wasn't a problem. On the way, I hoped to find some food that wasn't fast, fake, or fried.

It didn't take long to see that the town was lovely, if a little sleepy. I could understand its appeal if postcard-worthy mountain views and 18th century architecture top your list of must-haves in a community.

Within three blocks, I found a coffee shop with muffins that didn't look like they came from a factory in Pennsylvania and bought two in case the judge didn't take long recesses for lunch. I do not like to skip a meal. Hunger makes me cranky and stupid—a bad combination I have learned to avoid. I find it is counter-productive to getting work done or being a decent human being, both goals I usually try to achieve.

Today would be the start of jury selection. Even though I hadn't covered a trail in ages, I knew how they worked, thanks to experience, my mother, and, of course, television. *Law & Order* does get some things right.

As I got closer to the courthouse, I could see the antennas from the television trucks—I counted three of them. A small swarm of people was merging into the crowd that had already formed on the sidewalk and was snaking up the courthouse steps.

I looked around. It appeared I was going to be the tallest one here; where were Connor's teammates? Standing off to the side, a small group of Hispanic people looked like they could be Gina's family. Other than that, the crowd looked like a mix of reporters and townspeople with nothing better to do. Courthouse regulars, my mom used to call these folks, but not with disdain. No, my mother never expressed disdain for anyone. Emotions were not her thing.

The other reporters were easy to pick out. They travelled solo and were less well dressed. I planned to avoid my colleagues. Yes, it means I will miss out on any leads, but it also means I will get to form my own opinions. And there is the shame regarding my probation at the paper. Our tribe does not like colleagues who fake stories, which of course I did not do. Still. I was going to keep to myself. Get the job done and go home.

I parked myself against an unused bike rack on the opposite side of the street from the courthouse and ate one of my muffins while jotting down a few notes about the scene in front of me. My phone buzzed and as soon as I finished my muffin, I pulled it out and I saw it was a text from Sam the vet.

Charlotte is still alive. I named her. Couldn't help myself. Not very good at treating nameless animals. Hope you like it. It's for the spider in Charlotte's Web. Always loved that story and still cry like a baby at the end when I read it to my nephew. I know what you're thinking, but the spider dies of old age at the end. If our Charlotte gets to live long enough to die of old age, it will mean I did my job and she did hers. Sorry for the novel. More later. Bye.

Aside from the nightmares, which featured the newly named Charlotte in full Technicolor, I had forgotten about the poor dog. I can be good at shifting gears like that; I learned that survival skill at an early age. I texted back – "Thanks! Keep me posted" – and resolved to try and see Charlotte during the week, if she stayed alive. Now that she was back in my mind, I found it hard to shake the image of her face as I put her in the car. Such grit. Such acceptance. It seemed unnatural.

A bailiff suddenly appeared on the steps, so I gathered my things and trotted over to hear what he had to say.

"The courtroom is now open. Cameras are not allowed, and neither is conversation. Turn off all cell phones before entering the building and please follow me in an orderly fashion. There is plenty of room for everyone. We are in Courtroom One, on the left as you go in."

The old building has more than one courtroom, I asked myself? It seemed too small. I shrugged and joined the quickly forming line. An eager twenty-year-old under the supervision of an older guard who was trying to look bored and tough at the same time, but who as undoubtedly jazzed by the biggest trial Waynesville had seen in decades, rifled through my backpack then let me pass.

I took a seat in the next to the last row in the middle. While I liked quick access to the exit, it was easier to be in the middle than have people stepping over my legs.

Courtroom One was poorly lit, but beautiful. Hollywood beautiful. It seemed like Gregory Peck could walk out at any minute and start arguing for Boo Radley's innocence. The wood gleamed, and the ceilings were tall. I felt underdressed. Two of the windows—one facing east and the other west—were stained glass, adding to the church-like feel. Somebody cared about this place. There was probably a "Save the Courthouse" committee of concerned citizens. I jotted down my impressions. According to Alex, it's always good to have a story within a story in each piece you file, even if it is only a sentence or two long. It gives people a way in to the main story. I might have been a little rusty, but I was starting to remember how to do my job.

"All rise," the bailiff ordered, and we did.

The judge walked in, a gaunt, serious looking man who looked like he could use a sandwich or two. There's thin and then there is skeletal. Judge Branch Evans straddled the line.

"Be seated," the judge said, and we were.

"I have set aside two weeks for this trial, and I expect we will be done before that," he said, glowering at the lawyers. "I want no shenanigans. Is that understood?"

"Yes, your honor," both lawyers answered in an impressive harmony.

"We will begin jury selection then. I plan to take a short break at 10:30, a lunch break at twelve thirty, and we'll conclude at 5 p.m. Bailiff, please bring in the first group."

Now that the action had started, I looked around at the people and not just the architecture. Connor Braxton looked just as thin as he did in the photographs. More than thin, he looked diminished, altogether different. His blond hair was more of a beige, and he slouched as he sat. I picked out his father, Arthur Braxton, in the third row back, also from photographs. Mr. Braxton looked fully in control. Of what, I wasn't sure. It wasn't how I thought a father would look during the murder trial of his son.

The prosecutor, Madison Kupchak, looked like she could have walked onto the set of *Law and Order* at any moment. Shoulder length brown hair, black pumps and a neat grey suit with a pale blue blouse. The whole effect was one of pure, powerful competence. She started the show with general questions, then asked the pool of potential jurors if they could be fair and decide the case solely on the evidence and not based on anything they had read or heard before. Everyone nodded, except for one man who raised his hand and shook his head simultaneously. Uh oh.

"Sir … um … ," the prosecutor glanced down at the juror forms which were organized by chair number. "Mr. Clark, are you saying you can't put aside any pre-conceived notions and judge this case on the evidence presented?"

"Yes ma'am, that is what I am saying," said Mr. Clark, who wore a short-sleeved checked shirt and a tie. The summer uniform of serious, but practical men of a certain age. Mr. Clark was not quite that age, though. He looked barely 40.

"Are you saying that just to get out of service?" asked the judge, menacingly. "I've always known you to be a fair man, Bob."

The use of first names confirmed what I thought about small towns and everybody knowing everybody else—and their business.

"No, Branch—I mean Judge—I'm not saying it just so I can go home. I believe he did it and should die, no matter how good a player he was." He pointed at the defense table. "I don't even want to hear what that lawyer's going to say to try and get him off. I mean what he did to that girl and even…"

Heads in the audience nodded. The rest of the jurors clearly wanted to nod but refrained out of fear. The desire to move their heads showed mostly as widened eyes.

"You're excused. And will the rest of the jurors please disregard Mr. Clark's remarks," said the judge, clearly annoyed.

"Your honor, due to Mr. Clark's prejudicial remarks, I move this entire roster of jurors be dismissed and a new group brought in," said Connor's lawyer standing halfway up. Isaac Sutton also wore a gray suit, but it was wrinkled and had shiny elbows from wear. He looked fit but carried himself apologetically. Like tall people do sometimes, but he wasn't even that tall. Barely six feet.

46

"Goddammit Mr. Sutton, I said no shenanigans. Denied."

From such a narrow vessel, the judge could summon a very big voice. Mr. Sutton sat down and set his hand briefly on Connor's, as if to reassure. Connor flinched at the touch.

There was not a sound in the room. At least Connor's lawyer is fighting now, I thought. Interesting. Maybe the pre-trial silence was part of some too-complicated-for-me-to-understand strategy? Entirely possible given how rusty my instincts are.

"Go on Ms. Kupchak," said the judge.

The prosecutor nodded and resumed her dull but necessary questioning, and juror selection proceeded without any additional crises until the 10:30 a.m. break. Afterwards, the defense got to ask questions of the jury pool, some of which surprised me and one of which drew an objection. "Do any of you dislike wealthy people just because they have more than you?" brought Madison to her feet so fast it was like there was a string yanking her up. The judge allowed it, so the score was one to one between the lawyers at that point.

At twelve thirty on the dot, the judge announced a 30-minute recess for lunch. Although I was desperate for sunlight and fresh air, I needed to work. Finding an unoccupied bench in the hall, I ate my other muffin and pulled out my laptop to start my story. I typed in a few notes, but realized my mind was wandering. This always happens when I am tired and trying to process a lot at once, so I closed my eyes and let it wander. Maybe it would go someplace interesting.

After a minute it struck me that I hadn't seen any black people other than the bailiff. Where was Marcus' family? Surely someone would want to see his killer get what he deserved. I thought I read that Marcus was from Virginia Beach, which is not that far away. Just four hours or so. I opened my eyes and rifled through the print-outs of articles I had brought along and saw he had just an uncle left—Darrell Giminsky, his mother's brother. Darrell used to play in the NBA; he was the first graduate from Blue Ridge University to do so. He probably encouraged Marcus to come here and was now feeling a whole truckload of guilt. Marcus' parents died in a car crash last year, not long after the murder. Before that, they had threatened to sue the University for failing to keep their son safe. I wondered if that ever got filed, or if they talked to a lawyer? Maybe that's why the uncle wasn't there. I hadn't looked into civil suits, but I hadn't seen any mentioned in my research either. I should check with the clerk's office at the next break, I thought.

Now I had more leads to chase than columns inches for tomorrow. Not a good start. I stretched and twisted my back to try and relieve the pinch I felt. Two weeks of sitting on hard wooden benches was going to require high doses of Advil or some exercise—or probably both.

As I settled back into place, I saw a man in a wheelchair coming out of the bathroom.

It was Coach Haywood Ford, current men's basketball coach for Blue Ridge University. While he had coached in the NBA with moderate success, he had ended up at Blue Ridge at the twilight of his career. The party line was that because after a diagnosis of multiple sclerosis at 52—seven years ago—his doctors ordered him to leave coaching. Stress reduction is apparently the key to slowing the disease's progression. Haywood couldn't give up coaching entirely, so when the job opened up at Blue Ridge near his hometown of Charlottesville, he applied. The school was thrilled to have him, and he wouldn't have to give up everything he loved. It was the perfect compromise. There are no scholarships in Division III schools and no television contracts. In other words, no pressure other than just helping his players get better. Until now.

So much for the stress-reducing job. The MS had clearly gotten much worse after the murders. He wasn't in a wheelchair in the videos of Connor's games I watched. A couple of other coach-looking people were with him. Baseball caps and too-white sneakers and polyester shirts gave them away. I wondered if they would stay for the whole trial and when I should try and talk to them.

A kid walked over and waved his power cord and flashed me a big grin. He startled me out of my thoughts.

"Hi. Mind if I sit here? It's the closest bench to an outlet."

Back in the day, we would have called him a cub reporter. But they revised the personnel guidelines at the *Star* this year and a new rule said we could no longer refer to fledgling reporters as baby animals.

"Sure. I'm just leaving," I said and got up. His cologne or deodorant or hair gel or something was about to gag me.

"I'm sorry, if you'd rather I find somewhere else...."

"No, really, it's fine. I've got to go outside and make a call. See you back in there."

"Sure. Hey, who do you work for?"

"The *Star*," I said, flipping my press pass around for him to see.

"Wow."

"And you?" I asked out of politeness.

"The *Lynchburg Tribune*," he said, flashing his.

"And they have money to send a reporter and not just use the wires?"

"Not really. I'm an intern. I went to school here. Graduated last year. I'm staying with my parents," he said

"Ah. So, what was the mood on campus last year when this all happened?" I sat back down and held my breath.

"It didn't really affect the regular students. I mean it was an awful crime, but those jocks, who knows what they do." He looked me up and down and flushed. "Oh sorry, did you play basketball? I didn't mean to insult you."

People always asked me that, and I think they often meant to insult me just a little.

"Nope." I left out the fact that I was indeed a jock, just in a different sport. He didn't ask the broader question, though, and I didn't feel compelled to volunteer any information. People always assume that if I didn't play basketball, I didn't play any sport. Sure, swimming doesn't attract many non-whites, but still. I could have played volleyball or run track, both multi-colored sports, as I like to think of them.

"Oh, okay. Well anyway, so they live lives totally different from us. It wasn't like there was a crazed shooter randomly firing at people like at Virginia Tech. Or some serial killer."

Wow, I thought. That's a little harsh. But I kept my judgments to myself.

"Okay, well, that makes sense I guess," I replied instead. "So why are you here?"

"I want to make a name for myself and move up the ladder to more important stories."

"More important than life and death and justice?" I asked.

"Like there is any justice in a courtroom," he scoffed. "Anyway, I've got to send a couple of emails, and my battery is almost dead." He pulled his laptop and cord out of his flashy messenger bag.

"Okay. Well, it is important to have goals. Have a good day." I got up and left, feeling dismissed by the kid and a little ashamed. Something about hearing your own thoughts come out of someone else's mouth changes your perspective.

I walked over to the civil clerk's office to see if Marcus' parents had sued the University. Nothing had been filed. His uncle as next of kin could still do so, but I wondered if Darrell Giminsky had the appetite for it. He had a lot of loss to deal with and lawsuits often don't help with that.

The afternoon passed slowly, but by the end of the day, a jury had been picked and I had cobbled together an outline for my story. The lawyers ended up questioning almost everyone in the pool, which got a little more diverse as the day wore on. The judge kept everyone until a little after 7 p.m., despite his earlier announcement about ending at 5 pm, so the selection process wouldn't take more than one day.

"Court will convene at 9 a.m. for opening statements. Ms. Kupchak, I assume that you'll be ready and there will be no issues."

"Yes, your honor. That is my plan." She smiled.

"Court dismissed." Whack went the gavel.

It seemed like a decent jury for a small town; they had a mix of ages, jobs and education. One black juror, one Asian and one Hispanic. Nine whites of various shades and three white alternates.

I was starving, and everyone seemed tired. We slumped out of the courtroom. Connor was led back to jail, and his lawyer actually gave him a thumbs up. Arthur Braxton had already left. Maybe being in a courtroom gave him the heebie-jeebies. I had read he stood trial as a young man for running a gambling operation at Georgetown University. He, though, had a star lawyer that *his* daddy got him, and he was cleared of all charges. Maybe murder was harder to stomach for a parent. I set up camp on the same bench near that precious outlet and, using my outline, composed a quick 400 words for Alex on the town and the fact that a jury was already seated and that the judge looked like he was going to run a tight ship. I attached a photo of the courthouse. Nothing exciting, but a decent start. Enough to make the Star's readers keep an eye out for the next article.

Work completed, I walked back to the motel to get my car. Using my phone, I found an Applebee's and called Leo from the parking lot.

He answered before it rang on my end. "How are you? How's the dog?"

"I'm okay, and Charlotte is alive. That's all I know. Oh, and apparently, she is an American Staffordshire Terrier. A red nosed one."

"You found out her name? Does she have owners?"

Leo has a way of making everything dramatic and exciting and important, especially if it doesn't involve him. I used to think it was fake, but it isn't. He truly lives outside of himself and finds excitement in others, which I guess is why he is able to reach down and pull me up so often.

"Not that I know of. The vet just sent me a text saying Charlotte was alive. She named her. She told me I could name her before I left, but it was the middle of the night, and I wasn't too sure I knew my own name."

Leo laughed. "You could have named her after yourself and then you'd only have one name to remember."

I snorted. "That would be a little narcissistic. And confusing. It's not like I'm keeping her. I'll pay her vet bill and then..."

"Then what?"

I didn't know. "I'll see what Sam says and then I guess

take her to an animal shelter around here."

"Sam?"

"The vet."

"Boy Sam or girl Sam?"

"Girl Sam."

"Drat. I thought we might have a potential romance. Oh well. But you can't take her to a shelter."

"Why not?"

"If she doesn't get adopted, they'll kill her. Those rural shelters are overcrowded death camps, especially for pit bulls, which is what an American Staffordshire Terrier is called. Have you ever been to one?"

"No."

"I have. Trust me," Leo said with finality.

I didn't say anything. I needed a drink.

"You there?"

"Yeah, you just made me sad."

"I'm sorry. I bet the vet will help find her a home. Vets are soft-hearted."

"Not like me," I said, feeling ashamed.

"No, you are too, in your own way. You're just smart about what you can and can't handle."

We both sat there in silence for a while.

"How are you feeling?" I asked.

"I'm okay. My joints hurt a little worse than usual, but I think that's just because of the weather."

"You can come here. It's nice in the mountains."

"Nope! I am waiting for our weekend at the inn."

"Okay. Well, hang in there, and thanks for helping me

find that vet. You saved Charlotte's life."

"It was a team effort, and you're welcome. Has the trial been awful, by the way? I didn't mean to ignore your actual work."

"No, so far it's just been boring. They picked a jury without too much drama. No gruesome testimony and no tears. We'll see tomorrow, though. It's strange. I think Alex is right, there is a story lurking around here. But I don't know what it is, or how to chase it. It's like fog."

"Fog lifts with sunlight. You'll figure it out. Don't be in a hurry. Trust your instincts. And call me before the weekend and let me know when you are coming home."

"Okay. All good advice. Bye."

"Bye."

The problem was that I didn't really want to solve a mystery. I wanted to do my time, write my story and go home. Back to my life, such as it was. Writing obituaries had given me a new perspective. We will never know all the answers about a life. Or a death.

I went inside and found a seat at the bar. I watched the bartender make a half-dozen shooters from peach vodka and some slushy red stuff from a plastic pitcher. They looked disgusting. But he mixed them with flair and pride. He bore more than a passing resemblance to the blond one from *Starsky and Hutch*. I could never remember who was who.

"What'll you have?" he said, after he deposited the six shooters on a waitress' tray.

"Uh, just a beer, I guess." I wanted a scotch, but hard liquor on two muffins and no sleep wouldn't be the best idea. I scanned the taps. "A Sam Adams."

"Twelve, twenty or twenty-four ounces?" He wiped his

hands on his red vest in preparation.

It was like being at a Starbucks. "Twenty, I guess."

"Sure. No problem. Coming up." He whipped a glass from the rack above him and pulled my beer to the very brink of overflow but not beyond. It looked delicious.

"Thanks," I said, and he nodded back.

"Menu?" he asked.

"Sure."

I hadn't eaten in an Applebee's in years, but probably didn't actually need a menu. You don't get to be a grown up in today's world without knowing you can get a grilled chicken sandwich at any establishment that serves red slushy drinks. Still when the menu came, I took my time reading it and finally decided on that grilled chicken sandwich with a salad and French fries. When the food came, it wasn't bad, and I ate every bit of it.

At a little past 9:30 p.m. I pulled into the parking spot in front of my motel room. I drank a glass of water, rubbed a wet washcloth over my face, brushed my teeth, set the alarm and went to bed with an easy mind for once.

SIX

Wednesday, July 6

Awake before the alarm went off, I felt almost refreshed. There must be some truth in that old "early to bed, early to rise" saying, I thought, much as I hated to admit it.

I rolled out of bed in my underwear and T-shirt and did some sit-ups, push-ups and stretches on the only rectangle of carpet that could accommodate a full-sized human. Motel rooms are designed for short people, and it just isn't fair. I tolerate the fact that my head hits the top of my Corvette because it is a Corvette. The rest of the world is not as beautiful, so it should at least be functional. I headed into the bathroom, unwrapped a tiny bar of soap and tried not to bang into the shower head.

Still in my towel, I flipped on the morning news and checked my email. There was nothing interesting. Alex wrote that they ran the story with few changes and I clicked on the link to see it on the website. No photo. "Boring," she said of my image. "Looks like stock photography. People next time." She wanted 500 words for tomorrow. Easy enough, I thought. I sent an email to my colleague Jerry asking him if there were any fun places to eat in his hometown that didn't cost a fortune or push red fruity drinks. I didn't expect much of a response—Jerry mostly answers emails only when they are emergencies—but it was worth a shot.

I turned my attention back to the television in time for the weather. It was going to be identical to yesterday; clear and cool, but with a promise of an "afternoon warm up."

"You people don't know what an afternoon warm–up is," I said to the television. It didn't take an expert to notice that the mountains keep everything cooler here, plus there is no "city effect" from the concrete and lack of breezes. Washington, DC is lucky to have a lot of tree cover, but it doesn't do anything for the humidity. If I were at home, undoubtedly the air would feel like Jell-O. I resolved to at least enjoy the weather while I was here.

I took a second look at the talking heads on TV so that I would recognize them if I saw them at the trial. Calling the local people by name can charm them out of good information if it is done well. I rarely do things like that well, but it never hurts to be prepared. When I am reporting a story, I usually get my information the hardest way possible: by digging it out of piles of paper and piecing together terse answers and body language. If I got better at making people like me, it would make my job easier. Or at least that's what Jerry tells me. And since everybody likes Jerry, I guess I should take his advice.

I dressed in the same dark gray pants and a different shirt—short-sleeved turquoise linen that needed to be ironed—and headed out the door to my coffee and muffin place. Today, I didn't stop for motel coffee. It probably wouldn't taste as good after a full night's sleep. And I wanted a latte anyway. For me, some days are milky coffee days and some days are black coffee days. That always made my ex-husband Brian crazy; he said people should only take their coffee one way. That was the first red flag I missed. Two opinionated people probably don't make the best match. Someone needs to be agreeable.

The muffins at Sara's Kitchen – I noticed the name today - looked as good as they did yesterday, so I purchased two raisin bran ones along with that latte from the same college girl who was working yesterday. She must enjoy working the early shift, or else she's new and gets stuck with it. After eating, I headed over to the courthouse, and it looked like the same crowd was marching up the steps. None of the civilians were bored yet, and there were no other news stories big enough to pull the reporters away. Seeing everyone converge on the courthouse reminded me of those National Geographic specials where the zebras and wildebeests and elephants all visit the watering hole together.

I took approximately the same seat as before in the next to last row, and the bailiff called the court to order. We stood and sat again at the proper times—and I was reminded momentarily of church. The judge then took his seat, and I scanned the room. Connor's father wasn't there. I was floored. How could a parent abandon their child in a time of need? Well, come to think of it, my own father disappeared at a pretty bad time, but that was so much more complicated.

Maybe Connor really was a monster and yesterday was all his father could take. Although in my opinion it's more likely there was a crisis at the elder Braxton's office. No one gets as rich as Arthur Braxton by putting family first. Gina's family was still there in force, but again, no one was there for Marcus. I mean, I understand if you couldn't make the first day. Maybe you wanted to let things settle out. Maybe you hoped it was all a dream. But today; today the victims needed their people. If I were on the jury, I'd notice that.

I turned around in my seat as unobtrusively as possible. I also didn't see that cub reporter from Lynchburg; I guess he had better things to do to advance his career. So far, the only entries in the new people column were a pair of college kids in tie dyed T-shirts. Why the hippie look is back in style is beyond me. Face it, nobody looks good in a hurricane of blurry color. I am no snappy dresser, but at least my clothes don't have the potential to give unsuspecting passers-by a case of vertigo. The kids were taking notes, though, and looked quite serious. Then it hit me. They must be from the college newspaper. Good for them, I thought, and forgave the tie-dye.

I picked out the coach-type people again—three of them, but no Haywood this time. I made a mental note to try and interview them. One new addition was a concerned looking man in a suit, who had to be some unlucky administrator doing public relations duty.

My phone vibrated in my backpack and emitted a low buzz. It was another text from Sam the vet. Much shorter this time:

She's still fighting.

I smiled and slid my phone back into its spot. My heart was starting to root for Charlotte. My heart, though, I reminded myself, has regularly been an idiot in the past.

"All rise," intoned the bailiff.

We did, and the judge swept in. He nodded at the prosecution to begin its case. Madison Kupchak took her yellow legal pad, clicked her way over to the podium in her high heels and started the day.

Much like me, the prosecutor was wearing a copy of her outfit from yesterday: a navy suit and gray blouse with two-inch beige heels. Pearl necklace and plain gold studs for earrings, just like my mother always used to wear to court. As far as I could tell, Ms. Kupchak wasn't young, but she wasn't old. I'd guess around my age. Apparently, all the professional women in town that I encounter will be my age-ish. I wonder if they all feel like they aren't quite grown-up yet, even as they face the obvious deterioration of their bodies? Or is that just me? The way the prosecutor looked and carried herself revealed no doubts like that, and told me she'd present a competent, by-the-book case. She'd want to win fair and square. I never saw her glare at Connor, which would make me distrust her if I were a juror. In my opinion, how people look does tell you as much about them as what they say, if you look carefully and long enough. On the other side of the courtroom, the defense attorney looked no less wrinkled, although today he had more of a Colombo vibe, as if the look was on purpose. A way to distract and disarm. I sighed. We are all performing in life, whether we admit it or not. The trick is to be able to stop sometimes.

"Ladies and Gentlemen of the jury, my name is Madison Kupchak and I represent you, the people of this commonwealth, in their case against the defendant, Connor Braxton. Connor is accused of the premeditated killing of Gina Merguez and Marcus Walker on May 6th, 2015."

As I expected, she recited the facts with a minimum of drama and explained what the evidence would show. Some witnesses would place Connor at the scene, others would testify that his DNA was all over both bodies, and others still would report that he had a history of violence. The evidence would further show, she said, that Gina was Connor's girlfriend but that they were having trouble. Marcus was Connor's teammate who knew and liked Gina. A good student and a walk-on addition to the basketball team. Finally, the medical examiner would explain the details of the crime scene. It would be easy and correct to conclude after this evidence, that the crimes were gruesome enough to warrant "the state's most severe punishment."

The jury collectively swallowed and readied itself for the onslaught. They were all neatly dressed and skeptical. There wasn't one I'd want off no matter which side I was on. And I had no side, I reminded myself; the truth is not a partisan matter.

The prosecutor finished up after only taking seventeen minutes to present her opening statement. Then it was the defense's turn. Again, Isaac Sutton patted Connor on the arm as he got up, and again Connor flinched and then closed his eyes.

I really needed to find out what his prison medical records said. He just didn't look well. I fought the urge to leave right then and hunt down that story. If we as a society allow prisoners to be abused, we are failing.

In shoes that looked like they came from Walmart, Mr. Sutton walked to the podium with his own yellow legal pad. Unlike Madison, he actually flipped through it as he delivered his opening statement.

"Good Morning. My name is Isaac Sutton, and I am here today on behalf of the defendant, Connor Braxton. First, let me thank you for your service, ladies and gentlemen of the jury. Without you, our system simply would not work."

Oh brother, I thought. This will take forever. He's pandering, a quality I dislike intensely. I watched the jurors. Some looked pleased, even puffed up, at his compliment; others looked as if they wanted to roll their eyes. All he needs is one person on his side to get Connor off, though. One puffed-up ally.

"I apologize for the gruesome nature of some of the testimony you'll be hearing, but it is necessary. Connor is also deeply pained at the thought of reliving such a terrible night. Of course, he feels horrible about the deaths of his teammate and his girlfriend, but he, and I, do not believe they are entirely his fault."

The sound of a sharp inhale through clenched teeth came from the direction of Gina's family. I probably made a similar sound, but for a different reason. I mean, who starts out with "not *entirely* his fault?" The phrase is not very powerful, to say the least.

Isaac ran his fingers through his hair. "Alcohol, self-defense, and defense of Gina's honor, at least in his mind, all played a part in this tragedy for Connor. Yes, something snapped in him; all the testimony will show he wasn't himself the evening before the deaths. Why? We'll argue that Connor was worried about his relationship and his future in light of the ending of the school year. Everything was going to change, and this boy had already endured the loss of his mother only a few years earlier. He was confused. This situation was a tragedy, not a pre-meditated execution, which the state must prove it to be in order to get the extreme punishment they want. Look at Connor. He is a boy wracked with guilt. Yes, he is willing to spend many years in prison, but he should not have to pay the ultimate price. What purpose would it serve? There are far too many questions about what really happened in that room and the state will show you no evidence that these sad deaths were part of a plan Connor formed and then coldly executed. That is what you would have to find to convict my client of first-degree murder. And I do not believe you can find what isn't there. This was simply a terrible accident."

He looked at the jury for at least twenty seconds, which of course seemed like an eternity. Then he nodded, as if some compact was sealed between them all. "Thank you again for your service and for keeping an open mind as we move through this trial."

Isaac took his seat and flipped the pages of his legal pad back to where he started. There was silence for almost a minute. The motherless boy angle was a good one to introduce. I had to give him credit for that. But self-defense? Gina was five foot three and unarmed. I'd have to look up Marcus and see what was on his record. All I had read was that he was a good kid, but I was getting the feeling no one had done much digging on this case. I was going to have to work harder than I had planned.

"We'll take an hour and a half for lunch," the judge said without explanation and got up. The audience started funneling out the courtroom's double doors, which were held open by two large policemen.

An hour and a half. That is too long to sit by myself in a Wendy's, so I decided to try and catch some people for interviews.

Outside, Gina's family congregated at the bottom of the steps.

"Excuse me? Mrs. Merguez?" I said when I got near who I assumed was Gina's mother. She wore a new black dress, old brown oxfords and a purple scarf of indeterminate age.

"What do you want?" the woman asked with the kind of reflexive anger that comes with living with constant pain.

"My name is Gale Hightower and I am a reporter with the *Washington Star*. I wanted to ask you what you think of the trial so far and…"

"What do I think of the trial? That's your question? That's what you ask the mother of a dead girl? Why don't you ask me about what it's like to stand at the thrift store with a box of clothes and be unable to go in? Why don't you ask me what it is like to see your daughter's name dragged through the mud because she happened to love a boy who was a monster?"

I felt the slap of her words, as hard as any hand, and I was ashamed. I wasn't going to argue with her, although I certainly could have said I didn't ask you those questions because I know exactly how grief feels. But I should have been gentler. I should have started with an apology. An apology for being whole, for being alive.

"I'm sorry to have bothered you," was all I could say. It was too late to start over. All I could do was exit well. "Maybe, if you change your mind and want to talk later, to tell me about Gina, you can call me." I gave her my card. "Anytime."

She snatched it from my hand but at least she kept it. She would call, or stop me later this week, I guessed. She would want to have her say. Everyone wants to be heard, to be understood, in my experience. Gina's mother walked briskly away and her family followed in her wake.

"Why didn't you push harder?" asked the male of the tie-dyed pair of journalism students. They both appeared out of nowhere at my hip. Great. I didn't have the time or patience to be a teacher. I groaned silently.

"She's hurting, and there will be time later," I said, trying to sound wiser, and kinder, than I felt. "Plus, she still gave me a good comment."

"'Standing outside of the thrift store with Gina's clothes.' That does paint a strong image." He scribbled some notes. "I know who you are by the way," he said.

I turned around. "Okay. Who am I?"

"Gale Hightower. Olympic swimmer. Distance freestyle and butterfly."

"How do you know that?" I was truly startled.

"You stand out a little here. Also, my Dad swam. Albert Chin? And he used to talk about how great you were. He said you were coming up in the ranks when he was finishing his career. He swam a lot longer than most – the first man over 30 to swim in the Olympic trials. Anyway, when I saw Gale Hightower by-lines at the *Washington Star*, I wondered. Then I saw you today, and I took a leap of faith."

"What did you have to lose, right?" I said.

"Just a little face, and mine isn't my most prized possession. Of course, if my family still lived in Japan, I would be much more concerned."

"Assuming we all believe in stereotypes," I responded. I

64

liked his sense of humor, though, and decided to cut him some slack. "I remember stories of your Dad, by the way. An excellent backstroker."

Chin never made it to the Olympics thanks to the US boycott of the Moscow1980 Games. What happened to those athletes always broke my heart. I mean, I lost my chance to swim, but it was my own fault. They were political pawns. It was a sad, awful mess. Sports are supposed to be above politics. Above everything.

I pulled myself back to the present. "I'm pleased to meet you. What's your name?" I stuck out my hand.

"Bennett. Same last name as Dad." We shook.

"Hi Bennett. Who's your friend?"

"Jill."

"Stapleton," she said, sticking out her hand. I shook it, too.

"So, you two are working for the college paper?" I said. I wanted to change the subject.

"Yup. We've been on this story since the beginning. Some of Jill's articles have been picked up by the Associated Press." Bennett beamed.

They have to be dating, I thought.

"I thought I recognized your name," I said, lying a bit. Now she beamed. There was a whole lot of beaming going on all of a sudden. It felt nice.

"Well, I hope we can chat later, but I am going to run and try to catch a couple of interviews." I looked around and saw that everyone was mostly gone.

Bennett seized his opportunity like a seasoned pro. "Since there doesn't seem to be anyone left to talk to, why don't we give you a campus tour? I don't want the world to think we are just this trial. This is a good place to go to school."

He was right; everyone I might want to talk to had left, and a tour might be a very good use of a couple of hours. "Sure. Let's go," I said.

Bennett and Jill actually clapped their hands with glee. I raised my eyebrows, plucked my backpack off the ground and followed. As we walked toward the campus, Bennett gave me a rundown of the place as if he was chairman of the campus chamber of commerce. So much energy and optimism. I hoped he could hold on to both.

"You have a very practiced delivery. Do you give tours to incoming freshmen?" I asked.

"Yes, although they don't usually listen very well."

"They have other priorities," I agreed. "What's that building?" I pointed to a large brick building with columns and a dome that echoed Monticello. The dome was copper instead of white, though, and I liked it better.

"It used to be the library but now it's the foreign language building."

"It's lovely. So is the entire campus," I said. We could see most of it since we were on a hill and had a panoramic view of the valley, which cradled the main part of campus like a baby in a crib.

"You know, I think I saw him at a party once," Jill said.

"Who?" I asked, confused.

"Connor."

"Ah, yes, of course. I had forgotten why we were here for a minute. Anything to report?" I asked.

"He was by himself and he was just sitting there in a chair listening to the music. Then in the middle of a song, he got up and heaved the stereo against the wall and walked out," said

Jill. "I guess he didn't like the song, or he was stewing about something. But it was scary."

"Yikes. I'd read he had a history of violence. Nothing that got him arrested, though, right?" I offered.

"No one would arrest him whether or not he deserved it. His daddy practically built the new science building. After that, a couple of campus cops were assigned to kind of watch him and run interference. They were supposed to clean up messes and keep the city cops away from him if anything happened."

"I hadn't seen that. Did you report on it?"

"No, I'm saving it. I'm also kind of nervous about losing my scholarship if I make the administration too mad," she admitted.

I rolled my eyes. "This isn't China, for goodness sake. We have freedom of the press. If I give you a credit, can I use it? You'd need to show me your evidence, though. I mean if the school knew about Connor's behavior and covered it up, that is explosive stuff. They could be liable."

I thought of Mrs. Merguez and Darrell Giminsky. Money wouldn't stop the pain, but it would punish people who needed it.

"Plus, if it's in the *Star*, that would surely protect you from any scholarship problems."

Jill's eyes lit up.

"Deal!"

I hope I hadn't promised too much. We walked to the student union where the paper had its offices. On the way, we passed the pool, and the odor of chlorine was strong enough to penetrate the clear mountain air and the locked door to my own memories.

"Do you swim?" I asked Bennett.

67

"Nope. I mean I know how, but I don't love it."

"Fair enough." I dropped it. "Hey, why do you guys think Connor is so thin now?"

"I figure it's just the no-beer diet. There is a big drinking culture here," Jill said.

When Bennett opened the door to the paper's office, memories of my first journalistic baby steps at UNC came flooding back. Sure, there were more computers now, but the desks and bad lighting were the same. There was still the smell of ink and paper, and colored flyers for various activities and groups were taped up everywhere. The sense of possibility nearly overwhelmed me.

Jill handed me a file of notes. "These are copies," she said to my raised eyebrows.

"Excellent. I was going to lecture you about giving away your notes."

She smiled again. "They are the interviews I did with people who saw Connor being violent. A smashed chair at a party, an intentional car wreck, other stuff like that. No one actually got visibly hurt in any of them, so I think that's another reason he got away with so much."

I flipped through those notes. Things looked sound. Everything was dated, and the medium of the interview—in person, by email, or on the telephone—was noted. "I'll have to check in with these people, but I think we can run this. Definitely. Good work. How did you find these people?"

"One came to me, another is a friend of a friend on Facebook and I saw a post that I asked her about, and this guy," she pointed "is a teaching assistant. I was just in the right place at the right time, waiting for his office hours, and I heard a phone conversation. So, I asked him about it."

"And he talked to you?"

"I didn't tell him I was a reporter," Jill said looking at the floor.

"Uh. Questionable, but I don't blame you. Hey, I'm starving. Is there decent food in this building?"

"No, there isn't decent food on the whole campus," Bennett said.

Jill rolled her eyes. "Bennett is a food snob. There are a couple of better than average fast food places in the basement. The food won't kill you."

"At least not right away," added Bennett.

"Ok. Well, I'll manage. Want to come?" I asked.

"No, we'll work a bit and see you back in the courtroom."

I left and found a chicken sandwich that was edible. Is that all I'm going to eat this week, I wondered?

I made it back to the courthouse with a few minutes to spare. When we re-convened, the judge ordered the prosecution to call their first witness. The first officer to the scene took the stand. It was a boring recitation of facts. Then it was the defense's turn to cross, and it all got a little more interesting.

"Have you ever seen a crime scene with dead people, Officer Smith?" Mr. Sutton asked.

"No."

"Maybe it was a little traumatic, a little confusing this first time?"

"No. Not at all. I knew what to do, and I did it. We are trained for this with simulations and actors. I even went to a law enforcement conference with a virtual reality session of a mass shooting. I was able to rely on my training and cool my emotions and notice what needed to be noticed and record it."

This was going badly, was this all Isaac had?

Isaac decided to pull out a stapled stack of papers and showed it to the witness. "Is this your signature on the initial report?"

"Yes."

Officer Smith was proving to be well trained as a witness as well as a cop.

Isaac asked him to flip to page four. "Did you write the line there about halfway down that says: "It looks like there was quite a struggle?"

"Yes."

"So maybe Connor did have to defend himself, maybe there was a real battle?"

"I couldn't say. Maybe the victims didn't want to die and fought back. All I know is the defendant had no defensive wounds. I wrote that here," the witness said, pointing.

Ouch, I thought.

"But could there have been a struggle between Ms. Merguez and Mr. Walker; maybe Connor had to intervene?"

"Objection! Relevance! Speculation!" Madison was on her feet.

"I'll allow it."

Isaac waited. Officer Smith looked at Madison who nodded once.

"Maybe, but I don't think so," he said.

The rest of the cross went about the same, with Isaac possibly planting a seed or two of doubt in the jury's mind that Connor was not completely evil. I had seen better lawyers, and I had seen worse. Apparently, Officer Smith was going to be our only witness today. The judge banged his gavel.

"I have a one-day trial I have to hear tomorrow. We will resume on Friday."

Everyone seemed a little startled by the fact we had the day off tomorrow. I was too, but I was also thrilled. I was itching to do something more active than watch a trial. I went back to the motel and typed out a quick story and sent it via email to Alex. The first paragraph was a little dry but serviceable:

The trial of Connor Braxton officially began today with opening statements from counsel and testimony from the first police officer on the scene. The defense has chosen to admit that Connor killed Gina Merguez and Marcus Walker but that the crimes did not amount to first-degree murder. Connor looked much thinner than in his playing days, and the defense seems to be using that to their advantage by outfitting him in oversized suits. His father, Arthur Braxton, owner of Millennium Development, wasn't present at trial today.

I also sent a couple of photos I had taken of the exterior of the courthouse with Connor getting out of the sheriff's car in the bottom right. I quite liked the artistry of them, and the light was good, so they may run one. I told Alex we had the day off tomorrow and that I was going to do some real reporting.. She immediately wrote back:

"Don't do anything stupid. You are out of practice."

"Thanks for the vote of confidence," I typed. "I met some journalism students who may have some interesting leads, and I want to check out the prison."

"I know I sent you there to dig around, but keep focused on the trial," Alex wrote. "Don't forget the human-interest stuff. Watch the people. We may have to run something in the Style

Section, too. Too many people are on vacation, damnit."

I chose not to respond. The Style Section? My work wedged cheek to jowl with celebrity news and the TV schedules? No thanks. I think Alex just likes to keep me slightly pissed off. She knows I do my best work that way. We all do. It is a fine balance between not caring and having too much emotion that it blinds you.

Before I logged off, I decided to try You Tube for any more game videos of Connor and the team. Kids these days video everything, right? I typed "Blue Ridge University basketball" into the search engine and got dozens of hits, including a clip of Patsy Cline singing "Blue Moon" in case I didn't really want what I typed. Only about half a dozen looked helpful, and I clicked on the most promising. It was from 2013, Connor's sophomore season. I hit play and watched all three minutes and 18 seconds.

He was a skinny, rangy kid then. Not bad, not good, as far as I could tell. Nothing stood out in his play or demeanor. I clicked on another video from 2014, and he was much bigger, but then again so was everybody. Kids grow up, I guess. It was a four-minute clip, and I played it several times, so I could focus on different players and look for people on the bench and in the stands. I don't think I got much out of the footage, other than seeing Marcus alive. He was a nice-looking kid. In the last clip I watched, the announcers commented that Connor had become known for using his body: "As a freshman Braxton had a great outside shot, but his weakness was making plays in the paint. He has more than fixed that! Look at him claim his territory," the voice said with the same kind of excitement one might use to talk about a prize steer or a fighting dog.

I thought of Charlotte and winced. I watched the video over and over trying to look for Connor "claiming his territory."

This is a waste of time, I thought and shut down the computer. Basketball didn't kill Gina and Marcus.

I changed into knee length shorts – I think they were designed to be capri pants on someone more regular sized - and a T-shirt and went back to Applebee's. I started with a scotch this time. On the drive over, I decided I needed something stronger than a beer to help me puzzle through the past two days and my plan for tomorrow. It would just be one, though.

SEVEN

Thursday, July 7

I stayed far too long at Applebee's pretending to watch the baseball game when I was really watching the crowd. I did notice, at least, that the Nationals beat the Braves, four to one.

Sitting and watching people is a personal and professional passion. Leo calls it spying. There are always so many micro-dramas playing out in any public space. Flirtations, fights, and fake friendships abounded last night, and I was entertained. A guilty pleasure to be sure, but I also rationalized it as research. Some of which might even make it into a Style Section piece.

I decided to take a trip out to the prison to learn what kind of place it was and what kind of prisoner Connor was. My rusty instincts were arguing that his weight loss might be part of a larger problem at the prison. It was a bit of a tangent, but since I had the day off – and I don't like seeing people treated badly, even when they may deserve it – I wanted to check it out.

Since it was after 8 am, I called the main number for the prison and asked for the chaplain. In my experience, prison chaplains are the ones with the most information and are also the most willing to share it, if they trust you and you don't ask them to share anything told to them in confidence. I got a recording and left a message saying I would like to come by at 11 a.m. and gave my number in case that was inconvenient.

I ran through my mini exercise routine of push-ups, sit-ups, lunges and stretching, just to get the blood flowing. Then I showered and headed back to Sara's Kitchen for a coffee and a muffin. To get me through the day, I had settled on black jeans and an elbow-length light blue shirt with buttons all the way to the hem. It wasn't very summery, and it made my arms look ridiculously long, but I knew again from experience that I wanted a modest ensemble for the trip to the prison.

Sitting down with black coffee this time and a cranberry oatmeal muffin, I saw Connor's lawyer come in. He ordered and scanned the room as he waited. He looked at me with a blend of recognition and confusion, so I got up and walked over.

"Gale Hightower," I said, sticking out my hand. "I'm covering the Connor Braxton trial for the *Washington Star.*"

"Isaac Sutton," he said, shaking my hand with the appropriate amount of vigor. Like everyone else, I distrust weak handshakes, but I also hate those bone-crusher ones which a certain kind of man always feels compelled to throw my way.

"Would you like to join me?" I asked.

Isaac seemed conflicted – which made sense - but agreed to sit down. Some lawyers love to talk to reporters, and some think we are poison. The cashier handed him his chocolate chip muffin and black coffee, and he followed me to my tiny table.

"A guilty pleasure," he said as he sat down referring to the muffin.

"Nothing wrong with chocolate for breakfast," I said.

"Yet, you got the healthy one," he countered.

"It was a tossup."

"For me, too," he said.

"So, did the judge really have another trial today, or did he just want to play golf?" I asked to move the conversation off of food.

Isaac laughed so hard he snorted. I loved it. Nobody snorts on purpose. A snort is an honest reaction. I waited for him to gather himself.

"It is definitely a trial, but you do have him pegged. He will not hesitate to do what he wants. Good intuition. I guess that's why you make the big bucks," Isaac said.

"Not so much big, but it is nice to still have work in a dying industry. Speaking of which…"

Isaac laughed again, but he was ready for my attempts at humor now, so no snorting. I just waited. Sometimes you don't have to ask an entire question, a trick I learned from my father.

"The trial is going as well as can be expected," Isaac said flatly.

"Do you mind if I take a few notes?"

"Not at all," he gestured to my backpack. I pulled out my pen and notebook.

"Are you pleased with the jury?"

"Yes, I think so. I only hope once they see all the evidence, they will agree that second-degree murder is the only verdict that is just."

A standard question got me a standard answer. I'd need to go deeper.

"Why aren't you aiming higher?" I asked.

"What do you mean?"

"Well, I mean that you made a good point yesterday with Officer Smith about how the scene was chaotic and could support alternate theories—self-defense, or a struggle between Marcus and Gina. Maybe that angle could get Connor manslaughter or even acquitted on all charges?"

"I don't think many other people thought it was a very good point. And Connor's father and I decided it wouldn't be advisable to go for an acquittal. It would just make the jury mad if we argued his innocence. And an angry jury is more likely to impose the death penalty. It's like playing small ball instead of swinging for the fences. I occasionally can't help myself, though. Old defense lawyer habits die hard." He smiled, and I couldn't quite read what he meant.

"Huh. Okay. What does Connor think?"

"I can't really answer that except to say that he is very sorry that two people he cared about are dead."

We ate and sipped our coffee for a couple of minutes as I mulled my next question and waited for the caffeine to kick in.

"How much has Arthur been involved in the trial strategy?" I asked.

"I can't answer that. That's privileged information."

"Okay, well, do you like him?"

"Who?"

"Fair enough. Either one. Father or son."

Isaac considered his words, knowing as he must that they would find their way into print. "I like being a defense lawyer. No matter what the evidence looks like, everyone deserves someone by in their corner when the state comes after them." He paused. "I respect Arthur Braxton, and I feel sadness at the ruined life that Connor faces." He ate the rest of his muffin and picked up his trash and coffee. "It was nice to meet you Gale. I have to run, or I would be happy to continue our conversation," Isaac said.

"Okay. Nice talking with you. Thanks for your time." I said the last part to his back.

Happy to continue our conversation my ass, I thought. But I was pleased I got something. Covering this trial is as much about me getting back into Alex's good graces as it is the story, I reminded myself for the umpteenth time. Connor obviously killed Gina and Marcus. There is no killer running loose and no possibility of an innocent man going to jail. So, a few things seem strange. Life is strange.

I walked back to the motel to get my car and headed out Route 71 to the state prison. Strange or not, I had nothing better to do. There may or may not be a story there, but at least I would not have wasted a day of expenses. Connor should have been in the county jail, but they thought he'd be safer out here, plus I had read that the jail was undergoing renovations to remove lead paint. A state prison is a much scarier place than a county jail, but the defense agreed to it. Another confusing thing about Isaac's tactics, although I guess he didn't have many options.

With classic rock on the radio, the trip on the empty and smooth road was lovely until I got close to the prison. I *felt* the vacuum before I saw any other signs there was a prison nearby. Then the dense trees and undergrowth suddenly gave way to an unnatural vastness. I'm not a very spiritual person; dealing with what is physically in front of me at any given time usually takes all of my energy. But here the pressure of all those imprisoned souls butting up against the nothingness was crushing.

Shaking off the willies, I pulled into a visitor's parking space fifteen minutes before my appointment, which I hoped I had, given that I hadn't talked to an actual person. There was an enormous number of cars in the giant lot. It looked like the parking lot for Disneyland. Most of the cars had seen their glory days decades earlier. My Corvette may be vintage, but these cars were plain old. I checked my phone, and there was no call back. Which meant either the time was fine, or the chaplain hadn't gotten my message. Then I locked my doors and stuffed my CDs under my seat. No need to tempt anyone.

I counted five guard towers. Two guards were stationed in each tower. One had a gun and one had a pair of binoculars. It seemed most of the binoculars were currently pointing at me, but I was probably imagining it. There were a couple of dreary exercise yards fenced off from each other. They were just bare dirt and one concrete pad with a basketball hoop. No net. They were empty at the moment, which was 10:50 a.m. The cluster of buildings—one giant one, which I guessed was the actual prison and two satellite buildings which housed God knows what—seemed built to be depressing, even on a sunny day like today. Low-slung and gray, the prison looked a bit like a badly designed high school, if you took away the razor wire and guard towers.

The whole compound sucked something out of the air, and I couldn't tell what it was. Color, light, life, or a combination of all three. My father used to say I was like a wild animal caught in a trap when I didn't want to be somewhere—I'd chew my own leg off to get away. So maybe I was projecting a little. I couldn't imagine the horror of being in jail. I took a minute, gathered myself into a more professional and detached frame of mind and headed for the main entrance.

Getting through security was relatively painless, except for the full up and down stare from one of the guards. He needed to learn to be more respectful of women, but I couldn't think of a way to teach him that quickly without causing a scene. After I was escorted through the last in a series of locked gates, I felt a wave of panic, as if I was going to spend thirty years here and not thirty minutes.

The guard told me to wait in a row of plastic chairs in a hall and that "my party would be called." My party's name was Darius Hood, prison chaplain. I am not much of a fan of organized religion, but even before meeting Mr. Hood (Reverend? Minister? Sir? I hoped he would tell me which to use) I was ready to like him. Anyone who chooses to try and help people in this environment can use any tool they want as far as I am concerned. God, or the devil and anything in between.

About five minutes later, at 11 a.m. on the dot, the chaplain arrived. Mr. Hood had on jeans and a blue button-down with a very subtle white banded collar. It was just enough to signify his profession. No shouting about it, which I liked. He looked about fifty, but a young fifty. His hair and shoes were gray. He wore two diamond studs in his ears, and he was about my height. We could have been twins, except that he was white. With a name like Darius I had him pegged as a black man.

"Hello, Ms. Hightower. I'm Darius," he said as he approached. "I'm looking forward to showing you around. We don't get nearly enough interest from reporters."

"Ouch," I responded. "Call me Gale."

"I didn't mean it like that. Sorry. I just like to talk about what we do here."

"That's good for me," I said shaking his hand to ease the awkwardness. "So, are you a reverend, a father or what? My religious education was minimal," I confessed.

"I'm ordained in the Episcopalian church, but most of what I practice here is non-denominational spirituality mixed with a little self-help. I'm not sure I could go back to a church and a congregation. So, I just go by Darius. Would you like a tour, or would you prefer to go straight to my office for our chat?"

I'd be stupid to refuse a tour, but I really didn't want to walk through the prison. I took a deep breath. "A tour would be great."

"Nothing about this place is great, but I'll give you a feel for the layout in general population. Connor is in a separate wing, and we won't be able to go there."

"That's fine." I hadn't expected to be able to see him without Isaac present, and I was pretty sure I didn't want to even if his lawyer was there. Some things are easier to deal with in the abstract. "May I take some notes as we walk?"

"Certainly. I can't remember anything without notes, not at my age."

"How long have you worked here?" I asked.

"Eighteen years tomorrow."

"Wow. Happy anniversary."

"Thanks. If this were a marriage, in two more years, I get silver or china or something. Right?"

I laughed. Darius was being charming, but there was not enough charm in the world to make up for the rows of cages I could see when the hallway opened up into a large room the size of an airplane hangar. All I could think of was that this kind of place is where my father spent much of his youth. Maybe that's why I have such a physical reaction; he certainly passed on a lot of his DNA to me. I did my best to hide it, although I was sure Darius noticed. So far, he was polite enough to ignore it.

"Several of these guys actually do improve while they are here. That's what keeps me going. I mean, their lives were so awful outside that the routine of this place and the relative safety is a step up. It gives them enough stability to work towards a goal."

We walked up a metal staircase and came out into the medical area. Darius fumbled for his keys and unlocked his office door.

"I can't leave to go to the bathroom with locking the door. Prison policy. If there is one thing that frustrates me about this job enough to consider leaving, it's the huge number of rules." He sat down and stretched back in his chair, gesturing to me to take the chair across from him. "So, you want to know about our famous and tragic basketball player."

"I am curious about how he has handled his time here. He looks pretty awful in court."

"Rest assured, he is not being abused or neglected in any way. We keep him out of the general population, as I mentioned."

"And the guards?" I pressed.

"Our guards are pretty decent. There is the regular amount of race and class tension but nothing more. I would have heard if there was a plan to punish Connor."

I liked that he wasn't afraid to mention race. "What about food and medical care? He has lost so much weight."

"Well, we don't serve beer," he said, echoing Jill and Bennett's opinion on the cause of Connor's weight loss. "A lot of the guys lose weight in here, if they aren't specifically trying to bulk themselves up as a way of coping. The food isn't exactly tempting."

"Has he visited you? I'm not asking what you talked about, just if he's taking advantage of the resources…"

Darius looked at me, as if considering whether to answer. "He has visited me. Twice. Once in the beginning of his incarceration and once last month."

He volunteered nothing further, so I changed the subject.

"Tell me about some of your success stories." And the floodgates opened. He wasn't exactly bragging on himself, he just seemed to want people to know what was possible. I took some notes, he thanked me again for my time. I got up to leave. It was all rather anti-climactic. I was going to ask him about drugs, but I didn't feel I'd get a straight answer. At least not this time.

"Is it okay if I come back, maybe next week?" I asked.

"Next week I am on vacation, but after that, sure," Darius said.

I hoped the trial would be over by then. "Okay, well, thanks for your time. Maybe we can do a follow-up after the trial. A feature on your work here." It would be good for me and him. I would pitch it to Alex.

"That would be great. Just call and let me know."

"Will do."

We shook hands again and that was that. For now.

A new guard arrived to escort me out. I got to my car and pulled out of the parking lot and back onto the road as fast as possible without squealing the tires.

The afternoon slid by, filled by writing. I spent more time than usual on the craft of the sentences, which was both a treat and a giant pain in the neck. I mentioned that Connor was being kept separate from the general population, but I left the rest of my interview with Darius for another time. It seemed like a dead end, at least regarding Connor. Whatever caused his appearance to change so drastically, I didn't think it was mistreatment at the prison.

That evening, I went to visit Charlotte. I was excited and curious about seeing her. I had called the vet's office earlier, and they said she was conscious and stable and that Sam would be back after 6pm. When I got to the clinic at 6:30 p.m., Sam was at the front desk waiting for me. Her ponytail looked like it had been mauled by a pack of angry squirrels. I wondered how she manages to leave every night. She probably gets a case like Charlotte every day, or something worse.

"Hi Gale," Sam said without looking up for the chart she was working on. "She might look worse than when you last saw her. We had to shave part of her head and her skin is kind of mottled under there and she burst blood vessels in both eyes thanks to crazy blood pressure swings and well, of course, she's missing a leg now."

I cringed. "It sounds pretty bad. Nobody has looked for her?"

"Not a soul. And nobody will, I don't imagine. Out in the country, if a dog doesn't come home, people don't go looking for her. They know what happened to her, and they'll get another one if the kids cry too much. Otherwise, they are usually happy they now have one less chore."

Sam closed her eyes and rubbed her right one with the back of her hand. "Sorry. I try not to talk like that. It was a long day."

I didn't ask what happened because I didn't want to know. "I'm sorry. Do you have a partner, or is it just you handling all this?"

"Do you mean in life or in the practice? No, I know you mean here. I'm just messing with you. No need to get all in each other's private business, right? Stick with the animals." She smiled. "I did have a partner, but she retired last year. I get by on vet student interns and spectacular vet techs. Follow me to see your sweet, lucky dog."

I followed Sam through the swinging door past the exam rooms to a row of metal cages. The "your dog" comment didn't get past me, but I let it go.

"Here she is," Sam swept her hand out as if she were revealing a prize on the *Price is Right* instead of a pile of flesh held together by some fur and staples. Charlotte was lying on a raised mesh bed with what looked like someone's old mattress pad that had been bleached within an inch of its life as a blanket.

"Will you look at that, she's wagging her tail," said Sam. "She hasn't bothered doing that for any of us and we give her pain meds and food. Huh. That's amazing. She remembers you."

"Seriously? I'm the one who *hit* her." But damnit yes, that three-legged, half-shaved dog with an oversized head was wagging her tail and looking dead at me with her bloody eyes. It was disconcerting. She paused the wagging, which was slow to begin with, and lifted her head briefly to make sure I got the message. It clearly took too much energy to do both together. She set her head back down and resumed wagging for a few seconds until it exhausted her. If we weren't in a hospital, I'd say she looked almost content, like she was just waiting for something she knew would happen. She was biding her time and paying her dues. But... I couldn't have a dog. I needed help caring for a bird.

"You're also the one who saved her. Animals are very different from us; they remember the positive. Usually," Sam added. "This one seems special, and she seems attached to you. She's eating canned food and keeping it down. Her vitals have been steady for the last twenty-four hours, so we must have stopped all the internal bleeding. And she likes the chicken I brought her today," Sam said. "I think she's out of the woods." She cocked her head at me, trying to read my look. Good luck with that, I thought. I don't even know what my look says.

"I think you're just trying to pawn her off on me," I blustered. "A three-legged dog is a big responsibility. And that other hind leg still looks pretty bad..."

"Nope. Three legged dogs get along just fine, and she'll keep that other leg. She'll limp, but she'll have it. And three-legged dogs attract other people like flies to honey. You'll have so many new friends."

Oh God, I realized. Leo will love her. The more broken, the better. But Hawk? Hawk would dedicate himself to making her life miserable. The thought made me chuckle a bit.

"She should be smarter about cars now, too. That's a good thing," says Sam, as if that settled it.

"It seems a heavy price to pay for a little wisdom," I said.

"A leg for your life? Nah. That's a deal any dog would take, and any human should. Scarred but smarter, I say. If you don't take her, she'll have to go to the pound once she'd healed."

"You can't keep her here?" I asked.

"No, I wish I could, but no. We're lucky to not be too full now, but things can get crazy here. We run one step ahead of bankruptcy as well. Can't afford the mouth. If I kept all the sad cases, well, I'd never be able to help anyone else."

"But with her past...."

"Look," Sam said, getting a little exasperated. "It doesn't really matter. We try and figure out a dog's past as a parlor game. Dogs live in the present. What matters more for Charlotte is her future. That's should be true for people, too."

We stood there in silence for a while. I reached in to pet Charlotte on the good side of her head, and she wagged her tail again.

"How much will I owe you?" I asked.

"Let's call it $500, if you take her home."

"That seems pretty cheap for all the work you did."

"You're right. It is a $5,000 bill if you don't take her and I have a good lawyer and I will collect," Sam grinned at me.

"Does blackmail figure into your work often?" I asked.

"All the time. Don't mess with a pro."

I really liked this woman. "I'm in a motel now; I won't go home for good until the Connor Braxton trial is over."

"Ah. Okay. Well, she won't be able to travel for a few days anyway. Is that your car?"

My yellow Corvette was visible through the window.

"Yeah."

"Huh. We'll need to rig something for you so she'll be safe for the drive back. But there is plenty of time for that. Come into my office and we'll fill out the paperwork. I know the guy who runs the shelter. We'll make up a few things, but it will seem as if you adopted her from them."

"Sneaky."

"We do what we have to do."

I was adopting a dog. A damaged dog. What a pair we'd be. I wondered how she'd get along with Frankenpoodle, my nickname for the ancient tiny brown dog of indeterminate ancestry owned by my neighbor, Mr. Rivers. He was always walking her. Or him. Mr. Rivers already didn't like me. He said my car was too noisy.

"How do you think she'll be with other dogs?" I asked Sam, thinking Charlotte might want to eat Frankenpoodle.

"Probably fine, but a lot of that depends on you. Don't over-protect her, and don't freak out that she is a pit-bull. Other people might, and you just have to ignore them." She looked me up and down. "But you look sensible. Trust her and you'll both be fine."

"Okay." I felt complimented and admonished at the same time. I sat in the guest chair while Sam printed some documents and searched for a pen. The snowball was rolling downhill, and I apparently couldn't stop it. I guess I didn't want to. I don't believe in fate, but I do believe in happy accidents.

With everything settled and Sam doing the paperwork, I looked around and noticed a lot of basketball photos. "You like basketball?"

"Yup. And even if I didn't, I date the head coach for the

university – Haywood Ford - so I had better be able to fake it."

"I don't imagine you are very good at faking anything," I said. Sam grinned, shrugging her shoulders in agreement. "What's your take on the trial?"

She put the pen down.

"It all makes me so sad. For everyone. I mean I know it's the most awful for the victims and their families, don't get me wrong, but Haywood has taken it hard. The wheelchair wouldn't have been necessary probably for another couple of years. Stress speeds up the progression of MS, of everything really. I'm just hoping when the trial is over, we can go back to normal and the team can have a regular season this year. I see a lot of death. I guess I am a pragmatist. I know it sounds bad, but I didn't really know the kids he killed, and I tend to look toward the future, like I said. I mean, Connor needs to go to prison forever, sure, but then everyone needs to move on. It's been over a year. I just hope Haywood doesn't give up and retire. He's too young to sit around and that assistant of his—Kevin Battier—isn't ready to lead a fifth-grade field trip if you ask me."

My ears pricked up. "Why do you say that?"

"I don't know. I just don't trust him. There is something about the way he carries himself." She shook her head as if to wake herself up. "But I may not be a good judge of people anymore. I probably spend too much time with dogs. I hope I am right to like you."

"Some people say animals have the best instincts," I offered.

"I would absolutely agree with that."

"I guess you'd have to in your line of work."

"It helps. Anyway, back to Charlotte. I'll want to send you home with a course of antibiotics and a small dose of steroids to help with the inflammation and to build some muscle back. They will make her pee a lot and be hungry all the time, which is also good in her condition. I don't want her to lose her appetite."

I almost slapped my forehead. Steroids. Of course. How could I have been so blind? That would explain a lot about the over-the top violence of the murder scene, Connor's record of outbursts in college, and his change in playing style. 'Roid rage' it's called. Some people react badly to steroids or just take too much. I don't know the science, but anecdotally, as an athlete, we all saw plenty of roid rage. Usually in track and field or football, but anyone could be tempted. Connor's use of steroids also might explain the weight loss if he couldn't keep using in prison. It hadn't been mentioned in the jury selection; in fact, there were no questions about performance enhancing or illegal drugs at all. But Connor had to have been using steroids, I thought. It explains everything too well. It is the missing link! But why? Blue Ridge is a Division III school; there is minimal glory at this level and no chance of a pro career. No reason to risk your health.

Sam was waiting, staring at me. "Are you stuck?"

"No, no sorry. I mean, well, yes. I was just thinking about something else for a moment. Sorry. This all sounds good." I fumbled for my wallet.

Sam held her hands up. "Pay me later. We have a deal; that's all I was looking for today, although my accountant might disagree. I'm happy for you both," she said.

"Thanks. Me, too," I said. And I really was. I just had a little work to do now.

EIGHT

Friday, July 8

When I woke up, I was confused. Okay. Make that more confused than usual. If Connor was taking steroids, surely that would have come out already. If he was injecting, that is just too hard to hide. But, then again, he didn't have a roommate. No one shared his bathroom, so no one would find the needles. And Blue Ridge is in Division III of the NCAAs—they don't drug test in DIII. He wouldn't have to worry about getting caught, so he wouldn't have to fuss with masking agents, the additional drugs that can hide steroid use.

A trial is a game of hide the truth and whoever is better at it wins. Both Connor's lawyer and the prosecutor might know about the steroid use—but maybe they each decided it wouldn't help their case. I had to find out if they knew. Well, first I would have to find out if my theory was true. And for that, I was on my own until I figured out who to trust.

I showered and went back to Sara's Kitchen – I was feeling like a regular—and was happy to see a peanut butter oatmeal muffin. I never had one before, but it sounded filling and I was starving.

"Anything else?" asked the young woman at the register. A new one this time.

"A large latte."

"Sure. That will be $9.10."

I handed her $11.00 and proceeded to wolf down my breakfast. One of the benefits of being so tall is that even at 41 I have yet to see a need to watch what I eat. My body seems to take care of itself without much supervision from me. It's the head and the heart that need attention. Probably the liver too. But I knew I had to get my act together for Charlotte. With Sam's words about how she would follow my lead echoing in my head, I realized I had a responsibility not only to her, but to all those other creatures—human and animal—we interact with. This was going to be good for me, I told myself. Really.

Court was going to resume at 10 a.m., the judge had said, so I had about an hour. I went outside, found a bench in the shade and called Olivia to ask if Jerry had shown up yet today.

"Not yet. Must have been quite a bender last night. Do you want his number?"

"Yeah."

She read it to me.

"Thanks."

"Sure. How's the trial? Your stories are…"

"Boring?"

"No. Straightforward, I guess. Well-written of course."

"No, they are boring, but that may change," I said truthfully. "I'm going to check out a few leads. I might have something more interesting in the next couple of days."

"Ooh, that sounds mysterious and fun. Be careful, though."

"I will. How's life in the big city?"

"It's been pretty quiet here," she said.

I laughed. "It won't be for long, then. You know you just jinxed yourself. Enjoy it while it lasts."

Olivia laughed. "Good point. I gotta run. My other line is ringing."

"See? What did I say!"

I hung up and dialed Jerry and got his voicemail.

"Jerry, I have some questions about your hometown for a story. Call me when you can. Thanks."

I went back in and ordered another small coffee, found a worn-out armchair in the back, and pulled out my computer to take advantage of the coffeeshop's free Wi-Fi. Then I had another idea, and called Olivia back. She must have been done with her other call because she answered right away.

"Hey!" she said. "Long time no talk."

"Funny. Sorry to bother you again. If it's still not too busy, can I ask you a favor? You've got keep it quiet though."

"Sure. What's up?"

"Will you use LexisNexis to see if anyone has used—or tried to use—the influence of steroids as a defense to a crime?"

"Wait, you think Connor used steroids? There's been nothing about that…"

"I know. Keep it quiet, okay? I might be wrong. It's just an angle I thought of thanks to an encounter with an injured dog…"

I could almost hear Olivia cock her head in confusion.

"Anyway, it would explain the violence of the murder scene and maybe the weight loss from the withdrawal. And no, I have no facts, just a theory. I can research into the effect of steroids and the prevalence of drugs in basketball, but I can't access the legal stuff remotely…"

"Yeah. That's easy. I'll send you what I find. This is exciting."

"Thanks for helping. Now, I've gotta run, or I am going to be late to court."

"Behave yourself. Don't get thrown in jail for contempt. Alex wouldn't like that."

I laughed again. "No, but would she be surprised?"

Olivia was kind enough not to answer.

I pulled up photos of Connor from before the murders, taken both on the court and off, and looked with fresh eyes for evidence of steroid use. I enlarged one of the photos and looked at his face. It was disturbing looking straight at a killer, but I tried to ignore that and focus on the bones of his face and his hair. Keeping the photos open in one window, I pulled up kidshealth.org, one of my favorite science websites (it is written in language I can understand), on the other and searched for "effects of anabolic steroids." Bingo.

Anabolic steroids are artificially produced hormones that are the same as, or similar to, androgens, the male-type sex hormones in the body. There are more than 100 variations of anabolic steroids. The most powerful androgen is testosterone. Testosterone promotes the masculine traits that boys develop during puberty, such as deepening of the voice and growth of body hair. Testosterone levels can also affect how aggressive a person is. Anabolic steroids stimulate muscle tissue to grow and "bulk up" in response to training by mimicking the effect of naturally produced testosterone on the body. Anabolic steroids can remain in the body anywhere from a couple of days to about a year. Anabolic steroids cause many different types of problems. Some of the more serious or long-lasting side effects are: premature balding or hair loss, dizziness, mood swings, including anger, aggression, and depression, delusions, paranoia, problems sleeping, nausea and vomiting, trembling, high blood pressure, aching joints, weakened tendons, liver damage, cancer, testicular shrinkage, breast development, impotence and sterility.

Aggression. Paranoia. Yup. His hair even looked a little thinner. Connor could definitely have been using. But was he tested? Is there any proof buried in some file somewhere? He must have been drug tested when he was arrested, but they would have had to test specifically for steroids. They were probably looking only for street drugs and alcohol. And we know he was drunk. But if there is proof, does it change anything for Connor? Can or should it be part of Connor's defense? Or is it just another sign he was a bad guy? I ran my hands through my hair and decided I needed a haircut. I also decided I needed to go to court. My questions could wait until all this had a chance to settle. No one's life was on the line today.

I wanted to figure out why Connor would want to use steroids, though. He had to have been smart enough to know the side effects, not to mention the risk of getting kicked off the team if he was caught. A kid like him would have a career mapped out in banking or consulting or something similar by his father. Shoot, he would probably be a vice-president of Millennium Development at age 24 with a fat salary. He wouldn't need to take drugs to try and make it to the pros in order to make a living. He'd have better options. But maybe that didn't matter. It's so easy for an athlete to graduate from wanting to be better to being willing to do anything to be better. You reach the limit of your potential but not your desire. Desire doesn't crunch numbers or make rational choices. I saw that in swimming. I saw that in myself.

Packing up my things, I wondered, though, if anyone else on the Blue Ridge basketball team used. I would assume yes; it's a team. Teams do stuff together. There is no place for the lone wolf. But if that's what Connor was...Ah, my mind was wandering so far it needed a passport.

This is where I always get into trouble, and Alex says it makes me both the worst and the best journalist she has. Still, I know the outcome of any trial is only part of the truth. Now, I wanted to find *the* truth, not just report on *a* verdict, even though that was the initial plan. I never stick to plans, anyway.

Maybe I needed to head further back into the past. I remembered that Connor went to high school at Landfall Academy, a private prep school on the eastern shore of Maryland. From photos on its website, it looked like a dumping ground for rich kids, a beautiful kind of prison. I decided to look up his old basketball coach and call him at the first break. I checked my phone; it was nine forty-five, and I'd have to hustle to make it to the courthouse on time.

Everything seemed a little disorganized after the day off. The crowd was a little smaller. The jurors looked unhappy and took more time to get settled in their seats. Connor shuffled in, dead-eyed and slumped, as if he had been in prison his whole life. On the other hand, Isaac, his lawyer, looked eager. Good, I thought. Let the jousting begin.

I looked around and noticed Bennett and Jill slipping in. We all did the "chin lift of recognition and greeting," as Leo called it. I called it the reverse nod. Regardless, it is the thing you do to say hello when your hands are full, and you have to be quiet.

"All rise," said the bailiff precisely at 10 am.

We did, and Judge Evans walked in, took his seat, folded his hands and said "Proceed."

Madison Kupchak did as told, calling as witnesses neighbors who saw Gina and some who saw Connor that night. Isaac didn't cross-examine anyone other than one neighbor. A teenager who looked both scared and aggressive, almost feral like many teenagers do, if you look closely.

"What were you doing awake at 2:15 on the night of the murders?" Isaac asked.

"Playing video games. I looked out of my window when I heard a car drive up."

"How was he walking?" Isaac asked.

"What do you mean?"

"I mean was Connor moving quickly, was he weaving and stumbling, was he walking with a purpose or something else?"

To the kid's credit, he took some time to think about his answer. "He looked like he was in a hurry, but that he was too wasted to go real fast," the kid answered. "I guess he was stumbling, but he wasn't falling down or out of control or anything. He waited for the traffic light, even though there wasn't any traffic."

"He waited for the traffic light to change? I don't believe that was in your earlier statement." Isaac went to the defense table and picked up what I assumed was the earlier statement and flipped through it.

"No, but I remember it now. He parked across the street because that's where visitors park. If you live in the building, you get a sticker and can park next to the apartment."

"Okay. Well thank you. No further questions."

I wondered why he decided not to impeach the kid. That was certainly bad for Connor, I thought. Clearly Isaac was trying to plant the seed that maybe Connor was too drunk to know what he was doing, which would take first degree murder off the table. But if he had enough instinct for self-preservation, or if he was just taking the time to figure out a plan, he arguably had enough brainpower to form intent. At least that is what I would conclude if I were on the jury. I looked at them and couldn't tell what they were concluding.

It was 11:30, and the judge called a ten-minute recess. He also announced we would take lunch at 1:30. I got up and waved hi to Bennett and Jill. Then I headed out to make my call to see if someone was at Landfall Academy who I could talk to. Of course, it was summer, but it was worth a try. Googling on my phone I found the number for the athletic department, saw Barry Johnson was the head coach, hoped he was there when Connor was there, and called. Mrs. Merguez was smoking a cigarette and glaring at me.

The receptionist said all the coaching staff were all on break until August 1st. I left my name and number, said that I was calling about Connor Braxton, and asked that if he checked in for messages, would Coach Johnson please call me at his convenience.

My call finished, I approached Mrs. Merguez as she stubbed out her cigarette. Small talk didn't seem to be a good idea.

"Have you given any thought to speaking with me?"

"About what?" she asked with fire in her eyes, as if she were daring me to screw up again.

"About anything you want. Not much has been written about Gina. I'd like to give her a voice." That was not entirely the truth, but close enough.

She grunted. "What has written has been neither thorough or kind. How will your story be any different? Gina was not perfect, but she was going to graduate from college—the first one in our family—and make her own way in the world. I was so proud of her."

"Yes. I am so sorry. Maybe I can tell her side of the story."

"Beyond the fact that she loved a monster?" Mrs. Merguez almost spat out the words.

"Yes. It seems to me there is a lot that is not being told. A trial doesn't always bring out the truth."

"The fact that my daughter's dead at his hands is my only truth, and I want to see him die. That is the only reason I am here."

"Really? Don't you want to know what made him do it?" That was a stupid question, but it was all I could think of to keep her talking.

We stared at each other, and I could see wheels turning in her head. I couldn't tell in which direction, though. She walked off without saying anything. I chose to see our conversation as progress.

I turned around to walk back to the courtroom just as a tall man with white hair and a tan three-piece suit was striding toward me, his hand out. I did not like the look of him, but I had nowhere to hide.

"I'm William McFarlane, president of Blue Ridge University. You're with the *Washington Star*, correct?"

"Yes, I am. Gale Hightower," I said, shaking his hand. Something about him made me wish for hand sanitizer.

"This is all such a tragedy. I wonder if you'd be interested in hearing about the changes we're instituting in our sports programs to ensure these kinds of things don't happen again?" he asked.

Oooh. I am being courted. And murder has been reduced to 'these kinds of things.' I hate administrative language.

"Absolutely," I said pulling out my notebook. It is wise to let people talk when they want to talk, regardless of what you think of what they will say.

"Excellent. Would you like to come to my office at the conclusion of trial today? I believe Branch is going to recess early today."

He calls the judge by his first name. Interesting. "Certainly. You are where?"

"My assistant will give you directions. I look forward to chatting with you," he said and left, revealing a tall young woman who had been trailing him. She wordlessly handed me a parking pass and a map that had driving and walking directions on the back.

"Thanks," I said.

She gave me a tight smile and walked away. This was clearly going to be a very long day.

Back in court after our late morning recess, the prosecutor started the process of putting up forensic testimony on the victims and Connor. Apparently, Connor had a blood alcohol level of .18 and nothing else in his system. Or, I reminded myself, nothing else that was tested for. It's not like there is one test for all illegal drugs. You have to test separately for everything you suspect. If you don't suspect it, you'll never know. I was half listening because I was thinking about what I didn't like about President McFarlane. And I was trying to decide if Connor's use of steroids would help or hurt his defense, and what Isaac Sutton should know about that. I hoped Olivia would get back to me soon with her research.

I noticed some of Connor and Marcus' teammates in the audience—identifiable by their height, age and very new sneakers—and I decided to chase them down at the lunch break. Nothing much had been written about their take on the case. Or what they thought of Connor, for that matter. Maybe someone was telling them not to talk, I thought.

I also made a note to keep an eye on the thin blond woman whose reason for being at the trial I couldn't put my finger on. She had been there all week, alone. She looked like her future held lots of fancy charity events and a position of responsibility in the Junior League.

But at the lunch break, everyone scattered and the easiest person to reach was the prosecutor, Madison Kupchak.

"Ms. Kupchak? I'm Gale Hightower from the *Washington Star.* Do you have a moment for some questions?"

"I'm happy to talk," she said without meaning it, "if you'll follow me to my office. I have a sandwich there I'd like to eat while we conduct any interview. Of course, legal ethics prevent me from making any statement outside of court that will end up in the press and influence the outcome of the case. If your questions do not require me to violate the ethics rules, I am happy to answer."

Very by-the-book. And why wouldn't she be? I am a stranger to her. In D.C., over time, I built some good working relationships with prosecutors despite the constraints of our respective legal and journalistic ethics. And probably because of our human ethics. But it does take time.

"Sure. Thanks," I replied, with my most agreeable face.

Madison took the stairs with her arms full of files, and I opened the doors for her. She nodded her gratitude. When we got to her office, she slid the files onto her credenza and pulled out her lunch from a blue insulated bag. She motioned to a worn guest chair and I took it, even though I couldn't identify the stain on the seat. Clearly, not much money was spent on this building outside of its façade and the gorgeous courtroom.

"So. Fire away," she said, as she unwrapped her sandwich.

"How do you feel the trial is going?" It was another banal question, but a calculated one this time. With people like Ms. Kupchak—people whose professional lives are measured in wins and losses—I always like to start with a plain vanilla question. It allows them to feel superior, which in turn makes them more comfortable. Comfortable people are more likely to slip up and tell the truth.

"I think the judge is doing a fine job, and the evidence is supporting our case. I am pleased with the way the trial has been going."

Hm. That wasn't much. Maybe I had misjudged. I tried again.

"So, you think you'll get first degree murder?"

"That is for the jury to decide. I believe that, one," she held up three fingers and pulled down one, "the state has a strong case. Two," down went another finger, "Mr. Sutton is not mounting a vigorous defense because he doesn't really have one. Three, Connor Braxton needs to be removed from society."

Her fingers all closed into a fist. How appropriate.

"Has this trial been hard on the university community?"

"I wouldn't know," she took a bite of her sandwich. "I don't fraternize in that circle."

"Why not?"

"It's…it is a very tightly knit community."

"In what way?" I asked.

She just shrugged.

"Does the university bring a lot of crime to the town?" I tried the more specific route.

"Not really."

I waited, hoping she might add something. She did not.

She finished her sandwich in the silence, and I leaned forward in my chair.

"Aren't you curious about what makes someone take that step from fighting to killing? Why they don't stop. Don't you think there might be a reason other than anger? Your medical testimony proved it took a long time to stab each of the victims to death. I would think anyone in their right mind would stop short."

"One, I am not a psychologist. If that sort of thing interested me, I would have made it my profession. My job is to keep the community safe. Two, the defense has not submitted any insanity defense and there is no evidence of mental illness in the medical reports. Not every murder is so exotic."

No fingers this time.

"Was Connor drug tested?" I asked.

"Yes. Of course. I thought you were in the courtroom," she let her exasperation show along with a little condescension. "That's been in the papers and the testimony today. Blood alcohol of .18 as the evidence showed. Nothing else. For a man his size, that's tipsy, not drunk."

"What about other drugs, recreational drugs, performance enhancing drugs, things like that?"

"Nope. Nothing," she said.

"Not in his system or not tested for?"

"Stimulants were tested for and there was nothing," Madison said with finality, either ignoring the second part of my question or hoping I didn't really care about the answer.

I got the hint and stood up. I didn't dislike Madison Kupchak, but she didn't make me feel very good about the world.

She picked up her phone and smiled, and I waved as I left, pretending to be friendly. As I closed the door to her office, I saw a trio of very tall guys walking down the hall away from me. Perfect timing. This has to be easier than talking to Madison.

"Hey, wait up," I called, figuring that made me sound like I knew them and would cause them to stop faster than an 'excuse me'. They last guy turned around, and I closed the gap.

"Gale Hightower for the *Washington Star.* Can I ask you a few questions?"

"We're sad for Connor, but we really miss Marcus. He wasn't a big part of the team, but he was our teammate. We're sad for Gina too and her family. But we gotta move on and focus on the season. That's our statement."

The speaker – the last guy in the group – turned back around and took a few running steps to catch up with his friends and so did I. I caught my breath. My regime of occasional jogging was proving insufficient for chasing sources.

We all ended up outside.

"Is that what the coach wrote for you?" I asked.

No answer, which meant yes.

"Okay, can I get your names?"

They turned to each other, shrugged, and gave me their names.

"Who's the best player?" I asked, in a sideways move that might get me something.

They all pointed to themselves. I laughed out loud, and that at least got a smile.

"You ever play? You're tall enough," the spokesman said.

"No. I am not terribly coordinated on land," I answered.

He looked confused.

"I was a swimmer," I said. "Flat feet." I mimed flippers with my hands.

"Huh," he said and left with his friends.

That was the unremarkable end of our conversation, if you could even call it that.

I watched all four of them fold themselves into one very flash car—a black Camaro—which backed out in one sharp move. The expensive car made me wonder if there were some NCAA violations here. Division III schools can't give scholarships, but who knows what goes on behind the scenes, money-wise. Gifts to college athletes—who are supposed to be amateurs, meaning they receive no payment of any kind for their play—are illegal according to NCAA rules. But it goes on at Division I schools all the time. Well, not all the time, but at least one school a year gets caught for violations. And it is getting worse. Why wouldn't it trickle down to Division III schools like Blue Ridge? While I was thinking about who bought the Camaro, I totally missed the silver sedan that pulled out right after the kids.

Looking at my watch I saw I had twenty minutes before court resumed to find something to eat and then eat it. Back to the coffee shop it was, and luckily, they had a veggie wrap that wasn't too soggy. I ate it quickly and grabbed an orange juice to go.

Before we all filed back in to the courtroom, I caught up with Bennett and Jill and asked if they would look into something for me. I explained my thoughts about steroids.

"You think he was on steroids? I've thought that! Roid rage, right? I've read articles about lawyers trying to use that as a defense when athletes kill people. Like the South African paraplegic runner...they found boxes of steroids in his house after he shot his girlfriend." Bennett's eyes gleamed with excitement.

"Oscar Pistorius. I had forgotten about that," I said. "Yes, I have a hunch that Connor may have been using. It would explain the extreme violence of the crimes and the weight loss he experienced in prison after stopping the drugs." And probably the change in play style, I thought to myself.

"But would it matter to the outcome of the trial with all the other evidence?" Bennett asked.

"Maybe. Probably not. But it might matter in other ways. Like preventing other crimes if there is a lot of drug use going on among athletes at your school."

"I don't think there is. I mean, our other sports aren't very good," Bennet said.

"You don't have to be good to want to cheat. Let's just say I am curious, and it's good to follow your curiosity to see if it is something you can rely on." I felt professorial. "A reporter's curiosity, or gut, is the best tool you can have. It may lead to a different outcome for Connor if it is something the defense hasn't investigated, or it may lead to something else entirely. I don't know. I don't make the trail, I just follow it. You guys in?"

"Yeah definitely." Jill answered for both of them.

Good girl, I thought. "Okay. Start with prowling Facebook and Twitter and whatever that new one is—Snap Chat? —to see if there was any talk of performance enhancing drug use among the student athletes. People who use drugs talk about it. Or some do. Watch for slang for steroids. "Juice" is the one I remember. I am going to look into where someone might get performance enhancing drugs around here."

"Okay!" Bennett said.

"Great. Here's my cell number. Let's catch up Monday, or sooner if you find something."

Bennett took the scrap of paper that had my phone number. "Okay. Thanks. We are so excited to be working with you."

"I guess I am too," I said and surprised myself by meaning it.

NINE

Friday, later

Back in court, after more forensics testimony, Judge Evans recessed at 4 p.m. I dug out my map and made a beeline on foot for President McFarlane's office. When I got there in a full sweat 15 minutes later, the receptionist offered me a choice of water, tea or white wine. God, I wanted a glass of wine, but I am not that stupid.

"Water would be nice, thanks," I told the receptionist, a supremely well-dressed woman who looked about 70. I mean, where do you even buy clothes like that—a pale blue knit suit with ribbon trim and a silk blouse in a black and white stripe—in this town? She poured my water into a goblet that already had a slice of lemon in it. A minute later, the President McFarlane opened his door with a flourish as if I were his long-lost best friend and he wanted nothing more than to spend the entire afternoon with my amazing self.

"Ms. Hightower, come in, come in. Thank you for taking the time to visit us."

"Thank you for your willingness to be interviewed, President McFarlane," I said, pulling out my notebook.

"Oh now, this isn't an interview, is it? And call me William. It's just a nice little get-to-know- each-other chat. You sure you don't want some wine?" I noticed he had a half-full glass on his desk.

"No, thank you," I said through gritted teeth. This is going to be a huge waste of my time and a test of my self-control, I realized.

"So," he settled his long frame back into his chair, "did

you play basketball anywhere? The women's game is really coming along."

God, how I hate a patronizing asshole. "No, I swam instead."

"Oh, too bad. You look like you'd be good."

Because I am black, I thought and smiled. "Thank you," I said, instead of what was actually stuck in my throat trying to elbow its way out. No interest in my swimming either. He was not a sports fan, just a basketball fan. At least he didn't know anything about me, which might give me an advantage.

"So, this trial really has been a tragedy," he said, getting to his point.

Not as much as the murders, I thought. It was kind of fun having an imaginary conversation. It helped with the self-control.

"Yes," I said out loud.

"But you must cover this sort of thing all the time in the big city, sadly," he said.

"Not really. Yes, we have more murders, but they are usually gun crimes and drug-related."

"Yes, I see how that is different. No drugs were involved here of course. Just alcohol. So sad how some young men can't handle their liquor. Oh, but don't quote me on that." He waved his hands as if he could erase his words.

"Certainly not." Can't handle their liquor? What the hell kind of comment is that?

"What I'd like to make sure reaches a wide audience— through you, hopefully—is that we're still a good school. Blue Ridge University has a beautiful campus, a fine history, dedicated teachers, growing sports programs, and many cultural opportunities."

I am not your PR wench, I wanted to say, but I held my tongue. "I'm sure I can mention the history and academic standing of Blue Ridge."

"And our sports teams, too. We were quite good in basketball, before…and I am sure we will be again. We can't let this affect our recruiting. That would be sad for the young people who wouldn't benefit from Coach Ford's experience. Once…" his phone buzzed.

"President McFarlane," said the receptionist "Coach Ford and Assistant Coach Battier are here. And Mr. Wade is on line 1."

"Excellent. Send them in, and please tell Cyrus I will call him back this evening," he said to his phone. To me he said, "I thought it might be easier for you to speak with the coaches together."

Plus, you could control the conversation, I thought. Very smart.

"Who is Cyrus Wade?" I asked, just to be nosy. For all I knew it was his accountant or brother-in-law.

McFarlane answered with his back to me as he looked out his window. "Ah, Cyrus is an old friend and a big supporter of our athletic programs. He is the current chair of the Presidents Council for Division III schools in the NCAA and has held that role for several years. A terrific leader. He is most concerned about what we have been going through, on a personal and a professional level."

Huh, I thought. I wondered if McFarlane talked with his back to people when he was lying, or when he thought so little of them that they did not deserve to see his face. Could be either, from a man like him. I hadn't heard anything from "big supporter" Cyrus Wade in the press. I wondered if McFarlane was lying and old Cyrus was calling to chew him out. I would have to put Cyrus Wade on my ever-lengthening list of people to interview. I was getting tired just thinking about that list.

Before I could ask any follow up, the coaches came in. I stood and we all shook hands. It was hard not to stare at Haywood. He was a handsome man and clearly used to be tall, but he looked deflated. Seeing him in the courtroom was different. He was one of a crowd. Here, the setting was more intimate, and he looked out of place and uncomfortable in his wheelchair. On the other hand, Kevin Battier, the assistant coach, looked very comfortable. who was still very handsome and sculpted at what I estimated to be close to forty. Yowzah. Even with a suit on, and probably close to 40, you could tell that he could be an underwear model. Not my type at all, but still easy on the eyes.

"Beverages, gentlemen?" McFarlane asked.

"Nothing for me," Haywood said, and I wondered if it was hard for him to hold a glass.

"I'm fine, too," Kevin said.

He had a nice voice as well. This interview is looking up, I thought, until I remembered Sam's opinion of Kevin: *Not fit to lead a fifth-grade field trip.* Maybe Haywood was jealous of Kevin and she was picking up on that?

"I asked you each here because I thought it would help all of us for Ms. Hightower to have access to all the information she needs to write a full story on the university and our terrific basketball program. One bad apple can't rot the whole basket."

"Um, I actually am just here to cover the trial," I said, feeling railroaded. "No column inches for a feature," I said, shrugging and lying. But they didn't need to know Alex needed more articles.

"Well, certainly, of course, but I am sure your readers want a larger picture of what we are like here at Blue Ridge University."

People in Washington are mostly concerned about things in Washington, I said in my head. And all I wanted to know about was steroid use; if they knew Connor was using and if any other players were using. But this was not the time or place for that conversation. I needed more facts; shoot, I needed one fact. All I had was a theory. And President William McFarlane didn't seem the type to be put off his mission by a few unimportant details like other people's preferences. So, I played along.

"Certainly," I said.

He smiled and handed me a brochure. "This is what we give to prospective students. It gives a very good overview."

"Thank you." I can find this on the Internet, I thought, and smiled. He wasn't giving me anything to use to even write the story that he said he wanted. Could he be that stupid or was I missing something, I wondered?

"So now ask us anything you'd like," he said, relaxing into his chair with his hands clasped behind his head in the ultimate power position.

I smiled and got my notebook out of my backpack to stall for time. If I didn't stick with the suggested subject, I would never have a chance for another interview. I might need him or his office later. I was trying to decide what question would curry the most favor when my phone buzzed. I dug for it in my purse, grateful for the interruption.

"I'm so sorry," I said to them and got up, walking to the door. I looked at my buzzing phone and didn't recognize the number. "Gale Hightower."

"This is Barry Johnson from Landfall Academy. You

called me earlier about Connor Braxton?"

Shit! Not here. I looked at the three men and saw no sign anyone heard. "Yes, thanks. Can you hold on a minute? I'm in the middle of something."

"Sure."

"I'm sorry, I've got to take this. Can I come back another time?" I didn't have to take the call. I could have easily called Barry Johnson back later, but I really didn't know how best to play this group. And I didn't want to get played.

"Of course. I hope it's not an emergency," said McFarlane.

"No, no. Just an administrative detail from the office. Missing file. But they've got a deadline," I lied. "Next week? We can talk more then. I will confer with my editor and see how much space she can make for this piece." I smiled.

"Okay, that sounds like a great plan. Just call my office any time." McFarlane smiled, but didn't get up.

I grabbed my bag and backed out. "Sure, thanks!"

"Yes. Wow, thanks for calling me back so quickly," I said into my phone once I was in the hallway. "The receptionist told me you were on break."

"A coach never gets a real break," he answered.

"I know how true that is. Well, I am covering Connor's trial for the *Washington Star*, and I wanted to get some background on him."

"What can I tell you?" he asked.

"Well, anything really. What he was like, *was* he liked, any history of violence, was he a good player, things like that."

He paused, and I wondered if I should have gone with a softer and less straightforward approach. But I was fresh out of social niceties; I had used up my allotment for the day. Really, for the week.

"Connor was a decent player, and I'm glad he got to play in college. He wanted it so much and he worked hard enough to earn it. But he wasn't great. Maybe he could have become great if he stopped trying to be what he wasn't. Guys like him not blessed with loads of natural talent can still add to a team if they learn the finer points of the game, if they study defenses, if they perfect free-throws. But Connor didn't go for that. He always seemed young to me, so I thought maybe he could mature physically and mentally in college."

"You say he seemed young. What do you mean?

By now I had walked outside of the administration building, and I looked for a place to park myself and take notes. The best I could do was a bike rack, so I dropped my pack and fished out my notebook.

"He was small for his first three years. He grew six inches and bulked up a little in his senior year. A lot of boys do then. As for violence, we're a boy's school. We see a lot of minor violence. Nothing serious, but yeah, there are fights. They are like young bucks testing their antlers. Connor wasn't really that different than anyone else, at least not as far as I saw."

I scribbled. "I understand his father is a big donor to Landfall Academy."

"His family has been generous because they support our educational and athletic mission. What exactly are you implying?"

Might as well be honest this time and see where it gets me. "I guess I wonder if those donations affect your perception of Connor?"

He sighed. "I hope not. Most of these kids have rich families." He left it at that, and so did I. I trusted his tone of voice, probably because it was worlds away from the oily, velvety voice William McFarlane used on me.

"Did Connor's lawyer, Isaac Sutton, ever contact you?"

"No, he didn't. I've been wondering about what I would have said if he did."

"Meaning…"

"Meaning I don't know if I would have made a very good witness. Connor was a fine kid and an okay ball player, but I didn't really know him."

He sounded sad about that.

"How many of your players go on play in college?" I changed the subject.

"Only ten to twenty percent in any given year. These kids are more into golf, sailing and money than standard college sports."

"I've always seen golf as more of a hobby than a sport," I offered.

He laughed. "A woman after my own heart."

"Well, thank you for your time. If I have other questions, may I…"

"Of course," he said. "So how is the trial going?" It was like he was stalling, like he had something else to say but wouldn't—or couldn't—say it until I said the magic words.

"Normal," I said. "The prosecution is still putting on its case. The jury seems adequate and the defense is going for second degree."

"Yeah, I read all that."

I waited for him to ask me another question. He didn't, and I didn't know what my next move should be.

"Okay, well thank you for your time," I said.

"Yeah."

He had something he wanted to tell me, but until I could guess what it was, he could wait. Maybe he just felt. I had enough leads to track down. I also needed time to put the pieces I'd already found together.

That settled, I called Sam from my perch at the bike rack and asked after Charlotte.

"She's got a fever right now, and I am not happy. I've got her on IV antibiotics—Baytril. It is the king of all bug killers. I hate using the heavy artillery when I don't absolutely have to, but I can't figure out what is causing her fever to spike. Can you come see her at 6 pm? She needs something to make her tail wag"

"Of course."

Don't die now, Charlotte, I thought. I'd already imagined a future with her. And it was the first time I had imagined any future in a long time.

It was a little before 5 pm, and I had an hour, so I went back to my room and started writing. I put together a passable 500 words on the forensics testimony and the differing styles of the lawyers. It was filler until I got to the bottom of what I thought was going on. I still didn't have any evidence, but I was sure Connor had used steroids. What I wasn't sure of was whether it mattered. Connor has a lawyer and a father, what could I do? What *should* I do? There is no doubt he killed two people. Steroids or not.

I could always give Alex my suspicions and let her decide whether to assign someone else to do a full investigation. Someone not so rusty or ambivalent. Or I could send an anonymous letter to the NCAA. That would assuage my nagging conscience and allow me to write better stories on the trial. If my steroid assumptions amounted to nothing, I had sacrificed my opportunity to produce good work about the actual trial and might not be welcomed back into my old job at the Metro desk. I rubbed my temples. A weekend off would do me good, I decided. I can at least sort out what I want.

A little after 6 pm, I pulled into the parking lot at the vet's. Sam was in the lobby when I went in.

"You know, I really used to only think assholes and sad old men drove Corvettes. You are making me question my opinions," Sam said.

"I was probably a sad old man in my previous life." I tried to lighten the mood.

The creases between Sam's eyebrows were deep today. She rubbed them. "Sorry, I'm just tired. It is a gorgeous car. I'm probably just jealous. I do spay-neuter surgeries at the shelter on Friday mornings, and it was rough there today."

I didn't ask, and she didn't tell me, thank God. I hate sad stories about animals. I hate sad stories about anything I can't fix.

"So, Charlotte picked up a serious infection. That's not surprising considering how banged up she was. Come see her."

She looked horrible, all bloated and lethargic. I had hoped she'd wag her tail, proving that she was okay and that I was still her savior. All I got was a single thump that may have been more of a shudder. Apparently, the fastest way to know you love somebody is to come close to losing them. I was devastated, out of proportion to how I thought I should feel.

"She has fluid in her lungs. It's bad. But it's not over. Sit with her. I've got to check on a hound who just came out of surgery to remove a nail from his skull." My look of horror made her add, "He'll live, and it's not the worst case of animal cruelty I've seen. It may have even been an accident. Here, wash your hands and put on gloves if you're going to touch her."

Sam's ability to keep focused on her job and not wonder about what happened to land the animals in her care was almost unbelievable. I would get lost in their stories, imagined or real. I washed my hands as instructed and put on gloves and a gown to keep any germs from my clothes from infecting Charlotte and sat with her. I stroked her and talked to her about how great Washington is and how I'd always keep her safe. I knew a lot of what I was saying was just hope, and I bet she did too. What I needed her to understand was that I would always try, to the best of whatever ability I had. I put my head down so that I was half in and half out of the kennel, and I fell asleep.

"Jesus, I though you keeled over," Sam said when she came in. She was standing over me. "Then I saw your chest rise. I don't do humans, you know. So, if you do decide to have a heart attack, don't do it here. She switched out an IV bag for Charlotte and checked a few monitors. "That's better. Good. Okay, now go. You're leaving for the weekend, right?"

"Yeah." I rubbed my left shoulder and sat up. "Hey, sorry but can I ask you about Coach Ford, or is that mixing things up too much?"

"I usually call him Haywood, but sure."

She showed no sign of nervousness whatsoever. That was interesting and good.

"Um, what are his plans for next year?"

"For life or the team? And is this an interview for the record?"

"Either. And I'm not sure. If you don't want it to be, it isn't. I'm just having trouble figuring this whole thing out, and I like you and I figure if you like Haywood, maybe I should hear more from him."

"That simple?"

"Yeah, I think."

"You sound more like a detective than a reporter."

I felt like it, too, right now. "Sometimes you have to be both," I said.

She crouched down. "He hasn't decided whether he can keep coaching, health-wise. I think he wants to see how the trial comes out. But I also know he doesn't want to leave Kevin in charge, and he thinks that's what the administration will do if he leaves. I think he's mostly worried about Kevin because of my opinion of him. I can have strong opinions," she admitted. "Before I decided I didn't like him, Haywood thought he was a good coach. He thought they balanced each other well."

"What made you dislike Kevin?" I asked.

"It wasn't just one thing," she sighed. "Mainly, I don't like how he treats Haywood since he had to start using the wheelchair. Like he is the weak antelope in the herd. Haywood is not weak. Anyway, he's torn about retirement. He loves the kids and the game. That's what makes him a good coach. That's what makes anyone good at anything. I don't think Kevin loves anything other than success."

That was a lot of information for me to process. I didn't have a follow-up question, and Sam didn't volunteer anything else. We just looked at each other for a minute.

"Check with me next week. If Charlotte gets through this, she'll be fine."

"Okay. Thanks."

We both got up and shook hands like we were sealing a deal.

As soon as I got back in my car, my phone rang. I almost

let it go to voicemail.

"Gale Hightower."

It was Olivia.

"Hey. I found all sorts of interesting stuff on the steroids-as-defense angle. It turns out that steroid induced rage been used successfully as a defense many times. Well, not successfully—juries don't care—but it's been allowed by judges as a sort of diminished capacity, temporary insanity kind of thing. "

"Like when someone is too drunk to remember what they did?"

"It seems like that, yeah. I looked in state and federal courts. It's interesting. This one court in California allowed expert testimony on what a steroid rage reaction can do to a person. I'll email everything to you."

"Huh. Thanks Olivia. That's awesome. Hey, why are you working so late?"

"My air-conditioning is broken at home. I will be here all weekend," she said.

"Oh, that stinks."

"Yes, literally. Gotta go. My iced coffee is getting hot."

I laughed. "Okay, stay cool."

If I could find this out so easily—or rather, if Olivia could—then I assumed a lawyer could, too. And it might change the outcome of the trial, at least take first degree murder off the table. Surely Arthur Braxton would have enough money to hire the best experts out there for Isaac to use.

I went back to the motel to make a few notes, pay my bill, and get my things. As I was packing, I realized my timing was wrong. I needed to track down past players, the graduates. They would have been the leaders when Connor was a young and impressionable recruit. Where were they and what were they doing? Who was team captain Connor's freshman year? That sort of stuff. Man, if someone on my swim team who I looked up to had offered me drugs when I was a young swimmer, I might not have said no. I wanted to find whoever gave the drugs to Connor. Assuming there even were drugs involved, I reminded myself. That was still a theory. A very shiny, very enticing theory, but still a theory.

I went to the lobby and made a reservation for next week for the same room. Then it was off to the Shell station on the edge of town to fill the car up. As I was paying at the pump, a car pulled up on the other side. Low-slung and red, it caught my eye. Sure enough, it was a mid-1980s Vette. Maybe a 1986. Fifteen years newer than mine, but still worth a chat. Corvette owners are a tight group—most are old white guys who I would never talk to for pleasure in a million years. But cars—or any shared hobby I guess—can bridge the biggest divide. I was going to ask the owner about his car until I heard whoever it was screaming into his cell phone.

"Goddammit, do you know what kind of week I've had? Have you even thought about that?"

Geesh, I did not want to get in the middle of that. I pulled my receipt from the pump and ducked into my car, hoping the jerk didn't see my car and want to talk. It does work both ways. As I pulled away, the license plate caught my eye. "BALLR." That stopped me, and I stared at the guy for a minute. It was Kevin Battier, the assistant basketball coach. The voice matched too, now that I thought about it. Shit. I did not want him to see me looking at him. I couldn't get out of there fast enough, and I squealed my tires getting onto the highway.

Sam's words rang through my head; maybe Kevin was worth a second look. Everything about him said he didn't fit in here in this podunk town at a Division III university or didn't plan to stay here. Ah, but everyone had to start somewhere, I told myself. And who hadn't yelled into their phone for a little understanding? Maybe we were all just jealous of people like Kevin.

It was a long trip home. There was a wreck just outside of the beltway, and it brought everyone to a screeching halt. Literally. The Corvette does not like to stop quickly, even on dry pavement. We had a little fishtail fun but managed to avoid becoming a part of the problem. Then we all had to braid ourselves into one lane, which took forever.

It was 10:30pm when I pulled into the tiny garage my landlord lets me use. I trudged up the steps with my luggage and box of reporter gear. It had somehow gotten heavier in the five days in the motel.

When I got to my door, there were four of the big yellow sticky notes on it, all in a neat row:

Chicken soup is in the fridge. It's organic. Mostly.

I got the lemongrass from Mrs. Chen. She says hi.

It will heal what ails you!

Call me tomorrow. Oh, Hawk was fine.

For the umpteenth time, I thought, I love this man. Not romantically, of course, but maybe better. We should have multiple words for love, the way the Eskimo supposedly have for snow. I left the notes on the door and unlocked it, kicking my belongings into the room because I was too tired to pick them up again. Hawk screeched what I took to be "Hello, welcome home, I missed you!" I opened his cage and tried to pet him, and he tried to bite me. Things were nice and normal. I heated the soup to lukewarm because I couldn't wait any longer and ate every bit of it. This chicken tasted worlds different than Waynesville chicken. I chased it with some wine, a lot of wine, and went to sleep. I was so happy to be home.

TEN

The next morning, after I rousted the fuzz out of my head with two mugs of coffee, I called Leo.

"Once again, I owe you. You are my prince in shining Tupperware."

"Aren't I supposed to be a knight in shining armor?" he asked in mock puzzlement.

"I promoted you," I said, laughing. I had missed our banter more than I realized.

"Did you like the soup? I know July's kind of hot for soup…"

"I loved it; it was a tonic for the stomach and for the soul."

"Ooh, I love getting complimented by a writer!"

"You know, I'll never be able to pay you back for all the kindnesses you've shown me over the years we've been neighbors."

"Don't worry about it, and don't be maudlin. It's not like you. Plus, I'll find a way. Maybe you can promise to give me a kidney when I need one."

"You can have both, whenever you want."

"No, then I'll be stuck changing your diapers or something. One will do. How was the trial?"

"So far, more interesting that I would have thought. Do you like dogs?" I asked, knowing what the answer would be. Leo loves everything.

"I love dogs. Why?"

"I think we're getting a dog."

"You're keeping Charlotte? Yay! When do I get to meet her?"

I have never known a person so utterly comfortable with change.

"Maybe next weekend? It depends on when the trial is over. I didn't ask Sam when I could bring her home. She kind of strong-armed me into taking her, but now I think I'm kind of excited." That was putting it mildly.

"You're going to be a mother and I'm going to be a godfather!"

"Uh, I'm thinking we'll skip the religious education. Dog is God spelled backward, right? So, I think she's all good on that front."

Leo nearly busted a gut laughing.

"Careful, I don't want to have to give you that kidney now…"

He laughed until the hiccups made him stop. I was smiling. I never make Leo laugh. Dogs are good, I thought.

When he recovered, his thoughts turned to the dressing the dog and home decoration. "Collars and beds. You'll need several. And do you have a photo? We should match her coloring…"

"She's reddish-brown. Or will be when her fur grows back."

"Lovely. I am thinking a turquoise collar then."

It was my turn to laugh. "She's got some subtle gray and brown stripes, too. Kind of like a tiger. But the biggest surprise is that she has one blue eye."

"Mismatched eyes, like David Bowie? That's perfect!"

"Yup. Want to get dinner tonight?" I asked.

"I can't tonight. I have a date. Brunch Sunday?"

"Sure. But wait—a date?"

"Yup. Of the blind variety. Wish me luck. Mom set me up."

"Oh, you are a good sport," I said.

"Yes, yes I am."

"Have fun. He's a lucky guy."

"Good point. Thank you. Maybe we can go shopping for dog accessories after brunch?"

"Sounds perfect. Although let's not go overboard. I am not sure if I will be officially un-demoted after the trial. Bye."

"Oh, you will be. You are too good. And overboard is where the fun is at, darling. Have I not taught you anything? Bye yourself!"

I had to acknowledge that Leo probably had a point.

It was already miserably hot, but I decided to go for a run. I am not a very fast or graceful runner—a swimmer's flat feet don't translate to running very well—but I enjoy it. Plus, a week of sitting was making me soft. I didn't really have anything else to do, and DC is so flat and the Mall is so gorgeous that it practically begs you to run. The grade from where I live to the Mall, my regular running destination, is slightly downhill. Good for starting, bad for returning. But starting is the hardest part anyway.

After digging out some breakfast for Hawk, I pulled on light blue running shorts and a green T-shirt. Money and my key went into the pocket of my shorts, and I was ready to go at the stroke of 11 a.m. It was going to be sweaty, but that was the point. The first mile was easy, and I popped onto the Mall at the Washington monument. Circling the back of the monument I took a line to the Korean Memorial, my absolute favorite. Those ghostly white figures in ponchos look so unbelievably real. You feel like you are out of place, like you should be quiet so you don't startle them and distract them from their mission. As a work of art, it is the most powerful I have seen here. It's a war I know little about, but through this monument, I sense the horror of it and of all war. I finish paying my respects and take off again, too fast.

It takes me a few minutes to settle back into a manageable rhythm. Once the movement and breathing becomes automatic, my brain stops screaming at me to stop. It can then take on the job of sifting through the past week. I sift and run, sift and run for a few blocks.

I decide my next step is to talk to Coach Haywood Ford. If Connor was using steroids, Haywood had to know, didn't he? A coach's job is to monitor every little physical, mental, and emotional change in his players. My coaches knew when I didn't eat breakfast. And for God's sake, if Connor was using steroids, and the steroids made him more violent, and the coaches knew... then they are guilty of murder as well. Or of something. I hate cover-ups and I hate people who think they can get away with them. It's a requirement of my profession.

Turning around in front of the Capitol, I realized I could use some water. Thank goodness the museums are free. I dripped through security in the Hirschhorn and spent a minute slurping water at a drinking fountain. Back outside, I walked around the sculpture garden for kicks and to shake out my legs after the air-conditioning made them seize up. Then I dodged tourists on the Mall and headed back up the long gradient to my apartment. I stopped to walk about a half mile from home to cool down.

I called Alex right when I got home. She's almost always at the office on Saturday.

"I've got this theory on steroids. I think Connor was using and they may have played a role."

"What kind of role?" she asked.

"If he was jacked up on steroids he would have been more aggressive, more paranoid. Any little thing could have ticked him off, and under the influence, he would have reacted more violently."

"Have you talked to the defense lawyer about that?" Alex asked.

"Not yet."

"You're not litigating this case, you're just reporting on it, remember? Be patient. I imagine if there was steroid use, it will come out next week. I told you to be careful not to get distracted. You are still getting your sea legs back. Your radar may be rusty."

"All true, but how can I ignore a potential story? You said you needed more copy."

Alex sighed. "I don't want you to ignore it, I just don't want you to ignore your primary responsibility."

"I won't."

"You will. You always do." She sighed. All editors think reporters are impossible children. But we're not doing our jobs if we like each other all the time. "I have to answer to the publisher, remember?"

"I have a couple of college kids helping," I offered.

"Since when do you get help from college kids? You completely ignore the interns here. And you can't farm out your work."

"But they are good. And they are invested."

Alex grunted. That meant I was making progress.

"Fine. So long as you send me a story on the trial each night, you can pursue whatever else you want. I'm not saying I'll run it, though. And don't get the paper sued."

"Deal."

I stood in front of my window unit air-conditioner until my sweat froze, then I took the kind of shower you just can't take in a motel room. An hour later I went to the grocery story to get some fruit for Hawk and a steak and some wine for dinner. If I run, I get a steak. That is the deal I made with myself. Heart disease runs in my family on my mother's side, but I can't imagine getting old enough to get heart disease. Some days I feel lucky just to have lived this long. The steak was delicious, the wine was better, and after dinner Leo texted me.

"It wasn't awful. We may go out again. See you tomorrow!"

"Good for you. Sleep tight," I texted back.

Not awful translates into great when Leo is talking about dates. He is cautious in the affairs of the heart, and I don't blame him one bit. I had another glass of wine and watched *Jaws* on Turner Classic Movies. "We're going to need a bigger boat" is one of the best movie lines ever. It made me wonder if I am going to need a bigger boat. Metaphorically speaking, of course.

Sunday morning, I took my coffee out on the balcony and watched the birds hop around in our little garden. My left knee hurt, but otherwise I felt pretty good, probably because I held back on the wine. New running shoes would help my knee, so I added them to the mental shopping list. I was going to be seriously broke after today.

I went back into the kitchen to get paper and a pen. Above the junk drawer where I store half-used notebooks and stolen pens from the office is my calendar, and when I glanced at it, it did not have good news. I missed my appointment yesterday with Dr. Wilma Harper, my shrink. It's always the second Saturday of every month. Shit. I went inside and turned on the computer and e-mailed her my abject and profuse apologies. I always prefer to apologize in writing. It gives the apologizee a chance to forgive without pressure.

There being nothing else I could do, I grabbed my basket of dirty clothes and went downstairs to do laundry. The machines are in the back room of the gallery I live above. I love walking among the canvases leaning against the walls. They look like they are resting before their next big show.

I have a psychologist thanks to my mother. It was part of the deal that got me the car. I probably could have quit a few years ago, but I am used to Wilma now. I even like her. And I pick my battles.

My monthly visits to see Wilma usually consist of stern looks, jokes, huffs, and the occasional insight. I forget the appointments about twice a year. Wilma says my "forgetfulness" has more in common with a child's tendency to bury her new glasses than technical forgetfulness.

"You never forget deadlines for work," she said to me the last time I missed an appointment, something like six months ago.

"I thought we all knew I don't want to be here," I responded.

"Oh, that is a load of crap," Wilma said. "You love playing the role of long-suffering daughter. It's the only kindness—and I use the term loosely—that you show your mother. But we get a lot of good work done, and I see improvement."

"What exactly am I better at?" I asked, truly curious. I felt no different than I ever have.

"You are a tiny bit kinder, you are more aware of the destruction your drinking causes, and you don't slouch in the chair any more like a petulant teenager."

"Hmph. I'm not sure any of that translates to the rest of my life, but thank you, I guess."

"Progress is progress," she said firmly.

She was manipulating me with the compliment, but when I thought about what she said in the following months, I decided she was right. I was feeling less imprisoned by the past and, therefore, better.

I separated my whites from my colors and started the first load. Back at my computer, I had a response from Wilma.

"Next Saturday noon.

"Okay, I'll see you then. Thanks," I wrote back. Her brevity meant my apology was accepted. When she was upset, she didn't hold back.

Leo and I had decided to go to Dish, a new place only four blocks away. When we walked in, it smelled great. I love brunch because all that food and relaxation and Bloody Marys mean you can check out for the rest of the day. A good brunch can pass as a mini-vacation.

"So, tell me about the date," I said to Leo when we sat down.

"Oh, dinner was delicious. We went to the new place in Georgetown—*Bar None*. I had the mussels to start and a walnut risotto. Jack had an arugula salad and a steak. Everything looked so nice on the table, well matched, but different. I took that as a good sign."

"But what did he look like?"

Leo was torturing me on purpose.

"Tall dark and handsome, like you."

"He's black?"

"No. I guess you'd call him swarthy. He studied dance in high school, so we had that in common too. We'll probably go out again. I am supposed to call him."

"That's great," I said and meant it. Leo deserved someone to love. "I'll keep my fingers crossed."

"So, tell me more about Waynesville and the trial."

I told him everything this time; all my suspicions and all the players. Having an impartial ear was invaluable for me in sorting out facts and impressions. I learned that early on in my career, and I was ready to take advantage of it now. In the middle of my soliloquy the waitress came, and I ordered the eggs benedict with crab, a side of bacon from a farm just outside of DC and a croissant. Leo got an egg-white omelet with tomatoes— "hold the cheese"—and a fruit cup.

"Diet food? What gives?" I asked.

"Penance for last night's excesses," he said to my raised eyebrow.

I laughed and finished explaining the trial and my suspicions about steroids.

"So why would Connor have to do steroids if he already had a scholarship? I mean, he was set unless he got hurt, right?"

"Division III schools, which Blue Ridge University is, can't give out athletic scholarships," I explained.

"Well, thank God for that. There's always been something gross to me about giving athletes scholarships," Leo said.

"Really? Why?"

"I don't know. It just seems to me that the only scholarships a school should give out should be for academics. It's a school, not a farm team for the pros. It gives the athletes a false sense of themselves. It tells them that being an athlete pays when for the rest of their lives—for most of them—it won't."

"You know a lot of people are on the other side—that a scholarship isn't enough compensation for the athletes. That they should be paid because they bring so much money in to the schools. The shoe companies and hangers-on make a killing too. Why not the kids?"

"People who think that are idiots."

Ouch. I had never heard Leo speak that harshly about anything. I let it go. But he didn't.

"I mean they get a free education and so many other perks. Tutors, better food, travel, everything. And for what? Because they can run fast, hit hard, or jump high? What does that have to do with English literature or chemistry?"

"It might have a lot to do with chemistry," I joked. "Why does this bother you so much?"

"I don't know. I didn't know it did until we started talking about it." Leo started rearranging the flowers in the vase on the table.

"That's okay. Sports make people passionate."

"So, does art, but they don't give scholarships for that. Or not enough anyway."

"Good point," I said, wanting to make peace. "And that looks much better," I said, nodding at the flowers. Leo smiled.

Our food came, and we ate in a silence that relaxed rather quickly from tense into comfortable. It wasn't a real argument—more like a pebble being tossed into a lake—but it made me think about the ripple effect sports have. Sports do make people passionate, and passion can be bad.

"Let's go buy stuff," Leo said after paying the bill for both of us. "The cure for all that ails us." He took my arm and we sashayed out into a very humid afternoon. At Ruff N Ready down the street, we easily found a nice bed for Charlotte and a selection of harnesses.

"Sam said a collar can put too much pressure on a dog's neck. But with three legs, I don't know which will be most comfortable for her," I worried.

"That makes sense," Leo said. "I like the turquoise one—I think it will go nicely with her coloring—but the black one feels so soft."

"She's getting both," I said, heading to the cash register.

"She's going to be better dressed than you," Leo said, back to his old self. "And don't forget cookies and toys."

I grabbed a couple of bags of peanut butter and chicken flavored treats, two stuffed toys, and some bird food for Hawk, as well as a new perch. I paid the clerk and lugged the enormous bed back to my apartment while Leo carried the other bags. It is surprising how heavy foam can get in ten minutes.

With a home created for Charlotte and supplies restocked for Hawk, a few hours later I packed up my car again, said goodbye to Leo and Hawk and hit the road. There was no rain in the forecast, and I kept my eyes out for dogs and wildlife. It was an uneventful trip back to my motel where the clerk welcomed me back like family and gave me my same room as I requested. It was time to switch gears.

ELEVEN

The next morning, I was running late. I set my alarm as always but ended up hitting the snooze too many times. It is hard for me to transition from Sunday to Monday, even harder when I wake up in a new place. My mother always said the world needed a day between Sunday and Monday, but I think it would just delay the inevitable. Of course, that is exactly what I try to do with the snooze button, but please don't tell me I am just like my mother. Ever.

I showered and dressed in olive green pants and a red cotton blouse with short sleeves. I looked vaguely like the love child of a Christmas tree and a boy scout, I thought, unhappy with the effect, but not unhappy enough to bother changing. On the way to the lobby to get coffee, I noticed that the heat and humidity of Washington had followed me this time, so I decided to drive to the courthouse. Of course, there were no close parking spaces, and I ended up parking near the gym, almost as far away as if I had walked from the motel.

When I got out of the car, I could smell the pool. I was late, but not that late, I figured. And they could start without me. It had been so long; it would be okay just to peek, wouldn't it? I was curious if Blue Ridge even had a team. With the Olympics in Rio coming up next month, you had to live in a cave to avoid thinking about swimming.

I pushed open the door, and a man's head swiveled toward the noise. His eyes widened.

"Oh my God. Gale Hightower. In my pool!"

The whistle around his neck, the bleached-out hair, and

the fact he recognized me combined to give him away. He must be the swim coach.

"Hi," I said and stuck out my hand.

"Jesus. I thought you were dead. I'm sorry, I just mean you fell off the map."

He had fewer manners than me. "No, not yet," I tried to laugh and buy time to place him.

"I swam against you in high school," he said to help me out. "Well, not against you, thank God. I would have lost. I was distance free too. The two hundred and five hundred. I wasn't very good, but I loved the sport. I think that's why I still coach. And I'm sorry, I'm Ed. Ed Edelstein," he stuck out his hand and we smiled and shook. "What are you doing here?"

"I'm covering the Connor Braxton trial for the *Washington Star.*"

"Oh jeez, of course. That was so awful last year. Want to come in and have a look at our facility? I'm getting ready to coach a Masters team. Bunch of post-college people doing triathlons and a few decent swimmers. I can introduce you. It would be really inspirational for them."

"I better skip. I need to get to the courthouse." His swimmers wouldn't know me anyway. Most people only know Olympic gold medalists. America's relationship with swimming starts and stops with gold medals.

"Well, at least check out the pool." He stuck his thumb over his shoulder. "It's new. It took three years to raise the funds and two years to build it. Fifty meters by twenty-five yards and a diving well. It's an incredible facility for this place. Not that we're that good, but we're starting to attract some better kids out of high school. I've got some good divers, though, and they score enough points to keep us in the game regionally…"

"Okay thanks. Maybe next time. I should get going…I was just curious." I couldn't get away.

"Come back anytime. I can even get you a pass if you still swim?"

"Oh, no. I am fully retired. Thank you."

"Okay. That's too bad. Well, gotta run. Gale Hightower. At my pool. Wow." He muttered as he walked off.

I pretended to leave but then decided that maybe I did have time for a peek once he was gone. I followed my nose and walked down the hall and looked through the glass windows at the pool. One look took me twenty-plus years back into the past. I instantly felt at home and, at the same time, utterly unmoored from reality. Which is how I always felt when I dove in and why I loved swimming.

The pool was gorgeous, as all good pools are. Deep blue and clear, filled with possibilities. There was a big deck, stands, banners celebrating school victories, and a scoreboard. The lane lines could be set up to run the length of the pool, like in the Olympics, or they could be strung across the width of the pool making each lane twenty-five yards long. It was set up for yards today. I always preferred swimming meters; the longer the better. I was never good at turns; they didn't seem a real part of swimming to me. It made my coach crazy. *You'll never go faster than when you push off the wall if you do it right!* he would yell.

After five minutes of staring, I pulled myself back to the present and slipped out before Coach Edelstein could find me again. Then I hustled over to the courtroom where Bennett was waiting for me outside, scanning the sidewalks in sunglasses and shifting his weight from foot to foot. Jill walked up just as I did.

"I'm thinking now we should have told you about this before we ran it," he said sheepishly, pulling off his sunglasses and handing me the school paper. There, below the fold, was a story on me with a photo from the 1992 Olympic trials. I looked so young and so happy.

"Swimmer turned Reporter in Town for Trial." Byline: Bennett Chin and Jill Stapleton.

Twice in one day? Great. I started reading. "Our local murder trial has finally merited some attention from the big papers and the *Washington Star* was savvy enough to send someone with a connection to all aspects of the case. Gale Hightower..." The story jumped to page three, and I kept reading.

I stretched my shoulders and thought about what to say. "The facts are true," I said after I finished. "The grammar is fine. There's no poetry or music in the structure, but that may come later in your careers. If I were your professor, I'd give you a B. Maybe a B+."

"You're not mad?"

"No, I'm not mad." That was a lie. I was mad, but I needed their help. Plus, they looked so relieved.

"I still feel like we lied to you," Bennett said. "By not saying anything."

"No, that's not lying. It does feel like it, but in this business, get used to it. Your sources aren't your friends."

"But you have been so great to us," he said. "Letting us be a part...."

"And you have helped me in return. I may have some more requests as well. It will all even out. Look, don't be babies." I took a deep breath. "Okay, maybe I am mad. But I shouldn't be. Let's just move on."

"Your story is just so amazing. You went through so much and..."

"We're not on an episode of *Jerry Springer* are we?"

They shook their heads.

"Then let's. Move. On." I said and gave them The Look. The Look was part street thug and part disappointed grandma. The Look always worked.

"So, did I miss anything so far?" I asked.

"No. The prosecution is still putting up their medical case."

It amazed me how much time this was taking when there was no real question about how the victims died.

"Okay, I'm going in. I'll see you guys later, and we'll talk about what you found on social media, if anything. It's okay. Really."

I crept into Courtroom One and slid onto a bench. Scanning the crowd, I again didn't see Connor's father. Maybe too much was spinning in my head, but I was starting to really need to know why Arthur Braxton was not at that trial. Yeah, my father left me in my time of crisis, but that was because of his own demons; it had nothing to do with me, with anything I did. Was it the same for Arthur, or had he given up on his son? If the murders were a mistake, a fight that got out of control, a father would be there, particularly one who had made his own mistakes. Assuming I understood anything about normal families, which it could be argued that I didn't. But if Arthur had a reason to be absent, I needed to figure it out.

I slid back out of the courtroom and Googled the number for Millennium Development. I would rely on Bennett and Jill to fill me in on the trial. That is not entirely ethical, but I am hoping the ends will justify the means. Plus, they owed me.

"Millennium Development. How may I direct your call?"

"Is Arthur Braxton available?"

"Is he expecting your call?"

"No, but I am a reporter with…"

She hung up. Okay, that tells me something. What exactly, I am not sure. I needed to catch Arthur by surprise, I realized, and with no gatekeeper. I snuck back into the courtroom Madison was presenting more boring testimony about the accuracy of the instruments used to measure Connor's blood alcohol and that of the victims. I had to make myself take notes. It was hard to imagine anyone wanting to read this level of detail in this day and age.

At the break, I called the Maryland State Corporation Commission to see how Millennium Development was organized and who the registered agent was. Maybe poking around in the records would light a path to the senior Braxton. After being on hold for three and a half rounds of the same bad muzak version of some vaguely familiar song, a friendly sounding woman answered.

"Maryland SCC. How can I help you?"

"Excellent. Thanks. Hi, I am a reporter and I need some information on a company called Millennium Development, if it's not too much trouble." I can be friendly, too.

"Okay, what kind of information?"

"Well, what kind of entity it is exactly, articles of incorporation, registered agent. Just the basics."

Sounds of typing. "I see here that the total number of responsive pages to your request is seventeen. Please send a check for $8.50—that's fifty cents a page—and we'll mail the copies to you."

"Um, thank you, that was fast, but can't you answer my questions over the phone if you're looking at the records?"

"No ma'am, but you can go online and do it yourself. That's free."

"If I can go online, can't you just tell me what I would find?"

"No ma'am. I'm sorry."

"Are you really?"

"Nah. But you sound nice. So instead of just hanging up, I say I'm sorry. Would you like our address?"

I had to laugh. "No. I guess I'll go online later."

"Good idea. Bye, and thanks for calling the Maryland State Corporation Commission."

"You're welcome."

I like government in theory, but not when I interact with it. I would go on-line later. It probably didn't matter anyway. I am letting to many red herrings distract me. Arthur wasn't giving Conner steroids, for god's sake. I called Sam and she was there but about to go into surgery, so I got a terse update on Charlotte.

"No change. I'll talk to you later."

Come on Charlotte, I thought. You have a home to go to when you are up to it and I'm through with this crazy trial. You have to pull through. You have to.

Back in court, Isaac's cross examination of the medical witnesses was methodical. Everyone was getting frustrated, but to his credit, he seemed to keep to his game plan. All he needed was to plant one seed of doubt in one juror.

After we recessed for the day at 6:30, later than usual, I caught up with Isaac before he got in his car. "Mr. Sutton, do you have a few minutes? It's Gale Hightower for the *Washington Star*. We met at the coffee shop last week. Could you tell me how you think the trial is going now?"

He sighed. "How do I think the trial is going now?" He looked at me for a full minute. His face gave away nothing. He might have been about to explode at me or just walk away. I need a new question. I wasn't frightened, though; with us both standing, I could see I had at least three inches on him.

"I'm exhausted and I'd like a drink," he said. "Want to talk over dinner? I haven't had anything resembling a normal evening in weeks, and you seem nice enough."

That was not the reply I expected.

"Absolutely. Well, I don't know about the nice part, but I'll try my best. Name the place. I have only been to Applebee's." I made a face for Isaac's benefit, hoping it wouldn't offend him.

"*Black and Tan*. The owner—my friend Stan—went to England in college and thought the name would be fun. But luckily, they don't serve English food. Where are you parked?"

I pointed. "By the pool."

"I'm right here." He nodded to an old sedan, and I couldn't identify either the make or even the nationality of it. Poor guy. "Get in. I'll drive you there."

I got in. Three silent minutes later, I pointed to my Corvette and Isaac pulled in next to it.

"Nice car. The place is only about three miles away, but there are about a dozen turns. Stay close."

"You didn't seem to like me talking to me too much last week. What changed?" I asked before I got out.

"Everything and nothing. You've handled yourself well around here, not pissing anybody off and not writing anything sensationalist. And I am tired and hungry and a little lonely, to be honest. Lawyers are human beings, I swear. Really, the food is quite good, and I might give you a quote or two if you promise not to make me or my client look like a fool. What do you say? Are you still in?"

I'm a sucker for honesty. "All right. It does sound like an offer I'd be stupid to refuse."

I followed him through a maze of leafy small-town streets. Ten minutes later, we pulled up and Isaac let me have the space in front of the restaurant, which looked quite nice. It took up the main floor of an old Victorian house. I waited for him to walk the block from where he had to park.

"This is our little arts district. Refugees from big city life are trying to re-create the parts they miss of New York and Los Angeles, and we all benefit."

"I like it. I never would have found my way over here by myself."

The atmosphere inside was homey and a little edgy—like English pub meets Ikea—and the clientele diverse. It was not, thank goodness, the kind of place where every head turned toward the door when a black woman walked in. Big points for Waynesville's arts district.

Several seats were open at the far end of the bar. We snaked through the tables to claim a pair. They were red leather, with short backs, and they swiveled.

We settled in. My chair had an over aggressive swivel and in the process of sitting I spun into Isaac's knees. He winced.

"I think you were ambushed by a faulty bearing in that seat. Want to switch?" he said.

"No, I'm fine. I like a challenge. Sorry about your knees." I shifted my weight to better control the chair.

The bar was just crowded enough to feel lively, but not so much that you felt you had to defend your personal space from errant elbows and bags. A hockey game was on ESPN Classic on the bar television.

The bartender came over as he was wiping a glass and asked us what we wanted. "Scotch on the rocks, with a lot of ice." That should slow me down.

"Same for me," Isaac said.

I was relieved we had gotten over that hurdle and that he didn't drink light beer or martinis. I don't know why, but I don't trust men who drink martinis. Arthur Braxton probably drinks martinis.

"So how long have you been a defense attorney?" I asked. I was curious.

"Eight years next March."

"What did you do before that?"

"I was in college and then prison." He turned and looked at me.

Holy crap, I thought. I was stunned. This might be a little too much honesty even for me.

"Don't you want to know what for?" Isaac asked.

I tried to keep it light. "Okay, so what did you study?"

He burst out laughing. "English. I had a minor in math. And I went to prison for a rape I didn't commit."

It was like he wanted to get it out, rip the scab off, confess.

"Are you bitter?"

"Yes, but I am trying not to be. I was in for four years before the man who did it was caught thanks to DNA evidence. My record was erased, and my rights restored."

Isaac had his eyes locked on the bar, like he wasn't going to look up until I gave him the signal. I didn't know what I felt, beyond a glimmer of understanding. For years after my brother died, I felt as if I were in a kind of prison for something I didn't do. Living a normal life was impossible and wrong. So even though I was technically free, I wasn't really free. I often wondered what percentage of people like that are in the general population. I figure it must be around 50 percent. I pushed the peanuts over to him, and he looked up, smiling, and grabbed a handful.

"Didn't you have an alibi?" I asked.

"Nope. I was home alone working on a master's thesis. I finished it in prison, thanks to some kind professors." He paused. "Of course, then I decided to go to law school. I've only just started talking about it."

"I can see why. It's a lot to talk about." I sipped my drink. "Is that why you became a defense attorney?" I asked. "To save people from your fate?"

"Maybe. Sometimes. I do like the system in theory, even though it didn't work for me."

It was Isaac's turn to change the subject. "So," he said, wiping his hands on a cocktail napkin. "Stan's specialty is anything that swims."

"Sounds delicious. I used to live in Seattle, and I miss all the fresh seafood available there. Don't get me wrong, DC has its share, but it isn't the same."

"Nostalgia always tastes better. Are you from Seattle?" he asked.

"No, but I lived there for twelve years. I'm from North Carolina. You?"

"That's a little complicated."

"What does "complicated" mean?"

"I was born in Mexico, so I guess I'm from there, but I haven't been back since I was twelve. This actually feels like home."

"North Carolina doesn't feel like home to me either. But I haven't really found a place that does. I can't even imagine a place that would feel like home," I said.

"That's kind of sad," he said.

"Maybe. But at least I don't get homesick. And home has always been whatever I do, whatever story I am working on. A lot of people don't get that from their work. It's a trade-off."

Our drinks came. I took a sip and the scotch was delicious, cold, peaty, briny fire going down my throat, so I took another. "Why haven't you been back to Mexico?"

He took a sip of his drink, half the glass really, then stared at it for a while. "Family is why I haven't been back. One brother runs drugs, but he takes care of our mother. Another brother is a cop, but he's a jerk. On the take, they say. I idolized him as a kid. One sister has married into the coffee business and uses the first brother's services."

If I knew anything, I knew family wasn't your fault. "I like coffee," I offered. "A lot." Even more, I like people who handle their baggage well. This was starting to not feel like an interview any more.

Isaac laughed. "Thanks. So, what about your family?" he asked.

I looked at him, wondering if I could return the favor. What the hell. I took a deep breath. I would also have to get it out all at once. "My father grew up on the streets in Baltimore, hustling drugs while trying to nurture a poet's soul. My mother is from Louisiana. She was blessed or cursed with an IQ of 160. I don't know which. My claim to fame—if you can really call it that—is that my father shot himself in the head in front of my mother the night I was born. They were fighting, and she went into labor right after that. Apparently, it was an interesting trip to the hospital. Two ambulances and everything."

"I bet the EMTs still tell that story," Isaac said.

"I bet you're right," I said laughing. "So, Dad survived

– the bullet just grazed his temple - and they stayed together for some reason I'll never understand. He was my best friend until he disappeared when I was seventeen. I'm not too close to my mother. After my messy childhood, she went to law school and is now a big shot lawyer in Atlanta." I stopped and shrugged.

Isaac looked at his drink. "Wow. I think you win," he said offering his glass in a toast.

"Excellent. I like winning, although I think you are being generous. I assume there is a prize?"

"Certainly. You want the stuffed bear or the giant lollipop?"

"Bear," I said. "I think the lollipop would spoil my appetite."

"To honesty," he said, raising his glass.

"To honesty," I replied. "So what kind of cases do you specialize in other than…"

"Murder? I usually try and help people who have been screwed by the man," Isaac said.

"Ah, sort of a lawyer Robin Hood?"

He laughed. "Sort of. I don't need much money to get by here."

"I bet this case pays well." I couldn't completely shed my reporter's skin.

Isaac looked at me and didn't answer. I kicked myself for potentially blowing the evening. After a quiet minute, he nodded at the television. "I used to play a little hockey in college, but I was pretty bad." Isaac said to the TV as much as to me. "Not fast and not a fighter. But I loved the flow of the game, the way it could change in an instant. I had great teammates, too. God, that was a long time ago," he added, as if to remind himself as much as inform me.

"Where did you go to college?" I asked.

"At Brown. You?"

"UNC."

"Did you play any sports?"

"Not in college. I swam throughout high school, though."

"What was your event?"

"Distance freestyle. Some butterfly."

"You must be excited about the Rio Olympics coming up. Did you ever want to go to the Olympics?"

I guess he didn't read the student newspaper. "I actually made it there in '92 but didn't swim."

He looked justifiably puzzled. "Can I ask why?"

I wasn't ready. "Maybe another time?" I just couldn't, even after all these years, talk about it. I finished my drink and longed for another. As if reading my mind, Isaac signaled the bartender for two more even though he wasn't quite finished.

He didn't push. "Sure." He paused. "How about a primer on Seattle? I've never been farther west than Colorado."

My head popped up. "I did love Seattle. I wrote features, often about environmental issues. It consumed me. There were so many stories to write, so many things people needed to know. The *Seattle Ledger* hired me just out of journalism school. Occasionally I had to cover other science issues, but mostly my job was to report on the destruction of the water and the land. There was never a shortage of work. When I moved to Washington, I was able to stick with the environmental beat for a while until it was determined that no one cared. At least no advertisers cared. So, I got assigned to the Metro section, where I do a little bit of everything. In some ways, it suits me just fine."

"It got you here," he said smiling.

"Yeah."

"Isaac!" yelled a big man in a dirty apron who had just delivered two plates at the other end of the bar.

Isaac peeled away from me and got up to return the bear hug. "Hi Stan. Great to see you. Working hard?"

"As always. Been a long time since I've seen you in here. Who's the occasion?" he asked, tilting his head and wiggling his eyebrows at me.

"Stan, this is Gale. Gale, Stan."

Stan stuck a meaty hand across the bar and I shook it too. "Pleased to meet you." Stan turned his attention back to his friend, as if it wasn't odd at all that Isaac was in the bar with a black woman with mismatched eyes. "She's lovely," he said in a stage whisper.

"She's a reporter on the Connor Braxton trial, and this is a business dinner," Isaac said loudly back. "But I can't argue with you on that."

I blushed, dammit.

"You should have brushed your hair either way. Anyway, I'd love to cook something for you to honor this auspicious occasion," Stan said.

"Are you hungry?" Isaac asked me.

"Starving, now that I think about it."

"That's it then," said Stan, clapping his hands. "I'm making you dinner. Allergies? Anything you can't stand or got a crazy hankering for?"

I shook my head.

"Okay. Give me twenty minutes. I've got some delicacies from the Chesapeake Bay on ice." Stan jogged back into the kitchen, making the bar glasses rattle with his footfalls.

"Stan can be a little energetic…"

"He seems great."

"He is passionate about food."

"It's good to care about what you do," I said.

"We should drink to that," Isaac said and raised his glass. I clinked and drank. People were moving to tables, and the bar was emptying out. Another silence fell, but it was okay this time. I sipped my drink and we listened to music and watched the game. Like regular people.

"I couldn't decide, so you got both of my favorite dishes, so you can share," Stan said when he brought our order. He winked, too. "Bon appetit," he said with a flourish and then left.

Our meals were amazing. Shrimp and grits with grilled zucchini and goat cheese on one plate and rockfish in a pistachio crust with roasted sweet potatoes and spinach on the other. We did as instructed and shared everything.

"Oh my God. I haven't had a meal like this in ages. It's a symphony on the plate," I groaned.

"I'm glad you like it." Isaac beamed with pride in his friend's work.

Because everything was going so well, I decided to ruin it. "So, can I ask a trial question?"

"That was the original deal," Isaac said.

"Have you considered that maybe Connor was on drugs, that he was using steroids?"

Isaac's face showed no surprise. "There is no evidence of that. No blood test, no accusations. Nothing. I care about this trial, but I am not going to make up flights of fancy for the jury to get lost in. I think I can get Connor life, which is an excellent result for him. He admitted that he killed two people with his bare hands."

The subject was obviously closed. But sometimes I can't take no for an answer. Especially when I've had a couple of drinks. Some people are happy drunks, some are angry. I am a curious drunk. Some might say pushy.

"If I get you proof, will you use it?"

He looked at me then at his drink. "It depends. I'm not sure how you could do that at this late date. I haven't exactly been sitting on my duff. I did look into a few things. And unless someone was forcing him to take them, I am not sure it would help. Diminished capacity theories usually fall flat unless the jury is looking for a way to let the defendant off. I met a lot of guilty people when I was in prison, and Connor is guilty. Don't print that."

"I won't. I get it, but still. Something smells fishy."

"Says the swimmer," Isaac said with a rueful smile.

The steroids issue doused any potential flame between us, at least for the time being, and that made me sad. I was starting to like Isaac, and not just because he was honest and complicated. Although, those traits are like catnip to me.

"I didn't mean to be too pushy," I said.

"It's okay," Isaac said, although I could tell it wasn't really.

We walked to my car. "I'm not going to print anything from tonight."

"Thanks," Isaac said. "I don't usually let my guard down that far. Do let me know if you find anything. I can't share what I have looked into – it would spoil attorney client privilege – but I will look at anything you find."

"I understand. And thanks for a really nice evening," I said, extending my hand. He shook it without too much hesitation.

"You're welcome. I had a good time too. I'll see you tomorrow," he said.

Back in my motel room, I managed to write and send Alex a story summarizing the additional forensic testimony and speculating on what the rest of the week would hold in court. Then I just lay flat on the bed and thought about Isaac. And the past.

TWELVE

Monday, later

Sometime in the middle of the night, I woke up wet with my own sweat and utterly lost. Slowly, I realized where and, more importantly, when I was. Although it was just a dream, I was there feeling it happen all over again. I re-live it several times a year, and each time, it sucks a little more of the life out of me.

I was at the Olympics, about to get on the blocks and ready to swim my heart out. One second later, my world exploded.

Time is funny like that. A second can hold as little as a sneeze or as much as the gulf between first and last place. Death fits easily in a single second too. For a long time, I felt as if I'd never left that one particular second. Instead of expiring, it yawned and stretched to swallow the next twenty-four years of my life.

The day began magically. I swam well in the preliminary heats, going 4:08 for the 400 free. I had qualified at the Olympic trials a month earlier for two events, the 400 and 800 free. That wouldn't normally have been enough for my coach to be on deck—I was the only swimmer he had at the Games—but they made an exception because I was so young. Things might have turned out differently if they hadn't bent the rules for us. I try not to think about that. My 4:08 was the second fastest qualifying time and good enough to get me Lane 5. The middle lanes, 4 or 5, are always what you want; there is less turbulence there since they are farther from the walls. Smooth water means a better chance for a fast swim and a medal.

No one expected a gangly black-skinned 17-year-old

from a nobody team in Nowheresville, North Carolina to do so well, so I got a lot of stares. People were trying to figure me out. I didn't really want to be figured out, so I spent the time between morning prelims and evening finals in the pool as much as possible. The pool was home. Simple, safe, and clear.

I took one break from the water for lunch and a walk with my father. It was a gorgeous, cloudless day in Barcelona, and we had a good time just being together and taking in the strange sights of a strange city. Dad was too excited and proud to say much, and he didn't have to. I was relieved just to have him there and glad he was having fun. He always enjoyed new situations; he was a natural observer, and he made friends quickly. He just wasn't good at keeping them, but that wasn't entirely his fault. Mom and Trout, my little brother, couldn't come because we didn't have that kind of money and also because Mom was well, Mom. She was occupied with other things.

This was only my second international meet. All meets are the same in some ways, but this was the Olympics, and everything felt ratcheted up to the highest setting. The sense of possibility took the oxygen out of the air. You had to breathe more deeply, and then it was like the excitement entered your body along with the air. There were so many people and languages, so much color and noise, so many reporters and volunteers, and so many other events to watch.

Warm ups for finals went well. My stroke felt smooth and relaxed, but still fast and powerful. I was skimming over the water instead of pulling my body through it. Easy speed—the holy grail of swimming—is a glorious and rare feeling. To get it, you have to work incredibly hard and rest the exact right amount and be lucky. I dried off, and a volunteer handed me my sweats and Walkman and Gatorade. Coach and I had already gone over the game plan for the race: make each 100 faster than the previous one. It was always our game plan, and it usually worked.

The announcer called the Men's 100 free which meant it was time for the eight of us to go into the ready room. We jostled into the humid, windowless and nearly airless holding tank of a room. Everyone immediately created their own world in the tiny space, walling off the competition as best they could with headphones and jacket hoods and eyelids. You could still sense the different types of energy each person radiated—who was scared, who was confident, who was hungry, and who had the most to lose. Now that the moment was finally here, I realized I was hungry. I wanted it so much I thought my skin would split open from the wanting. I wanted to have the race of my life and touch the wall before anyone else. I wasn't just happy to be here. I wanted gold.

The announcer started the race right before ours, and the crowd went crazy the minute the swimmers hit the water. Forty-nine seconds later Alexander Popov took the gold. When the official opened the door for us to march out, we all walked in a perfect line, in lane order, one through eight, like obedient fifth graders going to a school assembly. I was right behind Janet Evans, my teammate and competition.

I stripped off my sweats and kicked off my sandals. Then I grabbed the edge of the starting block and twisted, first to the right, then to the left, always in that order, stretching the muscles of my back and shoulders to ensure that nothing would prevent me from getting the maximum distance per stroke and going as fast as possible. Then I did four slow motion jumping jacks. All that was left on the list was to splash water on my face and put on my cap and goggles. I didn't usually wear a cap because I kept my hair so short, but in competitions, I wanted the fraction of a second I could get from eliminating the last little bit of drag.

I easily found my father in the stands. I waved. He waved back, grinning with his arms outstretched, like he was scaring crows off the vegetable garden at home. I wanted to see the sign I knew he had; it was all part of the routine. But no sign appeared. Instead a volunteer leaned over him and put her head close to his, and my father twisted toward her, trying to hear whatever she was saying. I couldn't see his face. She passed him an envelope. It must be an invitation to something wonderful, I thought. It seemed like they created new events and receptions for finalists and their families every minute. I shrugged it out of my mind.

Lane 1 was announced as I put on my goggles. They fogged immediately, and I pulled them off. I told myself not to get anxious, I had plenty of time. I always had problems with goggles. I grew up not using them; it felt like my face fought goggles. For that reason, I wore my goggles outside of my cap, so I could rip them off in the middle of the race if I had a problem.

It was Lane 2's turn to stand on the blocks and hear the cheers of her countrymen. I spit in my goggles and tugged them on again. Now they were as clear as a bell. I looked for my coach one last time, just to see his crooked grin and trademark thumbs up. But instead he was looking down, and I saw an official cupping her hands around his ear like the other one did with my father. She bowed and handed him an envelope and looked at me. There was both fear and pity in her eyes. A roar started in my ears and grew to swallow my whole body in a bubble of noise.

The swimmer in Lane 3 waved to the crowd. I looked into the stands for my father again, and I couldn't find him. I got up on the starting block so I could see better and was immediately whistled down. They announced Janet in Lane 4. I looked back at my coach. He looked at me, and in that look in his face, in that half-second, I could tell my life was over.

Not knowing what was happening, the starter still announced: "In Lane 5, Gale Hightower representing the United States of America." The crowd still cheered for me. But I wasn't there.

It seemed to take forever to cross the 25 feet of deck to get to him. I didn't run. I couldn't. I was moving through molasses. I heard them call my name again, giving me another chance. Their accented English carried a mixture of encouragement, annoyance and desperation. One official, an older man with a pot belly, even chased me down, grabbed me on the shoulder, and tried to physically force me back to the blocks. They announced my name for the last time. More officials were hurrying toward me.

When I got to my coach he dropped his hands and started crying. He'd known my crazy family for a long time. His wife would cook casseroles for us when my mother was busy with law school. His daughter babysat Trout. Please God, let it be Mom, I thought, and hated myself.

"She woke up, and he wasn't in his bed. There was nothing your mother could do."

I stood still, not wanting to believe it.

"Trout?" My mouth formed the word, but no sound came out.

But my coach understood and just nodded.

"Is he dead?" This time aloud.

He nodded again, his shoulders heaving with his sobs.

"I'm so sorry," he said through tears.

"You must come now. Please, we cannot hold the race any longer," I heard an official say, her hand on my arm. This one was in a suit. They had called in management.

The crowd had gone silent. I turned around and saw three or four officials waiting like jailors to take me back into the race, back into the bosom of the Olympics. In the background, all of the other racers were turned toward me, toward the mess of my life. I turned back to my coach. He looked at me.

"Scratch us," he said. The words hit me like a hammer, but I knew I couldn't swim. I couldn't breathe.

He tried to draw me into a hug. I didn't resist, but I couldn't make my body respond. Everything inside my skin had turned to liquid. Trout was my baby brother. When I first saw him, only a few hours old, I felt a piece of my soul break out of my body and start living in him.

"Where is he? What happened?" I demanded. I was suddenly so angry I was rigid. At what I didn't know. I just felt a blind, burning rage.

My coach shook his head. "They can't be right. Something must have gotten mixed up in translation. Let's leave, try and find your father and get more details." He reached for my shoulder.

I shook him off. "What. Happened."

He took a deep breath and looked at me, as if sizing me up to see if I could handle it. I wish to this day I hadn't passed whatever test he gave me then. Maybe I could have recovered and swum the 800. Salvaged something bright from such an awful day.

"The message said he was found dead at the bottom of the neighborhood pool with a backpack of bricks locked to his body with a bicycle chain. Drowned."

Wet and nearly naked, I was defenseless against the horror of the news. I slumped onto the deck.

"Do they know who did it?" someone's voice asked. I guess it was mine. It was hard to hear with the roar still in my ears.

"A witness saw him walking to the pool weighted down by the pack. The guy apparently thought it was a stunt. By the time he got there, it was too late. And your mother found a note."

I started to wail like an animal, and the noise pushed the crowd away from us. Trout had asked me not to go. Begged me. I can still remember how he smelled when I left, like dirt and glue and grass and me. I told him I would be back in eleven days. I even circled the date I would get home on his calendar while he was sitting on his bed playing with his soldiers. Ten years old is old enough to understand, isn't it? But we were so close, and I should have known. We had never been apart for more than three days. I killed him. Swimming killed him. The water—my life—was his death.

The gun went off signaling the start of my race, and the crowd started cheering wildly. My drama was over for them. I turned to look and saw seven lanes of churning water and a single quiet one. I watched my lane as if something would appear out of it. Four minutes later, I could see Lane 4 won. WR flashed next to Janet's time.

The next day I woke up in a hospital room alone. The rage burned itself out overnight and left a hollowness that would remain forever. I vaguely remembered getting hysterical at the pool before the medics came and sedated me. I felt so heavy and weak, all I could do was lay there and count the slats in the blinds on the window and try to guess which flashing red light would flash next. Nurses came and went, but I wouldn't look at them. I could feel them smiling their sad, sympathetic smiles. I could sense they wanted to pat my arm, but they didn't. Then my coach came in.

"Your mom will be here tomorrow, Gale. Flights were

difficult to arrange. We haven't been able to locate your father. I am so sorry." He could only look at the floor as he recited his news. I couldn't blame him.

I knew my father was gone forever. This would have been too much for him.

I met my coach's eyes. "I'm sorry I couldn't swim," I said. He waved my words away and gave me a hug, but it was all I could focus on. I knew this was a disappointment to him; his career would have been made if I had gotten one medal. Any color. What didn't occur to me was how bad he felt for me.

It took me years to be able to see a pool without hyper-ventilating. Swimming and death became linked in my soul. I lost my brother, my father and my passion in one day. I couldn't stop thinking that I must be next, that crazy runs in my family. If I wasn't born a pessimist, I became one that day in a Spanish hospital room. I closed my eyes.

When I got back home, I stayed in bed for three months and in my mother's house for eight more. It took that long to develop enough scar tissue to be able to face the world. My coach visited a few times, but it was too weird. We had nothing in common anymore. The next fall, I went to college, but without a scholarship. I never swam again. I begged her, but my mother never showed me the note, and she wouldn't tell me what it said.

"I don't want you to remember him that way," she said.

For years I asked myself how I could have missed the signals that Trout was desperate enough to kill himself. I am not very proud of the answer.

THIRTEEN

Tuesday, July 12

At the first sign of dawn, I got up. I hadn't slept since I woke up from my dream, sobbing. I showered and went to the lobby to get a tray and as much coffee as I could carry.

The dream happened often enough that I knew what to do to survive. Switch off, batten down the hatches, and work. That horrible trip down memory lane might even have offered a clue to this puzzle. It took me back into the swimming world, which at that time was infested with drugs. In the 1980s, the East Germans got them from the government. Same with the Chinese in the 1990s. People don't usually do performance enhancing drugs on their own. They have to get them from somewhere. But in this day and age in America, they could come from anywhere. Gyms, mail order, doctors and trainers. I realized I needed to look off-campus. Why had I thought all the answers lay at the university anyway?

At eight, I packed my backpack and headed out for food on foot even though it seemed like it was going to drizzle. Rain doesn't bother me too much. I usually like it. It quiets every-thing. Back at Sara's Kitchen I ordered a small latte and muffin. The options were blueberry and something called the "Island muffin." Not feeling very adventurous, I went with blueberry.

At the courthouse, I slid into a seat a few minutes earlier than usual and watched the lawyers shuffle papers. Isaac hadn't noticed me yet, and I wondered if it was going to be uncomfort-able when he did. My stomach kind of did a little hiccup as I pondered the question. The jury came in, the bailiff said his part and soon after the judge took his seat.

We heard more mundane medical testimony for the first ninety minutes. At the break when I saw Bennett and Jill, I asked them if they were going to stay for the whole day.

"Yup. Do you need something?" Bennett asked with more than his usual quota of eagerness.

See, it was good to have them in my debt.

"I want to check on Charlotte. Could you take notes if anything important happens? I should be back after lunch. Then we also need to catch up on your social media research."

Their faces told me I hadn't mentioned Charlotte before, so I filled them in and they both got all soft-eyed. I figured that lie would work. And it wasn't totally a lie. I would call Sam, but I had a different plan for the next two hours.

"Sure. We'll see you after lunch and give you our notes. And are you okay? You look a little…"

"I am fine. Thanks." I thought about squeezing his shoulder, but that just wasn't me. So, I smiled and snuck out. Alex would kill me, but she won't have to know. Unless, of course, some witness dropped a bombshell, but that only happens on television.

Outside, I pulled out my phone and looked up local gyms. If I remembered anything from my athletic past, it was that the gym rats knew where to get steroids. And if I found the source, I may find out who else was using and try and save them. I couldn't imagine a college kid doing drugs on his own. I was sure of it. Kids ran in packs, especially in team sports and especially at this age and especially in a middle of nowhere town like this where there was nothing else to do. I found three gyms I wanted to check out and hustled back to my motel room to change.

I decided to work from the outskirts of town back in and

went to the one that was seventeen miles away on something called Turkey Foot Lane. *Pumpin' Iron* was the name. It seemed like my best shot. It clearly didn't cater to the leotard and iPod set. I doubted there would be yoga or cycle classes in what I assumed was going to be a sweaty concrete box. I pulled into a nearly empty parking lot and at the front desk, I introduced myself as a former basketball player who was new to town. I said I wanted to get back into shape quickly and maybe do some bodybuilding competitions.

"I have a sister in Cleveland who's been doing them, and it looks like fun." I said. "She even takes her little dog on stage with her." Details. Lies are all about the details. Keep talking until people stop really listening and let their guard down. "So, I thought maybe I'd come check out your place and see if—I don't know—it might be the right atmosphere. Maybe I could find a training buddy. I'm divorced, and like I said, I'm new to town. And man, I gotta spend that alimony somehow that my pricey lawyer got me, and I want to make that sonofabitch regret sleeping with that slut. Can you help me with my goals? I know it's all about setting good goals. I read that."

I stopped and smiled and waited expectantly for the girl at the desk to figure out what to do with me.

"Um, well, welcome."

"Thanks!"

"Let me see if Scott can show you around." She paged Scott who turned around from the water fountain six feet away.

Bingo. Bulging biceps—bigger than Kevin's—and tight clothes and a bowlegged walk.

"Hi, I'm Scott."

"Sylvia," I said, sticking out my hand limply. I repeated my goals to the very last detail, giving the dog a name—

Tamara—and a breed—Miniature Pincher, like a tiny Doberman you know?—And a pink collar. "Pink is my color, too!" I said.

"Well, I certainly think we can help you with your goals. It is amazing how quickly a committed person can gain muscle mass and lose flab. And on your frame, I am sure you could be ready for a competition in six or eight months. You don't have too much excess fat as it is."

Not too much excess fat? Thanks, buddy, I thought.

"Wow! Sounds great!" I said aloud.

"Let me show you around and introduce you to some of the trainers, and then you can go back and talk pricing options with the gals at the front. Sound okay?"

"Sounds perfect. I just wanna get strong and cut as soon as possible. I'm ready!"

Scott smiled, and we walked onto the main floor of the gym. It smelled like disinfectant mixed with old sweat and reminded me of my high school weight room. The equipment was probably from the same era too, which I liked. The few new gyms I'd been in—mostly by accident—looked like dentist offices.

We tested out a few exercises and Scott told me how strong I was. I wasn't even trying.

"So, what besides lifting weights can I do to get cut fast so I can do a competition and win? I like winning."

"Well, first, you have to enter the right competitions, and I can help you with that. Second, you're going to have to overhaul your diet." He looked me up and down like I was a piece of meat. Not sexy meat, just meat. "You probably have five to six percent body fat you could lose. I mean you're in good shape, but to stand on a stage, you've got to have nothing flopping over that bikini. So, eliminate carbs. All carbs. Alcohol too. It's a carb. Focus on lean protein, whey powder, canned tuna, things like that. We sell some great powders too."

"That sounds like a lot of work. I like my Cosmos and wine coolers! Are there, like any supplements? My sister, she works with some doctor…"

Scott's eyes narrowed. "Everyone I train trains clean. We compete clean." He folded his arms and looked at me. "Anything else is stupid, a way to blow up your tendons and your life. Your sister is getting some bad advice, and you should tell her to be careful."

I was shocked. I was sure, based on his appearance, that… Shit. I was flustered, not ready for this reaction. "I'm sorry, I didn't mean…"

"Now, if you want to lift weights here and learn how to support your hard work with the right diet, we can help you with that. Anything else, you're on your own, and you better not do it here. It was nice to meet you. Let me know what you decide."

We shook hands and Scott literally turned on his heel and left. All right, I thought, scratch this one off the list.

The other two gyms didn't look like they would fit the bill, but I tried my spiel anyway. At the second, they didn't even get my hint, and at the third, the guy took me into his office and tried to sell me creatine and a personal training package. So, no dice at the gyms. It was worth checking out, though. And I got a good little reminder not to judge a book by its cover. We have to form judgments in this life to get though the day and stay alive, but we also have to be willing to admit we are wrong.

I went back to my motel room and changed back into court clothes and caught up with Bennett and Jill just as the judge had recessed for lunch.

"Did I miss anything?" I asked.

"Not a thing. Here are my notes, though," Jill said.

"Thanks," I said and flipped through them. Basically, a repetition of yesterday's testimony. Repetition is the key both to building a case and boring a jury, I thought. I handed them back.

"How's your dog?" Jill asked.

Crap! I forgot even to call. "Oh, she's about the same. The vet says it will take a while, but she's getting a little stronger each day. She just has such an uphill battle."

Jesus, I was scaring myself. I was getting too good, I'd have to back off the lying. Although this technically was the truth the last time I checked. I would call Sam as soon as I got a chance to make sure it still was. But I had the sense, once I let myself think about Charlotte, it would be all I would think about. I needed to keep everything separate for now. I changed the subject to explore an idea I had driving back from the last gym.

"Do either of you think you can help me get into the college computer system?"

"You mean like you want to borrow our log-ons for something?" Bennett asked.

"No, something a little deeper. I'd like to see if there is any electronic trail, any evidence of steroid use. Internet orders, emails, whether deleted or not, things like that."

"We didn't have any luck on social media so far, and Connor would have had his own laptop, too, so I'm not sure..." Jill said.

She's nervous, I realized, and she should be.

"True," I answered, "but what about the athletic department computers? If Connor was using steroids, maybe someone here—a trainer, a coach—got them for him. And maybe others."

Since my foray for a source outside of the university

failed, I wanted to dig deeper on the inside.

They looked at each other, deciding.

"Is Adam back?" Jill asked Bennet.

"I think so," Bennett responded.

"Do you think he'll do it?"

"Maybe." Bennett turned to me. "There is a guy who may be able to help us, but we have a complicated relationship."

"Okay...what kind of complicated?"

"He's a jerk," Jill said.

"Oh, that can't be a problem. The world is full of jerks we have to work with," I said, although I did worry about expanding our little club too much, now that what we were contemplating was illegal.

"Okay, I'll call Adam and maybe we can meet at our offices later?" Jill said.

"Sounds good. Thanks." I mentally crossed my fingers. "Oh, and if Adam can get into the campus police database, that would be great. It would be helpful to see what has been reported regarding Connor."

"Two birds with one stone!" exclaimed Jill.

"Exactly. I would like to explore that angle more, possibly in a separate story. If universities think that violence doesn't leave their borders, they are crazy." If we found anything, I wanted to see if I could get it to Marcus and Gina's families for any civil lawsuit. This is all beyond my job as a reporter – and arguably outside of journalistic ethics. And outside of the law. But I could sort that out later.

We split up for lunch, and then I did call Sam.

"How's Charlotte?" I asked, fearful of the answer.

"Your girl is doing better. Not great, but better. This damn infection is delaying everything. But she's eating and doesn't seem too stressed. She is a patient girl. That is good sign. She is a good dog."

I was relieved, and it I know it showed in my voice. "Thank you."

"You're welcome, and don't worry. She's a fighter."

Fighting doesn't guarantee winning, I thought.

I went back to my regular spot to grab a sandwich—I was going to give Sara's Kitchen a glowing Yelp review when I got back—and decided to head into the past. I booted up my laptop and plugged in the Wi-Fi password. My goal was to find out what happened to every former player since Blue Ridge started becoming competitive. I should have done this kind of methodical research sooner, but between being rusty and having my attention diverted by Charlotte, I was a little slow.

Working backwards in time, I found team rosters for each year, added the names to a spreadsheet, got rid of duplicates, and then searched each name in Google. It was quickly apparent that there was not a lot of post-college success for these kids. The few players that had a shot at the pros overseas, where the bar to entry is much lower than for the NBA, got injured, and there was one suicide.

After lunch, Madison put on the state's last witnesses. The volunteer coordinator from the local YMCA was up first. In a pale pink blouse with a bow at the neck and librarian glasses on a chain, she was the spitting image of prim and proper. She testified about how gentle and great Marcus was with the kids.

"He just had such patience. His job was to teach them basketball, but he took time to laugh and didn't get upset when their attention wandered. I think he was teaching them more than basketball. He was showing how a certain kind of man can behave. With kindness. He was a saint."

Isaac tried to cross-examine her, but given her testimony, he didn't have too many options.

"Did you socialize with Marcus at all?" he asked.

"No?"

You could tell she didn't see the relevance of the question, but I did.

"So, you only saw him once a week for the school year?"

"Sometimes twice."

"Okay, thank you very much for your time."

Doubt planted. A lot can happen in the other days of a week. It was a smart move, a surgical strike. If he went too far, she would have caught on and defended her opinion. That line of questioning also answered my question about whether Marcus had a record. If he did, Isaac would have brought it up.

At the afternoon break, the thin, blond, current or future Junior Leaguer finally came up to me and offered her hand. She was the one whose reason for being at the trial I couldn't figure out.

"I'm Caroline Wilcox," she said.

"It's nice to meet you. I'm Gale Hightower from the *Washington Star.*" We shook hands and she kind of squirmed, as if she had touched something she'd rather not, but knew she had to. I can spot racism a mile away—the talent is a gift with purchase kind of thing when you're born with brown skin.

"I know who you are. I wonder if you'd come out to my house for dinner tonight?"

I was confused. She was clearly not the type to socialize with my type. She wanted something from me and was trying to make friends first. I should go along for the ride. Never say no when someone wants to talk, that's the first rule of reporting. Plus, I was hungry as well as curious.

She sensed my hesitation - not that it was that hard to sense – and tried to sweeten the pot. "I am a good cook, and my father wants to meet you. He's ill, or he'd be here at the trial. We may have some information that could help you tell a more complete story." She clearly could say more, but she was waiting to see if this would be enough.

And it was. "Okay. When?" I asked.

"6 p.m. Here's the address."

She handed me a piece of monogrammed stationary with a street address written in the most elegant handwriting. My handwriting, even I can't read it. I almost laughed.

"Okay, thanks. I'll see you then," I said.

My mother would have killed me for not offering to bring something, but what could I bring? Beef jerky from the 7-11? And this was clearly a business dinner. I decided I was off the hook.

Back in court, the prosecution finished presenting its evidence at a little before 5 pm, and the defense moved to dismiss the case. It's a pro-forma motion, but it seemed particularly out of place here. The judge denied it with a look that would put the best I could muster to shame.

"Will you be ready tomorrow to present your case?" the judge asked.

"Yes, your honor," Isaac replied.

Everyone packed up, and I waited for Isaac outside. I wanted to gauge how upset he was with me for raising the steroids issue on what might have been a date.

"Thanks again for dinner last night," I said.

"You are welcome. It was a nice diversion. I was thinking

more about what you mentioned," he didn't say the word steroids, "and I'll do some more digging. I'll talk to Connor's father. You may have a point. I've got to run and get ready for tomorrow." He smiled. Why the turnaround? I was suspicious. Either he likes me, or he is trying to put me off a scent. I truly had no idea which it was.

I had just enough time to hurry back to the motel, grab my car and head to dinner.

FOURTEEN

Tuesday, later

Afraid I was going to fall asleep in the middle of dinner at Caroline Wilcox's house, I stopped for some coffee at the 7-11. It was burnt and weak, but it would do the trick. After a short drive west that took me into a very nice neighborhood—and seemingly fifty years back in time—I pulled up to the Wilcox mansion a few minutes after six. Just fashionably late, I figured.

When I rang the bell, a middle-aged black woman, heavy but fit, wearing an actual maid's costume opened the door and stared at me in confusion. Apparently, my type used the back door, and her employer hadn't warned her that their guest tonight was also black.

"Hi," I said. "I'm Gale. I think I was invited for dinner." And for something else, although I wasn't sure what exactly.

"Welcome to the Wilcox residence. My name is Athena. Come in. I will take your things." She recovered quickly like a true professional and asked me to wait in the hall. She took my backpack and put it in a closet. A minute later, she came back with Caroline and then slipped away soundlessly.

"Thank you for coming," said Caroline.

"Thank you for having me. Something smells wonderful," I said, because it did.

"I told you, I am a good cook."

"Is this your house?" I asked before I would help myself. She looked too young for so much house.

"No, it's my father's. I only recently moved back."

"It looks like it has a lot of history."

"Yes, most of it bad. I'm sorry about earlier. Other than Athena, I'm not really around black people very much and they—you—make me unsettled, I'm embarrassed to say."

"Well, I appreciate your honesty. You make me unsettled too."

"Why?"

"Money, I guess. Your nervousness. It's a vicious circle. But I can put that aside if you can," I said. "We don't have to be friends to have a common cause."

"Good, because I think I need your help. My husband committed suicide, and I believe it was because of what went on in that team," Caroline said.

"The Blue Ridge basketball team?" I asked, as if there could be another team at issue right now.

"Yes. He graduated in 2013, and he shot himself two years later. I've had my suspicions that it was related to what was going on with the basketball team, and now I want to see if they are real. If you'll help. That is why I have been at the trial."

Her husband was the suicide I found. "Why didn't you say something to me last week?" I asked.

"Around here, we like to know people a bit before we trust 'em," said her father, who just appeared, leaning on his walker. "Caroline said you seem to be no-nonsense, and your stories aren't full of lies. I'm Bob Fisher." He didn't offer his hand, probably because he needed both of them for his walker. "I'm all Caroline has left."

"Okay, well, Caroline, why don't you tell me the whole story, and I'll take some notes if that's okay."

"That's more than okay. Thank you. Let's sit down in the library," she said.

Caroline walked past a staircase that looked like it was

borrowed from the set of *Gone with the Wind* and turned right into a small room with floor-to-ceiling windows on the far side and bookshelves filled to the brim on the other three walls. She sat down in one gold leather wing chair and her father took the other. I sat on the sofa. It had a royal blue and white garden print. The whole effect was tasteful, but heavy. Caroline smoothed her dress to buy time, took a deep breath and met my eyes.

"My husband – Billy Wilcox - was the team captain when Connor was a freshman. Billy met Connor when Connor was still in high school on a recruiting trip in the fall of 2011."

She paused, and I just waited.

"This was before we were married. He told me about him; he said that Connor was a wild kid, but he had potential, and that the team was lucky if they could get him to come. Maybe they could even go to the tournament. The university had hired a new president and he was very interested in sports. The players were excited about the future."

"William McFarlane?" I asked.

"Yes. He came on in 2008—a year before Mack, the old coach, died—and started to steer money into the sports programs. This was the reason the team could invite kids for recruiting trips. They never had money for that before. President McFarlane said it was the key to setting the school apart. He brought in big money somehow and didn't just give it to the basketball team—he spread it out among all the sports. And even purchased new equipment for the student gym. He was fair with the money. People were happy. I mean professors weren't really, but the students and alumni were."

I took notes, trying so hard not to jump to conclusions. William McFarlane felt dirty from the first time I met him.

"There was money for conferences, too. Coach Ford

and Kevin went to the NSAA conference in January 2011. I remember the dates so well because it was when I was planning our wedding."

"What is NSAA?"

"National Strength and Athletics Association. It was new. After that, the team changed, Billy said. It became a 'win at all costs' culture. Kevin and Coach Ford split the practices. Coach Ford focused on the game and Kevin focused on strength training and nutrition. Billy said it felt like boot camp, not basketball. He really liked Coach Ford but wasn't sure how to handle the changes. Connor thrived in the new system, though, and so did a lot of the other players. They got bigger and stronger and started winning, when they didn't foul out. Billy got hurt and lost his starting job. He was always more of a thoughtful player, not super athletic. That fall, we had our worst fight ever and he came close to hitting me. I think the coaches were forcing the players to do something that was making Billy really uncomfortable, but he couldn't tell me what it was. He was raised to get along and pay your dues. So, he bottled it up until he couldn't."

She stopped and took a big breath, clearly trying not to cry.

"Let's eat," Mr. Fisher said, stopping the tears before they could start. "Caroline made the chicken and vegetable things, and I made the wine. If you can handle it."

We got up and went across the hall to the dining room. The table was set with fine china and crystal and fresh flowers. I felt like I was in a Ritz-Carlton. Athena served us.

"Everything is delicious." I said. "I've never had homemade wine before."

"Big city folks tend to look down their noses at it," he said. "But once you stop thinking it should be like some French chateau de whatever, it is good. Better, I think—especially with Caroline's chicken. Be careful though, it's pretty strong."

"Thanks," I said, instead of 'I think my tolerance for alcohol could take yours outside and pin it in a wrestling match. No contest.' I don't like condescending old men. But I liked Caroline. She was complicated.

"What do you want me to do?" I finally asked. "Not that I am not sure I can do anything."

"I'd like you to clear my husband's name," Caroline said.

"And take down those smug bastards," her father added.

"Who are the smug bastards?" I asked

Caroline threw her father a look. "Billy never would have committed suicide if something or someone didn't drive him to it. He changed when the team changed. And I think the same thing may have had something to do with the murders of Gina and Marcus."

"You think the team—the coaches—are responsible for your husband's suicide?" People don't make other people kill themselves, I thought. I spent my adult life forcing myself to believe that.

"I think they provided access to steroids and maybe other drugs and encouragement to take them. I think the administration and the coaches had stars in their eyes. I think they used the players. I know Billy never would have come up with the idea by himself. The team was his safe place, and then it changed. That was confusing to him. From what I have read—and what I saw in my husband—steroids made everyone stronger and faster and able to tolerate those crazy practices. That's what people want to see now, athleticism. Even at this level. No one cares about a bounce pass or a lay-up."

"You know the game," I said.

"I loved Billy. He loved basketball. I learned. I mean he wanted to be the best guy on the team, but he knew he wasn't. Deep down that was okay with him, or so I thought. I think Connor was caught in the same trap Billy was; he just handled it differently. They made it about winning and they forced the players to go along."

"Forced?" I asked

"I just know there shouldn't be so much death associated with one team," she said with finality.

"Hear, hear," her father said and raised his re-filled glass.

"Do you have any proof?"

"No, just my instinct. I was hoping you could find some. I don't know if I'm right or not. I don't know who started it. Or why, other than money and glory, which is why everyone plays sports. I just know something is very wrong. Or was. Can you help me?"

"I don't know," I said. "I am a reporter, not a detective. I am definitely not the police. I have the same sense you do, but intuition can be self-reinforcing." I didn't want to give too much away. "Do you have anything of your husband's that might be helpful? Old diaries, calendars, a computer?"

Caroline shook her head. "I, I kind of lost my mind for a while after Billy died. I threw away everything of his. I was so mad. At him. At the world. I wish I hadn't now, but I can't go back."

"Even the computer?"

She shook her head. "I drove over it with my car."

"You should see her when she gets a notion," her father said. "A regular little firecracker."

I looked at my watch. "I'm afraid I have to run. Thank you for sharing your suspicions with me. And I am so sorry for your loss." I really was. This whole mess was getting sadder and sadder. I needed to leave before I made too many promises.

"I'll look into a few things. Call me in the meantime if you have any other ideas or come across anything you didn't throw away." I handed her my card and she nodded, tears welling up in her eyes. "It's okay. It's okay." It wasn't, but what else could I say? She would have a lot of work to do to make a new life for herself, but I know from experience it can be done, as many times as are necessary.

It was only 8:30 and still light when I left. I sat in my car and checked my phone. Bennett had texted me with instructions to meet him at the newspaper's offices in the student union at 9 pm. He must have found something. I got back to campus, parked, and hustled to the student union by 9. I never noticed that a car was following me.

I opened the door to the student newspaper office and saw three heads bent over one computer. Only Bennett looked up.

"So, Gale, this is Adam. Adam, this is Gale, the reporter from the *Washington Star* who kind of started all this."

Adam certainly looked the part of computer hacker, with skin that only sees the light of a computer monitor, a flabby body and greasy hair. But I was so happy to see him, I could have kissed him.

"What exactly are we looking for?" he asked me.

"Any evidence that any athlete at the university was using steroids."

He turned to look at me.

"That's a very broad search."

"I know."

"We'll start with Student Health then go to email

accounts," he said, his fingers flying.

Leo's advice ran through my head. 'Make friends, *then* ask for something.' I had it backwards, but maybe I could make up some ground.

"Uh, can I order you a pizza or anything?"

"I don't eat pizza. And I don't need bribes. This is work. And for a good cause."

"I really appreciate your time. And talent." I was humbled by his candor.

"It's cool. I hate sports."

"How can you hate sports?" I asked, truly puzzled. "I understand hating a sport or a team, but the entire concept? That's like hating art or music. There is so much diversity in sports and so many great things about moving and doing."

"I'd say the bad outweighs the good," Adam said, still typing as he looked at me "Money, cheating, injuries, turning a generation of kids into wanna-be ballers so they don't apply themselves to anything else. The sheer perversity of having an academic institution provide support for athletic competition. And don't forget a governing body like the NCAA that tolerates all kinds of abuse and neglect to further its own brand."

"Sports have always been a part of education. And the big money sports support the smaller teams so more people can compete," I countered. But he sounded like Leo, and I understood his point.

"But should sports be a part of education in the twenty-first century?"

"Maybe not," I said, deflated and troubled. I had never fully thought about the issue – probably because I was athletic and enjoyed my physical body. I never played college sports either.

"I'm just saying I'm happy to help you if I can," Adam said. His fingers flew over the keyboard, punctuated by aggressive strikes of the enter key. "I'm not finding much in Student Health. Those records are locked tight. Connor's email accounts have been de-activated. Totally scrubbed. Huh. That takes a lot of work. Someone better than me maybe could find a trail…"

So, nothing, I thought. I go computer hacking for the first time and get nothing.

"Any other ideas of where to look?" I asked Adam.

"What about the coaches' email accounts?" Bennett offered.

"Of course. Yes," I said.

Adam answered by typing.

While he worked, I asked Bennett and Jill about any local places that took old donated computers. If this has been going on since 2008 when McFarlane became president, then computers have surely been updated in that time, especially with the influx of money.

"Computers 4 Kids is the only one I know of. I volunteer there," said Jill.

Of course you do, you sweet soft-hearted thing, I thought.

"Have you had donations of computers from the university, especially the basketball team?"

She bit her lip and thought. "Not that I know of, but Alma has been there forever, and she keeps track of everything. She tags the computers with the date received and who it came from, in case the IRS ever comes calling."

"Do you wipe them clean when you get them?"

Jill was starting to get the picture. "It depends on how busy we are. Do you think…"

"It's worth a shot, isn't it?" I asked, grinning.

"Bingo," Adam said. "I'm in."

"Where?" I asked.

"Coach Ford's university email account. From there, I can find his personal account which is what I imagine he would use to do whatever it is you think he did."

"What about the assistant coach, Kevin?" I did not want him to find anything suspicious about Haywood, because I did not know what I would do with the information given his relationship to Sam. I like Sam; she saved Charlotte. I did not want anything I did to cause her pain.

"Okay. Give me a minute."

I was getting excited. We were moving forward. I tap-danced around Adam, which could not have been pretty because I cannot dance. Then there was an explosion and everything went dark.

"Shit! That must have been a bolt of lightning hitting a transformer!" Bennett said.

I hadn't even heard the thunderstorm. But now it was pouring rain.

The glow of Adam's computer screen caught my attention and I realized Adam was still working. The rest of us were still a little shell shocked.

"The hit must have knocked out Internet service. I'm at a wall. Can't do a thing 'til it comes back on. I'm tired anyway," Adam said. "Can we get back on this tomorrow?"

"Sure," I said, hiding my disappointment. Nothing was going to happen overnight anyway.

"I'll text everyone a new meeting time and place," Bennet said.

I got back to my motel room very late and realized I gave Alex nothing today. What is wrong with me? I have never missed a deadline. I texted her an apology and said I would make it up. The only thing saving me was that there was little other press interest, so the *Star* wasn't getting scooped. And if this steroid thing checked out, I would have the story of the year for her.

FIFTEEN

Wednesday, July 13

I woke up late and drove to the courthouse with just two cups of motel coffee in me. I had trouble finding parking and ended up in front of the basketball gym. It was high time I checked it out for myself anyway, so I walked in. It was quiet and seemed small. I tried to imagine the team playing here. Sitting on the bleachers, I spied Haywood in his wheelchair coming out of an office with a ball in his lap.

"Can you play?" he asked without looking at me.

"Not as well as I should. And nice peripheral vision," I added. What I hadn't told anyone was that I could shoot a decent free throw. I played basketball for a while in junior high school, before my swim coach forbade it due to the risk of injury. 'Can't risk a sprained ankle or a twisted back. Sorry.' He was right, but it was still frustrating to be denied anything you liked as a kid.

"Fair enough. I understand you can swim pretty well," he said.

"At one time."

He rolled himself into position and heaved a shot into the air. Swish.

"How do you think Connor's trial is going?" he asked.

"That's usually my question. It seems to be progressing like everyone thought. My guess is that Connor will get second degree and a life sentence. You?"

"I think you're right." Swish.

"Is that the outcome you'd vote for if you were on the jury?" I asked.

He scooted his chair over to the ball and picked it up.

"I can't even think about it that way. Logically. I mean. I just wish it never happened. I guess I'm living in the past. The present isn't my cup of tea right now, and I don't have much of a future. I doubt I'll be here much longer. I'm tired."

Ouch, I thought. "I understand that with therapy MS is highly treatable, and you look great."

He laughed. "No, I mean here, at Blue Ridge as head coach."

My ears pricked up. "Why?"

He took another shot and missed, so I got up and trotted across the court to get the ball for him.

"Shoot it," he said, avoiding my question. "Let's see what the world missed."

I dribbled for a minute and then shot from the baseline, my favorite place. It bounced off the rim.

"Good mechanics. Flat feet though. But as a swimmer, I guess that helps. Flat feet make good flippers."

I laughed this time. "You know swimming?"

"Just a little. As for your question, I just don't really want to do the job anymore. The job and the game have changed so much. I don't have the energy or the desire to ask the kids to give so much to a sport that won't be with them for life. I mean swimming, that you can do forever."

"You are still shooting the ball," I offered.

"Yeah, but that is less than ten percent of the game. The rest is getting into position, reacting to your teammates and the other players. It's keeping track of nine other guys and running your butt off. Shooting is nothing."

"I hadn't thought of it like that. Of course, now that you

say it, it makes sense."

"I am going to miss it, but I think it's time, for the team and for my health. Sam wants to move to Washington anyway. She says I can get better treatment in a big city."

"She seems like she knows what she's talking about, medically. She has done wonders for my dog." Already *my* dog.

"She's told me about you and that crazy dog. She is very good at her job."

"And are you?"

"I was. I am not anymore. I think the game left me behind. I think this school left me behind."

"No more Princeton offense?" I had read that was his signature. The Princeton offense is all about patience and getting the right shot, not the one that will attract the most attention or make the most noise. It is a style of play anyone can learn and find success with regardless of athleticism. Taken to its extreme, it was the Four Corners practiced by Dean Smith at my alma mater before they killed it with the shot clock.

"No more Princeton offense. Exactly."

I decided not to ask anything else until I had more information. But he certainly gave me some confirmation that Caroline's suspicions had some legs. We took turns shooting the ball and didn't talk, except to celebrate when my shots went in.

"I guess I've got to get over to the trial," I said, "now that I'm nice and sweaty."

"You look fine. I was going to go today too. I'll go with you if we can stop by my office first."

"Sure." I followed him down the hall. We passed Kevin's office. I tried to peek in, but the shades were drawn tight. Haywood's office had no shades and the inside held a mash-up of old school coaching debris—whistles, tape, half-inflated balls, boxes of jerseys, and spare nets for the hoops—and photos of Sam. Candy dishes and handouts from the student health office covered the rest of the available surfaces. In my opinion, this was not the office of a man who had anything to hide.

"So, you came to Blue Ridge in 2009?" I asked.

"Yup. September."

"You had a lot of work to do, I hear."

"It's always a challenge to be new, to take over a team, especially after a sudden death. But Kevin staying on as assistant coach provided a good bit of continuity. That is one reason I kept him on. I didn't want it to look like I was cleaning house."

"How did the former coach die?" I asked.

"Car crash. Alone. He ran into a tree on campus. They think he just fell asleep. The university police found him. He was the sole caretaker for his wife, and she had to go into a home. It was all so sad."

Haywood grabbed a file and his jacket. We walked and rolled over to the courthouse, and I pushed Haywood up the wheelchair ramp. When we slid into the back, Isaac had Darrell Giminsky, Marcus' uncle, on the stand. Finally. Where he had been hiding?

"Marcus and Connor were great friends," he said. "I can't imagine he would have meant to hurt him like that. I think something just set him off, that it all got out of hand."

"Your witness," Isaac said to Madison without a trace of smugness even though every juror looked rapt. This was a man they seemed to believe. Madison was wearing a pantsuit today, rather fashion forward for a small town.

"Mr. Giminsky," she smiled just by moving her lips, not her eyes, "I understand you played basketball in the pros?"

"Yes, that's what I said."

"But you were injured quickly, correct? A career ending injury?"

"Yes, I blew all the tendons in my left knee."

I couldn't help it, I winced.

"And there was speculation at the time that this injury was due to steroids, correct?"

"That's correct."

"Was it in fact due to steroids?"

"Objection. That's asking the witness for a medical opinion," Isaac argued.

"I'll allow it," said the judge. "Please answer the question, Mr. Giminsky."

"Yup."

"Yes, it was due to steroids?" Madison asked to clarify.

"Yes, in my un-medical opinion. Steroids do bad things to your body."

"No further questions." Madison sat down.

Holy cow. Does she think she discredited him, I wondered? That was confusing, to say the least.

Isaac got up to re-direct. "Darrell, please explain more about your use of steroids, so the jury can put it in context."

"When I was signed to the pros, everyone did drugs. Everyone, at least on my team. It was kind of a condition of playing. They paid you a lot of money, so they owned you. They helped you with doses and masking agents and all that jazz. No one was looking at basketball players. They still aren't. I mean, I'm mad, but I'm not that mad. It was still my choice. I was a grown man. I could have walked away. After my knee exploded, they paid for my medical treatment and bought out my contract. But yeah, I blame the drugs for my career ending so soon. Although some would say I might not have had a career without them." He shrugged. "When it was all over, I was happy not to feel so stressed out all the time. You know to have anger like that, like Connor did. I think he could have been on steroids. That would explain why he overreacted to whatever he did."

The jury gasped. It was like something out of a movie. I peeked at Haywood, and he looked like he was going to be sick.

"Objection, your honor…" Madison said, leaping to her feet.

"Overruled and sit down. You brought it up," said the judge.

"That's, that's just speculation about Connor though, correct?" Isaac asked.

"I don't have any proof, but I've been around the block a few times. But yeah, it's speculation. Do I think that means anything to whether or not he's guilty? No, I do not. I mean no one else killed my nephew. But it does make it all even more sad for some reason. I don't know if he could form intent with all that in his system."

"Objection," Isaac said, weakly

"Overruled. Look. I think we're done with this witness, correct?

Isaac and Madison nodded. Darrell limped off the stand and out of the courtroom.

"We'll recess now for lunch," said the judge with a bang of his gavel.

"Are you okay?" I whispered to Haywood.

"How could I not have known? That explains so much."

"Well there is no proof," I said, playing devil's advocate.

"No, but it explains a lot like he said. It's a possibility, and that's enough for me. I mean…," he stopped.

"Do you want to get out of here?" I asked.

"Yeah."

I got up, and we left too quickly to see who was watching us. I pushed him back to the gym and into his office. A phone rang as somewhere as I walked down the hall.

"I've got to go. Are you okay?" I asked Haywood. I probably should have pressed him for some answers, but it didn't feel right. Trust your gut, I always said. I'd rather be wrong than violate that rule.

"Yes. Thanks," Haywood said absently.

At Sara's Kitchen I had a turkey club for lunch and wrote and filed a piece on the steroid claims and the potential for a coach shake-up – hopefully without violating Haywood's confidence. I touched on Giminsky's accusations about the Warriors, his old pro team. Alex would have to put another writer on that, and she would be bursting with glee since she was a Stingers fan and those two NBA teams have hated each other since the 1970s.

I looked at my phone and saw that I had a text from Adam saying he had something come up and could we meet tomorrow? I texted him begging for tonight, but heard nothing back. The cat was out of the bag. We had to hurry.

While my phone was in my hand, I called Sam and got her voicemail. I left my message asking about Charlotte and then headed back to the courthouse. After the jury filed back in, Isaac said his proposed witness was ill and asked for an extension until tomorrow. The judge granted it, but I think we all wondered if Isaac just wanted the afternoon to process Darrell's testimony. I know I would have.

I went back to my coffee shop for the free Wi-Fi, ordered a tasteless herbal tea to rent my seat and pulled up the Maryland

State Corporation Commission website. I typed "Millennium Development" into the search box and got dozens of hits. Great. On closer examination, there was only one active Millennium Development, and it was registered as a limited partnership. All the shares were owned by the estate of Arthur Braxton's wife and Connor. No other partners were listed. Rats. But, the registered agent was Barry Johnson, Connor's old coach. That was very, very interesting.

I went back to Google and saw that Millennium Development had bought a biotech company a couple of days ago. Their main product was a drug based on resveratrol. No FDA approval yet, but it was supposed to allow people with heart failure to exercise. Huh. Sounds useful and possibly performance enhancing. Sure, buying a company probably takes some hands-on time, but his son was on trial for murder, for God's sake.

I spent the rest of the afternoon researching and making lists and an outline of next steps. I tried to get a hold of Adam or Bennett, but it was like they had disappeared. I berated myself for thinking I could rely on college kids.

That night, the local news was breathless. I watched it at Applebee's with a beer and plate of chicken and broccoli pasta that was not half bad. The news showed footage of Haywood, Kevin, and President McFarlane all dodging microphones until they were trapped and ultimately forced to deny there was a steroid problem at Blue Ridge. Haywood looked as devastated as he did when I left him, Kevin looked tense, and McFarlane looked distracted. No one had gotten Darrell on camera though.

"But we will take a hard look at our practices to make sure there are no athletes who are tempted," said McFarlane.

Ah, smart. Throw the blame on the athletes.

It felt like something had been set in motion that I would have to run to keep up with.

SIXTEEN

Thursday, July 14

The next day, after a fitful night of sleep, I scanned the web to see how the major news outlets were handling the steroid story. It barely registered as a blip outside of Waynesville. It would, though, I thought, it would. The clock was ticking, and I had some choices to make. Originally, I wanted to see what was behind Connor's weight loss and why there was such a tepid defense. Now I feel I have an answer to the first – steroids pumped him up and without them in prison, he dropped the added bulk - and that the second isn't really the right question anymore. The right question, I thought, was where did Connor get the drugs and who else was involved.

I called Alex and told her my suspicions about who else was involved, starting with the assistant coach, Kevin Battier.

"Get me proof," she said.

"I will," I promised, without knowing quite how, especially given I had lost my computer hacker.

I stopped by the courthouse without planning to stay for long. The story outside the courtroom was bigger than the story in it right now. I had to make a list of what I needed to prove and who I needed to talk to, and I couldn't imagine another shocker like yesterday.

Isaac called Kevin Battier as his first witness. I had been surprised that Madison never called him, but this trial was surprising in many ways. Connor's reaction was fascinating. He didn't mind the gruesome medical testimony, the YMCA lady testifying about Marcus' amazing character, any of it. But Kevin; Kevin he hated. Connor's neck was tense enough to pop.

After swearing to tell the truth, Kevin settled himself in the witness seat as if it were the most comfortable chair in the world. He had an easy, leonine grace. Isaac started with preliminary questions but didn't take long before he got to the heart of the matter. Isaac certainly was not a time waster, nor a showboat who loved to stand in front of the jury. I liked that about him. I liked a lot of things about him.

"Coach Battier, did you see any signs of tension on the team in that spring of 2015?" Isaac asked.

"Well, to be honest, I think I did. I mean, with the benefit of hindsight, some of the interactions between Connor and Marcus looked off."

"What do you mean?"

"I don't know. I mean Connor never seemed like a racist, but things were escalating between them."

Isaac's head snapped up from his legal pad. This was not the answer he was expecting. Damage done, I thought. Isaac looked flustered, like he knew it would be fruitless to continue down his planned path but couldn't see any new paths and couldn't turn around. He gathered himself.

"What is your personal workout routine?" he asked to everyone's surprise.

"Objection!" Madison yelled. "Is defense counsel looking for a new exercise program? This has no relevance."

"Sustained. Move on to something else, counselor."

Isaac didn't want to ask what made Kevin think Connor was a racist. That would allow Kevin to slam Connor. But his workout routine? That was odd. Maybe it was an attempt to make everyone forget what they just heard.

"Did you socialize with the players?" he tried next.

"Not much, and not in the evenings. Sometimes we'd

grab coffee, talk about how practice went, that sort of thing," Kevin said.

Isaac worked around the subject, trying to show all the things that Kevin didn't know about the players. It was slow going and didn't seem to have much of an impact on the jury. I felt a little sorry for him.

At 11:30, the judge said he would recess for the afternoon to hear another matter. How many matters did this small town have I wondered. But it helped me—nothing would happen in court while I went digging.

I decided to go to Landfall Academy to see Barry Johnson, Connor's old coach. His connection with Millennium Development opened up a new can of worms. I thought Arthur's business dealings were just what kept him too busy to attend his son's murder trial. But what if it meant more? What if Arthur and Barry were more deeply involved? The Millennium Development connection puts Barry and Arthur on the same team, so to speak. But in what way and why? It could be innocent – the Braxtons did have a vacation home near Landfall. But talking to Barry on the phone had left me with the feeling he had something he wanted to tell me, if I asked the right question. Maybe this was it. And maybe I should ask it in person. No one can hang up on you in person.

It was a risk, sure, but the drive would give me time to think. It would be almost a five-hour drive, so long as the Bay Bridge wasn't backed up. I could get there by 4:30. Luckily, I do drive the greatest car in the world, and I think best when I am in motion.

I was sure Kevin was involved in Connor's choice—and maybe those of other players, like Billy Wilcox—to use steroids. But I wanted to make sure I wasn't missing anything. And I needed actual proof Connor was using. Proof that would stand up in court if Isaac wanted to use it and if the *Star* got sued. William McFarlane certainly seemed like the type who would file a libel suit against the newspaper. I could come back to Kevin tomorrow.

I called Sam before I left.

"How is Charlotte?" I asked.

"Definitely better," Sam said. "Want to come see her today?"

"Can I come tomorrow? I'm going to take a little trip."

"Sounds secretive. Tomorrow is fine." She paused. "Haywood says you are nice, by the way."

"I like him, too."

"Good," she said and hung up.

I tried to figure out what tone of voice she was using—threatening, satisfied, motherly?

As soon as I got in my car, my phone rang.

"Gale Hightower," I answered.

"This is Claudia Merguez, Gina's mother."

I was astonished. "Mrs. Merguez. Thank you so much for calling."

"You don't know what I am going to say yet."

That was true. "No, I don't, but I imagine you have a good reason for calling." I wasn't flattering her. The hairs were standing up on the back of my neck. She had something.

"I found Gina's diary. I read it, and I want you to read it. Can you meet me soon before I change my mind?"

"Absolutely. Where and when?"

"Now. At the McDonalds at exit 118. Go south out of town and take the first exit."

"I am in my car. I will be there in 10 minutes."

Mrs. Merguez was at a table near the bathrooms in the back. I sat down across from her, avoiding the ketchup on the seat. She turned her eyes from me to her purse and rummaged around until she found a small pink notebook. She handed it to me.

"Have the police seen this?" I asked.

She shook her head. "I just found it. It was in a box of her clothes."

"And the police never searched her apartment?"

"They kept it cordoned off for a week, then they let us come and pack things up. I couldn't bear to do it, so my cousin's moving company did it. They just put everything in boxes. I don't know if the police searched her apartment and just ignored it, or if they never searched."

"I assume it would have been evidence."

She nodded.

"Would you like it back?"

"No." she said and walked away.

I turned the notebook over in my hands. What was in there? I didn't want anyone to see me, so I went straight to the bathroom and locked myself in a stall. I flipped through the pages. Only about half of the notebook had writing on it, and there were a few ticket stubs and other memorabilia taped in between. Gina had dated every entry; it looked as if the diary covered the five months before her death. The first entries were about schoolwork and contained some decent poems. She must have started this for a class, I thought.

Then Connor hits her for the first time. He cries afterwards and admits to her that he is scared and confused. That he has been taking 'supplements' provided by the team. I read every page, through multiple flushes of the adjoining stalls. I was starting to have to pee, but I didn't want to put the notebook down.

There were only six more pages and the last entry matched up with the end of classes. I closed the notebook and tucked it in my backpack, so I could use the facilities as they were designed. It was too late to go to Landfall now, so I went back to my motel room. Should I take this to Isaac now? I didn't know. I went back through all my notes, added new ones and tried to put together the puzzle of what I thought happened with the Blue Ridge University basketball team.

I thought back to what got me started on this trail. Connor Braxton and how he had changed. It sounded like he didn't even know what he was taking. Or that he wouldn't tell Gina. That says he knew it was wrong. What would have happened to him had he gone to school somewhere else? What kind of lives would Gina and Marcus have made?

I got up and left the stall and restaurant. It was after 1 pm now, so a road trip didn't make any sense. That would just have to wait.

Back at my motel, I figured lunch or a quick run were my two options. I picked a run and then a late lunch. Gina's diary called to me again, so I spent the afternoon re-reading it and making notes. It was so desperately sad to hear the voice of someone dead. I didn't know how to work it into any story yet.

Gina's diary scrubbed any desire I might have had to be around people, so I found a supermarket nearby and picked up some deli items and a bottle of wine for dinner in my room. Tomorrow was a new day, and one thing I wanted on my list was an interview with Darrell Giminsky.

As I was figuring out how to approach him, my phone

rang.

"Gale Hightower."

"It's Sam. How are you?"

"I'm fine. How's Charlotte?" I panicked a little; it was late for a social call. After 9 pm. If she had bad news....

"She's all right. She's great actually. It's you I am worried about. Haywood said he was hearing some grumblings about the fact you haven't done a nice glowing article on how great our little university is."

"Sam, do you think I should?" I was surprised.

"No, and what I think doesn't matter. You need to be careful. Haywood wouldn't tell me anything more, even when I threatened to neuter him on the spot, but I just got a sense."

"Thanks."

"I just don't need to be stuck with your dog."

I laughed. "I don't think it will come to that," I said, with more confidence than I felt.

SEVENTEEN

Friday, July 15

In the courtroom the next day, the jury was getting that glazed look, like they were all waiting for a bus in the rain. Isaac paraded some former teammates up to testify for Connor, which they did with all the enthusiasm of jocks taking a math test. They gave only the blandest testimony. "Connor was a good guy. A hard worker. I am sure he didn't mean to kill anyone." Interestingly, Bennett and Jill were still missing. I still hadn't heard from Adam either. I was getting an uncomfortable feeling, but it was summer break.

When the judge called his morning recess, I saw Bennett and Jill outside the courtroom. They looked distressed.

"What's wrong, and where's Adam?" I asked.

"He decided to go to Philadelphia for a concert. He said he would be back Monday," said Jill.

"I told you he could be a jerk," said Bennett.

"Shit." I needed him.

"I am sorry we were gone too. I was sick," Jill said "and Bennet had to drive his mom to visit her mom."

"It was a last-minute thing. My grandmother can be a little demanding."

"I get it. Being demanding is a privilege of old age. Life still happens. Okay, well, I have a Plan B. If we can't get into the computer, we need to go old-school. I need to get into Kevin's office and I need lookouts."

"Isn't breaking and entering a crime?" asks Bennett.

"Yup," I said. "Breaking and entering is a classic reporter

tactic."

"How do you propose to not get caught?" Jill asked

"Well, first I actually worry about getting in, then I worry about getting out." Why was I saying this as if I had done it hundreds of times?

"Can you pick a lock?" Bennett asked.

"With a credit card, sure. I also think a lot of people don't lock offices. It's a matter of getting in the building when no one is looking. I'd like to go tonight." Kevin is probably one who locks his office, though, I realized.

"I'm in," Jill said.

"I'd rather not," Bennett admitted.

"You have to come," Jill said. "Otherwise how do we know you won't tell?" She looked to me for approval. I trusted Bennett, but I had been wrong before, and I wanted to encourage her adventurous and bossy spirit.

"Yup. You're coming," I said with The Look.

"All right, but I am not touching anything. I don't want to leave fingerprints."

"Oooh gloves," Jill said. "I'll get us some."

I smiled. Visions of disaster fitted through my head, and I chased them out. We would be fine.

"Okay, let's meet at 10 o'clock. Wear dark clothes and meet me behind the pool." I just remembered where I could get in, assuming there were no locked doors between the pool and the basketball gymnasium.

Back in court, the lawyers were squabbling over a piece of evidence and the judge called them into chambers. We all twiddled our thumbs for thirty minutes and when they came back, he recessed for the day. This trial felt like it had the same half-life as plutonium; it would never be totally over. I wondered if that was part of some plan.

I packed up my things. The television cameras had chased down Madison and Isaac and they were continuing their squabbling, but it seemed half-hearted. Everyone was tired.

On my way back to my car, I spied a catering person coming out of a building with a cart full of sandwiches.

"Would you like a sandwich?" she asked. "They are just going to a board meeting for something. Never can remember what." She smiled.

What a happy accident. I was thrilled. I had forgotten lunch.

"Yes please," I said and took one off the top.

"Oh, those are bologna. You want bologna? I hate the stuff. Here," she pulled out a tray from the bottom. "I have some extra tuna salad left with pickles and celery and carrots. It's especially good, if I do say so myself. My mother's recipe."

"Fine. Thanks."

"You can have two if you want."

I wanted. "Thanks again." I walked off happily with my two sandwiches.

"Have a nice evening," the woman said.

"You too," I called over my shoulder.

I called Leo while I ate my sandwiches in my motel room.

"I'm going to wait to come home until tomorrow. I've got a little project for tonight. How is everything?"

He wasn't easily distracted. "We're all fine. What kind of project?"

I told him, and he let out a big breath that he sounded like he had been holding for the whole story. "Are you sure that is a good idea?"

"No, I'm guessing it's not, but it seems to be the only idea I have. Got any others?"

"Call in the police?"

I grunted. "I'm not so sure the local police are super interested in anything to do with this case or the university. The campus cops seem to handle everything, and I do not want to call them."

"Really? You think they are in on something?"

"Maybe. I am not there yet, but they certainly kept some incidents of Connor's violence out of the press. And that is not right. How are you?"

"Relatively healthy and happy. Hawk is in my shower having a big time. I figured out how to leave it on mist, and he loves it. He is literally singing."

"That cannot sound good!" I laughed.

"No, it doesn't, but it does sound happy, and since there is no one here but me..."

"I know, I know, I can't wait to come home tomorrow."

"Huh," Leo huffed. "You should come home tonight. Nothing good can happen in the dark."

"Nothing?" I chided him.

"You have a dirty mind," he admonished. "Be careful."

"I will. See you soon."

Speaking of dirty minds, I found myself wishing I could see Isaac again. Maybe after the trial. Maybe if he would come to Washington. Maybe, maybe, maybe.

Sandwiches devoured, I got a drink of water and typed up some notes. I also put Gina's diary under the bed for safekeeping and then doubted myself. That is the first place anyone looks.

So, I just put it back in my backpack. Then I changed into black khakis and a navy t-shirt and watched TV until it was time to leave.

Bennett and Jill were waiting for me when I got to the pool.

"Hi. Are you ready for this?" I asked them.

"Yes." Jill's eyes sparkled. Bennett nodded.

The outside door was open as I had hoped, so we all crept in. It was dark, but we felt our way along the halls until we came to the first door, which was also unlocked.

"Nice security," I said to no one in particular.

It was a piece of cake to find Kevin's office again, but that was where we hit our first snag. Not only was his door was locked and his shades drawn, I could hear him—or someone—on the phone. All six of our eyes widened; this was not part of the plan. I pulled us into the women's room across the hall.

Kevin must have finished up his call quickly, because he left his office a minute later. I could hear the door shut. I waited five more minutes in case he came back, and then we all stood outside his office. He had sadly not forgotten to re-lock it, so I pulled out my credit card and worked on the lock. It took a few tries, but I was able to push the latch back in and open the door.

"Voila!" I whispered with more confidence that I felt.

"So, what exactly are we looking for?" Jill asked.

"Communications with players. Allusions to performance increases. Promises. Receipts. Drugs. Anything really."

We all pulled on the gloves Jill bought, and I tried the computer mouse. Kevin had turned everything off. I booted his computer back up, but it asked for a password, so I turned it off again. We looked in a file cabinet and found nothing. I stood there for a second and looked around, willing myself to be inspired. The décor was distracting, though—superhero action figures and lots of signed photographs of famous players. Michael Jordan, Larry Bird and Julius Erving. Obvious picks, all of them. You would think an insider might have a favorite player or two who was less well known. The whole office was a study in second-tier wanting. There was nothing academic at all, no sense he was coaching student-athletes.

There were expensive touches, particularly a lot of expensive looking glass. A couple of pieces looked like they were done by that Italian guy I had seen in the Renwick Gallery. I took some pictures and figured I would send them to my landlord Kathleen to see if they were real. That would mean a lot of money was flowing through here. More than you would think William McFarlane could squeeze from donors to an athletic program

I was deep in thought and frustration when Jill said "Aha!"

"What?"

"Oh, never mind. I thought I found a file on Connor, but it the file name is "Corvette." Corvette, Connor. I can't see well without good light. I'm sorry to get everyone excited."

"Huh. Anything else?" I asked.

"Nothing. I mean nothing. It's weird," Jill said, perplexed.

"He must keep all his files on the computer. I wish Adam were here," Bennet added.

I nodded and looked around the office again for hidden compartments, freshly painted spots on the wall, anything odd.

"This must not be where he does his real work. This has got to be for show," I said, finishing my scan.

"Okay, well that was a bust. Let's go home," Bennet said.

When I got back to the motel, I sent my photos to

Kathleen thinking she would see them tomorrow, but she was up. She answered right away by text.

>*"Those are copycat Dante Marionis. The artistry is good, but the ideas are tired."*

>*"Thanks! I appreciate the fast response!"*

>*"Sure. I'm at an art fair in California, so it's not so late here. And I'm bored. Art fairs aren't what they used to be. I miss the 1980s."*

>*"That's funny. I do not. BTW, how much cheaper are the knock-offs?"*

>*"Not that much cheaper. Maybe half price. A real one is $35,000 and a copy would be $15,000."*

>*"Jesus Christ, that's still a lot of money."*

>*"Glass is expensive. But I could get him something much more lovely but less well known for a third of what he paid. But people who buy that don't want quality. They don't want art. They want to show off. They want fame. I have to run. Glad I could help."*

Another little piece of the puzzle that made up Kevin's personality, and it did not make a savory picture. Fame over quality. He had too much money and wanted to make it look like he had more. People who want that aren't the comfortable ones. They aren't the ringleaders. They are the ones trying to move up in the world. And that makes them dangerous to anyone who gets in their way.

EIGHTEEN

Weekend, July 16-17

Around 2 a.m., what started as a garden variety unhappy stomach—I had figured it was just too much coffee and unpredictable food—transformed into what undoubtedly was the worst case of food poisoning in the history of the world. I never should have trusted old tuna salad from a catering cart, no matter how special the recipe. I lost count at five trips to the bathroom. At 6 a.m., I got up to brush some of the vomit out of my teeth. The movement sent a new wave of nausea over me, but I didn't have anything left to throw up. Once that passed, I felt a little better and was soon dying for a ginger ale. But there was no way I could make it to the vending machine yet. I felt as weak as a kitten.

I fell back asleep for a few hours and when I woke up, I turned on the television and lost myself in morning show silliness. The local news came on at 9:50 and they did a segment on the trial. Since it was Saturday, they were rehashing the whole week and showed several clips patched together. It is always fascinating to watch how people react to having a microphone shoved in their mouths. Isaac and Madison said the trial was going 'as expected,' and Mrs. Merguez wouldn't talk to them.

Dig deeper, I wanted to shout at the television, but digging is not a television reporter's job. It is my job, but I was too sick to do it.

Just then, Sam called.

"I understand you're still in town."

"Yeah, I feel like crap. Food poisoning." I didn't think to ask her how she knew.

"Good. I mean I am sorry. But I'll bring you some nausea meds if you take Charlotte for the weekend. She's getting depressed in here."

"I though you said she was better?"

"Physically yes. Emotionally, no."

"Okay. That makes sense. You know, speaking of her mental state, I was wondering. Will a country dog adapt to life in the city? It's so much more confining."

"Dogs adapt. People do too, they just take longer."

"I am not moving to the country, if you are implying anything"

"Just saying, if you did, we could go drinking together every now and then. I like to blow off a bit of steam, and you seem like you would be a fun person to do it with."

"Thank you, but I am really not much fun at all. I am a lazy, cynical, workaholic homebody."

"Huh. Poor Charlotte."

I laughed. "When are you coming?" I asked.

"After lunch. I'll come back and get her Sunday night. Do you have bowls and a bed and a leash and things like that?"

"No. At home, but not here. Can you bring some?"

"Sure. And you guys can be bedridden together. It's good for bonding."

I hung up and stood up, and immediately sat down back on the bed with a thump. The room was spinning wildly. I took a few deep breaths and tried again. Better. Just low blood pressure. I was dehydrated. I drank a little water and held it down. Then I went to the drink machine and they had no ginger ale, of course. I got a Coke instead, and it helped.

I showered and called Leo. The original plan was for me

to come home today, but I couldn't see driving that far. Plus, I was kind of excited to have a trial run with Charlotte.

"Sam is going to bring Charlotte since she is depressed, and I am too sick to drive. Food poisoning."

"Rats. I was looking forward to seeing you," Leo said.

"How's my angry bird?"

"He's fine. Have you thought about getting him a girl-friend? He's actually been a little overly affectionate with my shoe."

"He likes shoes, and I think he's just hoping you'll take him in."

Leo laughed. "You know, we could pool our resources and get a house together. It would be good for Charlotte to have a yard."

A house? But then I would have to commit to a place, a life.

"Interesting concept," I said cagily.

"At least shopping would be fun," Leo pointed out.

"Are you fresh out of other things to shop for?"

"Decorating myself and this tiny apartment is getting a little old," Leo admitted.

"All right. I'll think about it. I'm flattered you think you could handle living with me," I said and meant it.

"One, we almost do now, and two, it could be a big house."

I laughed. "Ow, that hurts my stomach."

"I hope you didn't break a rib throwing up. That happened to me once."

"Nah, I'm too tough," I said.

"How's the sleuthing going?" he asked.

"Still mostly suspicions, but they are getting stronger. I think I am going in the right direction. I'm sure Connor did steroids—I know that much from Gina's diary, Caroline's suspicions and Darrell's testimony—and I am pretty sure it was part of a bigger plan. It was not just his idea. I just don't know how far up it goes." Or how far out, I reminded myself. The connection between Connor's father and high school coach was eating me up, because it didn't make sense.

"You mean the coaches were giving it to them?"

"Or turning their backs. I don't know which. And I can't print anything until I know." I told him about my unlikely hacker friend and Caroline's husband.

"That is so sad," he said.

"Yeah, it might be more sad if she didn't have a black maid who has to dress like a character out of *Gone with the Wind*."

"You have less sympathy for racists than murderers?"

"I guess so. But I do kind of like Caroline, despite myself. What she is doing takes guts."

"Ah, you are a softie. Be careful. And make sure you re-hydrate and eat something as soon as you can hold it down. Your brain needs food to work properly."

"Yes, Mom."

"I would make such a good Mom. Want to get a kid when we get a house?" Leo teased.

"God no."

"Huh. Think about it. You can be the Dad. You'd be awesome."

"I'm not sure if that is an insult or not."

"That says more about how you view gender roles than

about my comment."

"My head hurts," I said, in an effort to escape the conversation.

"Okay, then. My work here is done. Bye. Love you."

"Love you too."

I did take Leo's advice and get some food, just a plain donut on the way to the pet store. Sam said she would bring some things, but my addled brain decided Charlotte deserved new things for her first night with me. I ate half of the donut and it stayed down.

Almost a hundred dollars later, I had a bed, a leash, a collar, poop bags, a bowl, some treats and a stuffed squirrel. Sam said she'd bring food, so we wouldn't have two creatures in one room with bad stomachs.

I got back, checked with the front desk and they said yes to dogs with a deposit. So, I paid the $75 and beat Sam to my room by just a minute. Charlotte seemed happy to see me, but tired. She headed straight to the new bed.

"Here's some anti-nausea stuff. It works for dogs and people. You just need to take two now and one more tonight. Since you seem to have everything you need," she looked around, "I'll keep the old ratty blankets and leash I was going to lend you. Here's some food, though. Don't overfeed her. One cup, twice a day."

"Thanks," I said and took the bottle of pills and the food.

"Make her walk, but not too far. But mostly just enjoy her for a while. I think she needs the quiet and the bonding time. Hospitals are noisy, smelly, cold, awful places. Full of fear and death."

Perfect. We could hang out together. I had some things I could check out on the computer. Not all reporting has to involve shoe leather. "I will."

"Well, if I don't hear from you, I'll come back Sunday around 5 p.m."

"Okay. Thanks."

"No, thank you. This is good for everyone. Bye."

I put the pillows on the floor and snuggled up with Charlotte in her dog bed, and my plans for computer research. There was time, I figured. Nothing could happen over the weekend, and no one was really chasing the story other than me. Sure, the other papers ran Darrell's claims, but no one else knew about Caroline or Gina. I wouldn't get scooped. Other than Isaac and my college kids, no one knew I was investigating this story, so no one could hide anything or destroy evidence. Yes, I had time to take a little break.

That evening, Charlotte and I walked a little—well, I walked, and she limped—and I put her in the car, so we could get some plain rice from the Chinese take-out place I found in the phone book. She sniffed the passenger seat carefully. "I have definitely been here, and it wasn't very nice," she seemed to think. "But this time seems okay."

The trip was quick, and I ate half the rice and mixed the other half with her food. She ate it gingerly, chasing rice kernels as her tongue flicked them out of the bowl. We both fell asleep on the floor as soon as it got dark. I eventually made it to the bed, but Charlotte never moved.

The next morning, I got up early; probably because I had slept for 12 hours. I took Charlotte out, fed her breakfast, which she wolfed down, and went to get some coffee for myself. I had just booted up my laptop when there was a knock on the door. Charlotte let out a low growl. Before I had a chance to decide whether to take her advice into account, I opened the door.

Thankfully, it was just Caroline Wilcox with a basket of fruit.

"I bet no one officially welcomed you to town."

"No, not officially. Reporters don't usually get a red carpet. Or fruit. Thanks."

Charlotte was waging her tail, apologizing for her mistake. Food apparently made a visitor okay.

"This is Charlotte, a dog I hit on the way into town two weeks ago. Come to think of it, I guess she was my welcoming committee."

"I like dogs," Caroline said, as Charlotte limped over to give her a good sniff. "What happened to her leg?"

"Like I said, I hit her. The vet had to amputate it."

"She looks like she has forgiven you."

"To forgive is divine, isn't that a saying?" I asked.

Caroline squinted her eyes, unsure what to make of me.

"How did you know I am staying here?" I asked.

"When you came over the other night, I had Athena check your bag for your laptop and put a tracker on it," Caroline said. "She has many skills, as do I. Skills people wouldn't imagine by looking at me. My grandmother was a code-breaker for the Navy," she said. "She taught me a few things. I want to help if I can. I haven't slept well since our dinner."

I thought for a moment.

"Do you have time now? I have some things I would like to check out, but I have been a little hamstrung. I don't have your skills and my previous assistant is AWOL."

Ah, I am becoming just like Alex with the military lingo.

"You're not mad about the tracker?" Caroline asked.

"Yes, but I can use the help. I might have done the same

thing if I knew how. And it's the newspaper's laptop anyway. It's all a means to a good end, right? So never mind. I've got a code- breaking job for you, if you think you can handle it. Or more of an electronic breaking and entering."

"What are we looking for?" She sat down on the bed and looked like she could handle it.

"I'm not totally sure, but I think I know who was involved in getting drugs for the players and why." I explained my theory about Kevin. "I think this guy wants to satisfy his ego through the team. I think McFarlane's influx of money made his dreams a reality."

"Kevin was so nice to me after Billy killed himself," Caroline said wistfully.

"Nice guys can do bad things," I reminded her. "We were in his office and there are no files, no records, nothing. I think he's operating all electronically, but I don't know how to get into his computer files without his passwords. Can you help me?"

"I'll try," Caroline said, and she opened her laptop and started typing furiously with very nicely manicured fingernails.

"Okay, specifics." I nudged my foggy brain into gear. Sometimes too much sleep is as bad as too little. "Here is what I am looking for. We need to find recruiting letters and medical records," I said. "Spreadsheets, I would think."

Charlotte positioned herself so she could see both of us.

"Do you know if he used Dropfile? Sorry, that's stupid, how would you now that," she said to herself still typing.

"What's Dropfile?"

"It's a remote password protected program for storing documents. Popular in this new cloud computing world, particularly if someone wants to stay off a network. That has to be what he was using. I'm going to try and crack his password."

"How do you do that? Guess?"

"Yes. I also have a program that helps me make educated guesses. Any ideas for a starting point from being in his office?"

"Let me think," I said, remembering with some effort last Friday night a week ago. "I saw him – he drives a Corvette like me – at the gas pump. He had a personalized plate. It read BALLR."

"Spelled like that?"

"Yup."

She tried it. "No luck."

"What about that plus his number from when he played?" I flipped on my computer and searched his name. "He was 14 in high school and college."

Caroline typed.

"I'm in!" Caroline shouted. "BALLR1414. Okay, now I need to poke around."

She worked. I paced. Charlotte had her head on a swivel.

I walked around the bed and could see her screen as a list of files popped up.

"There are folders on every player," She said. "Going back to when it started."

Caroline started typing and I knew what she was thinking.

"Caroline, wait a minute," I grabbed her arm. "I know you're going to want to look up your husband's file, but can we start with Connor and Marcus?"

"Of course. I can get back here any time," she said with a flippancy that I was sure she didn't feel. She shook her head a little and was poised to click on Connor's folder when I saw one marked "Recruiting."

"Wait. Open that one," I said, pointing. "Recruiting."

She did and there it was. A form letter inviting the kids to hell.

> *Dear _____:*
>
> *Congratulations on your impressive athletic achievements to date. As an admirable student and outstanding athlete, we at Blue Ridge University would like to encourage you to attend our school. Our basketball program, while relatively new, is growing and extremely well-respected. We use every tool at our disposal to help our players develop to their fullest potential. While we cannot offer scholarships, we can offer a future in the sport. With cutting edge science and nutrition, you will leave our program a better athlete with the ability to use your honed basketball skills. More of our players have gone on to basketball careers than from any other Division III school. We want to help you, and in the process field an excellent team. In this day and age, the only way to compete is by using all available tools, and we will give them to you along with an education that is one of the best. Our body mind spirit program plus our mountain air plus our tailored basketball program will make you feel strong and focused. If no one else believes in you, we do. By now you've undoubtedly heard about the tragic case concerning former student Connor Braxton. Please be assured this unfortunate situation and Mr. Braxton are not representative of our program and our values. As you know, we can't give scholarships, but we can give experiences, which will form you into a*

potential career athlete. Our goal is for the NBA
to take notice of our kids. No one is as focused on
your future as we are.

"Cutting edge science and nutrition? Nice code for drugs, right?" Caroline demanded.

I got a lot of recruiting letters my senior year, and they did not look like this.

"It could be. The letter is certainly making promises the program can't keep. It's just a slimy letter," I said. I couldn't become too convinced this was the proof I needed before I was totally sure it was the proof I needed. "College sports is becoming a slimy business. Slimy isn't illegal."

"Okay, let's look at the other folders, starting at the top with the *A*s," Caroline said, fully invested.

For each player, there were subfolders with their basketball stats, nutrition plans and supplement use, and a folder marked injuries. A few players had subfolders marked "Incidents." They documented infractions liked missed practices, low grades, and one attempted assault. We opened all the folders and examined every incident. It took all day. We ate lots of fruit to keep going. Connor and Marcus did not have any subfolders. Neither did Billy Wilcox.

"So, the biggest incidents have no folders. This is either fake, or he deleted the important stuff," I said, rubbing my neck. "Can we copy this stuff to my computer?"

"You can't use it, can you? We didn't get it legally…"

"No, but I can ask some much better questions." I wondered why she was balking now.

"Shouldn't you go to the NCAA or someone official?" Caroline asked.

"Maybe. I don't know yet. I need to play out this trail. I

can't give them half a story or half the facts. I can't do anything until Monday anyway, so I'll think about it." What I was really thinking about was Connor sitting in jail with all this in his head. I didn't know who to contact at the NCAA and I didn't want to get scooped. Plus, a Division III school? I'm not sure an organization focused on big schools and big sports would care.

NINETEEN

Sunday evening

About ten minutes after Caroline left, there was another knock on the door. Charlotte was drinking water and raised her head.

"Did you forget something?" I asked before I fully opened the door.

A tall man with a balaclava over his face and a gun in his hand shoved his way in and clamped his hand over my mouth before I had a chance to scream. Charlotte's bark quickly turned into a growl that raised the hair on my neck. The man turned his gun toward her. I heard the click from the hammer being pulled back, and I lost my mind. I threw my body into the path of the gun. The bullet hit me in the shoulder, but I wouldn't realize that until later. I grabbed his gun hand and Charlotte was on his leg in a heartbeat. He screamed as Charlotte's teeth hit bone. She smartly let go, and he crashed back out of the room as quickly as he came in. With the door open, I could hear him thudding down the stairs.

The man in the room next door came in a second later, and soon after the motel clerk appeared.

"What the hell?" my neighbor said. He was in jockey shorts and a bathrobe. The clerk just stared, wide-eyed. I don't remember what he was wearing.

This is when I realized I was shot. It was also when I realized I could have happily killed whoever that was. I didn't even need steroids. He was going to shoot my dog. Charlotte was cowering in the corner looking at me for reassurance that it was okay to bite that man. I cooed at her and she bounded toward me, wagging her tail madly enough to make her lose her balance.

"I'm calling an ambulance," said the clerk, breaking the spell.

"No, no, wait."

Everyone waited. When you are shot, apparently you have a lot of power. I didn't want an ambulance. Where would Charlotte go? I wasn't that hurt either. Or at least I didn't think so.

"Would you just call my vet?" I got my phone and gave the clerk Sam's number and laid down holding a pillow ever my shoulder. Charlotte launched herself on the bed with me and put her head on my other shoulder. Between us, we were down to six useful limbs. I almost laughed. I closed my eyes because my shoulder was starting to hurt awfully bad. The clerk left to make the phone call and the man from next door stayed.

"Can I get you anything? Water or ice or something?" What a good Samaritan.

"No, but please stay until the clerk comes back." I was becoming very needy.

"Of course, of course." He went back to shifting from foot to foot. Each time he moved, Charlotte pulled her lips back in a silent snarl. Good thing he didn't notice. I patted her.

Sam drove up about a minute later, just as things were feeling awkward.

"Is she okay? What the hell happened?" Sam scowled at the man and looked at me, her scowl softening a hair.

I knew 'she' was Charlotte.

"She's fine. I got shot, though. Someone broke in and Charlotte growled, and he tried to shoot her, and I attacked him." That was as concise a version of events as I could give.

"Bastard. Let me see." She poked around my shoulder, grabbing it like it—and I—was a piece of meat. "Barely more than a graze. It went clean through, and that is good. You don't need to go to the emergency room. We'll take you to the clinic."

"It is starting to feel like more than a graze," I argued.

"That's just the shock."

"Um," said my neighbor.

Sam gave him a look that could rival the best I had to offer. "You can go. Thank you for your help."

He left.

When we got downstairs, I saw Haywood in the passenger seat.

"We were going out to a movie when I got your call," she said. "I would never have gotten here so quickly otherwise. And he makes a decent nurse." She jerked her thumb towards Haywood.

"The more the merrier," I said and Charlotte and I piled into the car. I closed my eyes.

"Shit, you need pain meds. I am sorry. I was just so focused on getting you out of there. Our local hospital is not the best, and they always ask so many questions in the ER. Okay. Haywood, grab my bag. It's on the floor."

He did as instructed, while Sam pulled into a 7-11. She went in for a bottle of water, came back, got a bottle of pills out of her bag and gave me two.

"Are you always this prepared when you go to the movies?" I asked.

"Yes. I carry around a full vet kit just in case, and some human meds."

I blindly swallowed what she gave me and almost immediately felt my consciousness drifting.

TWENTY

Monday, July 18

I woke up on a strange couch with my arms pinned. As consciousness came, I started to panic. Feeling my breathing change, Charlotte started licking me. Then I realized that I wasn't tied down, I just had a three-legged dog draped across my bandaged right arm and a left arm that was asleep. The memory of last night started to trickle back. I blinked several times, and Charlotte jumped off and whined. I sat up. My shoulder didn't feel too bad. Charlotte looked ready to go. Go where, I wanted to ask her. She started trotting into a room with a light on. I pushed myself up and winced and followed her. Sam and Haywood were sitting at a round kitchen table.

"Hi," I said

"Hey," said Sam. "Those pills still helping?"

"It doesn't hurt so bad, so they must be."

"Want some more?" Sam asked. "We should change the bandage too. I put some stitches in, so it would heal faster."

"You did all that? I didn't feel anything. No more pills," I shook my head. I wanted to have some of my wits about me. "Have I been kidnapped?" I was having trouble piecing everything together.

Sam laughed. "Yes and no. Haywood wanted to talk to you anyway, and it seemed that we might be short on time. We couldn't wait for the hospital to admit you and then treat you, and then have the police come and everything. It all takes too much time."

"Any particular reason we are short on time?" I asked. They were making me a little nervous.

"I don't know if what happened to you in your motel room is related or not—I hope not—but I think we have a big problem in the basketball team and possibly beyond," explained Sam.

"I have been piecing some things together," added Haywood.

"Me too," I said. I explained about Kevin and the DropFile documents, my belief he started a systematic doping program to build his own career, and that Connor was a casualty of that. And Marcus and Gina of course, I reminded myself.

Haywood sighed. "Kevin has a good basketball mind. I don't know why…"

"William McFarlane?" I suggested.

"He had a lot of specific expectations for us. We were supposed to win seventy-five percent of our games. Seventy-five percent! With no scholarships! So, Kevin came up with a plan." He paused. "And I got sicker, so I wasn't noticing things." Sam reached for his hand in such a tender way.

"Anyway, Kevin suggested that we use the latest nutrition science to help our players get stronger. But what he meant by nutrition changed over the past couple of years. He started getting us deals on shipments of supplements he called them. I believed they were supplements, but now, now I'm not so sure. And because I didn't stop it, I was a part of it."

I felt for him, but I didn't have time for emotion. "Do you know where he kept the pills?"

"No. I just know he brought them to practice in a duffle bag."

"You don't have any with you…"

"No. If it were in season, maybe I could get my hands on some, but now…"

"Let me think. Does he still trust you?" I asked.

"I doubt it," Haywood said with an odd mix of pain and pride.

"Do you remember an NSAA conference in 2011?" I asked, thinking back to what Caroline saw as a turning point.

"Absolutely," Haywood replied. "Kevin was pretty excited, and so was I. Not so much about the conference itself—I have been to so many over the years—but about what it meant that we could do."

"Did you attend the same sessions?" I asked.

"No, we split up."

"What about players? Do you have any special relationships with any?"

"On last year's team? Only Marcus. The rest did what I said, but that was about it. They weren't my team anymore. Not these guys."

"Do you remember Billy Wilcox?"

"Very clearly," Haywood said. He was about to say more when Sam interrupted.

"We don't have time for regrets now. Tell her later. Now she needs facts."

"Sam's right. I can't print accusations. Not in the *Star*. I need another source."

"What about me?" Sam asked.

"An unbiased source," I said.

"But if you print something, even if it's not totally right, maybe it will stop. Maybe they'll get scared. And stop," said Haywood. Even he didn't seem to believe his argument. It was just hope.

"And maybe the paper will get sued and maybe I lose my

job. My editor is already giving me a long leash." And I couldn't waste it.

We fiddled with the coasters on the table waiting for inspiration.

"I'll make more coffee," said Sam.

"Oh, thank God. That's got to help," I said, and everyone laughed.

"Coffee. The secret weapon of do-gooders everywhere," said Haywood.

"I'd lose my will to live, much less fight for justice without caffeine," I offered. Or alcohol. But I kept that part to myself. And I hadn't had a drink since, what, Thursday? Huh.

"Do you think the players knew what they were taking?" I asked after I had my mug.

"If I had to guess, I would say some yes, some no."

"Connor?"

"Probably," he said.

"Have you spoken to Connor since his arrest?"

"I went to see him a few times, but I got some flak from the administration. They wanted us to distance ourselves from Connor. He stopped coming to the visiting room when I was there."

"Why do you think that was? I mean I would think prison would be such a lonely, horrible place you'd talk to anyone decent."

"I guess he thought I wasn't decent. I am sure he blamed me in some way."

"Or he was depressed," Sam said. "Charlotte didn't much like living in a cage, so how could a person?"

We drank our coffee.

"I don't like Kevin, and I know he's hiding things, but do you think he is the entire problem? He certainly wasn't the one who shot me." I could tell by the body. I couldn't have wrestled Kevin and won.

"I don't know if he is the whole problem, but he is the part of the problem we might be able to solve," Haywood argued.

"Your shooter could have had nothing to do with the trial. He could have been a garden variety junkie. Meth. Heroin. We have a lot of drug use around here. And you drive a flashy car," Sam said.

"Great. Did anyone consider warning me?"

"Well, the opioid crisis has been all over the news. Would you have done anything differently?" asked Sam, ever the pragmatist.

"No, probably not," I conceded.

"I don't believe Kevin is capable of violence, anyway," said Haywood. "Cheating, yes, assault, no."

He set his mouth firmly as if that were the end of that. But belief is not truth. And supplying drugs is a form of violence in my book.

Later that morning, when it was fully light and decent people were up, I went to the police station with Sam and gave a statement. They agreed that it was bad luck, a random robbery. Afterwards, we stopped by the motel so I could get my things. I took a half a shower at her place. I wasn't supposed to get my shoulder dressing wet, even though I didn't think I really needed it anymore, so I had to hang that whole side of my upper body out of the shower. Her floor got a little sloppy, but I figured it was a bit of payback.

I called Leo as I was walking to the courthouse. I couldn't take my car even though I was exhausted because driving a stick shift seemed out of the question right now with my bad shoulder. Well, it wouldn't have been impossible; just painful and unnecessary. Even at the glacial pace I was walking in the heat, I would still get there right before the lunch break.

"I think they tried to kill me." Leo was the kind of friend with whom you could start a conversation this way.

"Seriously? Who? Why? Are you okay?"

"It is a really long story. I don't know. I need to find out. The cops and Sam are saying it was a random robbery because of my Corvette. But I think he—or she or they—were following Caroline." That insight came to me as I was showering. Something about water always makes me think better, or at least differently. I didn't tell Sam or Haywood, partly because I didn't want to worry them, but mostly because I didn't want to put them in danger. Knowledge is power, but it can also make you vulnerable.

"If I hadn't reacted right when I heard the click, Charlotte would have gotten shot." I bragged.

"Wait, a click?" Leo asked. "Guns these days don't have clicks. They are all automatics. That had to have been an antique or something. That is not a meth head's gun."

He had a point.

"I'll ask the cops if there were any reports of stolen antique guns, but I'm not holding my breath. I think you're right though. This was not a drug crime. It didn't feel like that. This was about my investigation. Someone was trying to stop me from asking any more questions. Someone who doesn't usually use a gun." And it wasn't Kevin, I knew that much. So Kevin wasn't working alone.

"I'm guessing it's going to have the opposite effect," Leo said.

"Exactly. I just need to keep Charlotte hidden. I don't think so clearly when I am protecting someone."

"Do you want me to come get her?" Leo offered.

"Maybe. I'll see. Thanks."

"Be careful."

"I will. I have too much to live for." Now.

When I hung up, I called Caroline to warn her. Maybe her computer hacking had been discovered. I assume that leaves a trail to an experienced eye. She wasn't there, and I left a message with Athena. I tried to get across the urgency of the situation without setting off a panic, but when I hung up I wasn't sure if I succeeded.

The security guard at the courthouse just raised his eyebrows when he saw my arm but didn't ask a thing. He did help me lift my backpack back onto my good shoulder after he rifled through it. Then, I walked down the hall and pulled open the door to the courtroom as quietly as I could. The first thing I noticed was Arthur's presence. This was only the second time he had been at trial. Why today? Was he going to testify I wondered? Then it clicked in my head, or rather my gut. Arthur is the one who tried to kill me. The height was right, and I always say trust your gut.

"Mr. Braxton? Can I ask you a few questions?" I called to his back at the lunch break. He was standing at the water fountain as if he had just finished taking a drink. I saw that he was weighing his right leg more than his left. Charlotte bit him on the left.

Arthur winced, then quickly recovered, although I could see the effort in his upper back. Even though it only took a second, and the man who turned around was smooth and polished when he faced me, I was sure.

"Of course, but I am late for…"

"Why did you try to kill me?"

The smoothness broke. He wanted to run but knew that would draw more attention. But I wasn't the only one who wanted to see him.

"Arthur! There you are!"

The voice came from over my shoulder and it belonged to William McFarlane. Kevin Battier was with him. The two were together an awful lot, it seemed.

"How are you holding up, Arthur?" William asked. "Can we get you anything? Mary would like you to stay at the house while you're here, or at least come for dinner."

I had the three musketeers right in front of me. All my suspects. But what to do with them? Arthur didn't let me decide.

"Thank you, thank you," Arthur muttered. "But I need to do this interview. It has been scheduled for a while. I promised, you know? Ms. Hightower has said she will mention the foundation we are working on. And she has promised to work on the more general piece on the University. I assume we are all thrilled about that. That will be valuable press, of course. Long time in the works. Should have told you, of course. I'll call you, though. Thank you."

"Okay, well we'll call you too," William clamped his hand on Arthur's shoulder in a proprietary way and Arthur grimaced.

William McFarlane glanced at me. "What happened to your shoulder, by the way, Ms. Hightower?"

"Fell down," I answered.

"Ah, we all get clumsy as we get older," said that oily voice.

When they left, Arthur turned to me.

"Please, let's go outside and you can ask me whatever you like."

I was not at all scared. First, he couldn't shoot me here at the courthouse. The security guard would tackle him, or so I hoped. Second, *he* looked scared. His actions at my motel room were clearly those of a desperate man, not a calculating one. I am also enough of a competitor—all reporters are—to rejoice when we see weakness. My arm hurt, and I was pissed, but I wasn't scared. Surprised, yes, but not scared.

"I'll repeat. Why did you try to kill me?" I asked as soon as the doors closed behind us.

"I was just trying to scare you off. For your own sake. But it all went very wrong. I am afraid of dogs. I am very sorry. I didn't mean to. Look, we don't have long, or it will look suspicious, and they are certainly watching. Is your dog…is she okay? How is your shoulder?"

"Charlotte is okay, and my shoulder is fine. What were you trying to scare me off from?"

"Connor was caught up in something much larger than himself. And so was I. Yes, Connor is responsible for his crimes—I have always been a little frightened of him, I am ashamed to say—but I am also responsible for not protecting him. And so are…"

"Kevin Battier and President McFarlane?" I finished his sentence before he could wriggle out of it. This would be my proof, if he would go on the record. I needed him to know he had no way out.

"None of this would have ever happened if…if certain people were not in charge." He looked around. "But they are my business associates and there are some debts," he stopped and looked around again.

"Look, let's meet somewhere where we can talk freely," I said, hoping he wasn't playing me, but he looked and sounded sincere.

"Where? I think my movements are being tracked. That's why I keep going back to DC. I want them to think I am not a threat, that I am not investigating," Arthur said.

"Smart. Who are they?" I pushed.

He didn't answer, just looked around again.

"Can you meet me tonight? Despite the delays the judge is adding in, I don't think we have a lot of time before this trial ends. And then there is not much we can do for Connor. There is a Waffle House near my motel. Don't come in your regular car," I said, trying to protect him. If only I had heeded my own advice. "After dark. 10 p.m.?"

"Okay." He just got up and left before I could tell him where it was. Then I realized he knew my motel, of course, having shot me there.

The pieces are coming together, but now how I thought. This is not about getting justice for Connor anymore. Or even Billy. Or even Gina or Marcus, I had to admit to myself. This is about taking down people who abuse power. It is my favorite hobby. I'm aiming for the top. The people in power need to pay. They are the ones who pull the strings. We are all just flawed puppets in their play.

Arthur left, and my phone rang.

"This is Detective Oliver from the Waynesville Police Department. Is this Gale Hightower?"

"Yes, it is."

"We have a suspect in your shooting in custody. The Blue Ridge University police apprehended him on campus. We'd like to see if you can come down to the station and take a look at a line-up. I will send a car."

Huh, I thought. This is an interesting development. The perpetrator just left. I wondered who the 'suspect' was?

"Certainly," I said. "I will be at the courthouse."

Ten minutes later, Officer Stuart dropped me off at the police station. I went in and Detective Oliver identified himself and shook my hand.

"How is your shoulder?"

"Healing nicely thank you," I said, which was true. The rest of what I was going to say might not be.

"If you could, step into this room. The line-up will be behind one-way glass and you just need to let me know if you recognize any of them as the man who shot you. Drugs are a big problem around here. With your fancy car, you were probably a target. Fancy cars equal fat wallets to them."

I played along. I examined each of the five young men in the line-up. Sad creatures all of them. I pretended to really study their faces and even be a little bit frightened.

"Gosh, it could be any one of them. He had his face covered," I said shaking my head in disappointment.

"Are you sure? No one stands out?"

"Yes, I am sure."

Detective Oliver was not pleased with me, but he mumbled some words about continuing the search, and I thanked him profusely.

I went back to the courthouse and got there just as the judge recessed for the day. The bailiff lead Connor away. I watched Isaac gathering his papers and decided to see if Isaac wanted to talk. I figured I was on a roll.

"What happened to your arm?" he asked as we walked

out together.

"I fell. I was running this morning and took a bad tumble off the curb. Just sprained, they say," I lied.

"Ouch. Tough for a swimmer, I would think."

"Yeas, but I don't really swim anymore," I reminded him. "Can I walk with you?"

"Sure. I'm headed back to my office. I could give you a lift back to your motel after I drop off my things, if you like."

"That'd be great."

We walked until Isaac got curious.

"What did you want to ask me?" he said.

While I did want to take down the ringleaders, I couldn't help but think Connor could get—and maybe would deserve—a lesser sentence if drugs were involved, drugs he was never really given a chance to refuse. I hope Isaac would agree to work that angle into his defense.

"If Connor was coerced into using steroids, doesn't that lessen his responsibility for his actions under the law, like if someone drugged your drink with PCP and you went crazy?"

"My office is just up there," he pointed to a red brick building that looked straight out of the old TV show *Mayberry RFD*.

He unlocked the front door. I followed him into a very tidy, if shabby, office. He settled into his desk chair and pointed to a loveseat for me. I sat gratefully, and when I did, I realized how exhausted I was.

"You think I don't know the law?" he said without rancor.

"No, of course you do. But I'm thinking you didn't know that you might have a set of facts that would support a very different tactic. I am discovering there may have been," I chose my words carefully, "a more complex situation."

He looked dead at me, and I stared back.

"You think someone at the school was forcing Connor to take steroids? Holding his nose, bending his head back and jamming pills down his throat?"

"Not quite like that, but I think an eighteen-year-old can be coerced to do a lot of things if shiny trophies are dangled in front of him."

"Why? Why would the school do that? Why?"

"Same reason anyone cheats. Money. Fame," I said. "A black heart."

"It's just speculation. Do you have anything I can give a jury?"

I didn't tell him about Kevin's files. It didn't seem wise. Yet. And there would be time. Not much, but some. I wanted to meet with Arthur first. Isaac didn't seem terribly receptive, or maybe he was just tired like me.

"No. I guess I just thought I would play lawyer. See you tomorrow," I said.

"Do you want to get a drink?"

"No. Some other time, though," I said and meant it. I liked Isaac.

After he dropped me off, and I got my car, I went back by *Pumpin' Iron,* the first gym I visited when I was pretending to be looking for a steroid dealer so "me and my little dog could do some competitions."

Driving didn't feel great, but it wasn't impossible. On my way, I called to see when Scott—the body builder who rejected my oh-so-subtle request for drugs—got off work. I was in the back parking lot when I saw him lugging a giant gym bag out of the back door.

"Please let him be alone," I whispered, and he was. The door closed behind him. I got out of my car.

"Scott! Hi, can I talk to you for a minute?"

He walked over. "You lied to me. I saw you on TV."

"On TV?" I was confused.

"In the background when the local news was interviewing someone about the Blue Ridge murders. You're hard to miss. You're a reporter."

Ah crap. I always tried to get out of shots. "I'm sorry. I had a reason. I have a reason. Will you come with me, so we can go somewhere and talk about that reason? I think you will care, given what you said to me the other day."

"Let me throw my bag in my car," he said.

When he managed to fold his wide body into the small seat, I put the car in gear and headed back toward town for lack of a better idea.

"I am sorry I lied to you," I said.

"It was a great story, though." He said. "I mean, I could just picture the dog and your no-good ex-husband. Are you married?"

"No, but I do have a no-good ex-husband."

"Maybe we could set him up with my cheating ex-wife. What is your connection to the trial?"

"You guessed correctly. I'm a reporter for the *Washington Star,* and this murder trial is getting weirder by the day."

"The trial seems kind of superfluous. I mean, the kid clearly did it, and my money is on him being jacked up on 'roids. The things I have seen guys who take steroids do, they are just not things regular people would do."

"I know, that is what made me start digging around. I had

the same thought, especially when I saw how much weight he lost in prison. I think something else was going on. I think there is a larger problem with steroids at the university, and I think someone knew and let it go. Do you know anyone I could talk to?"

Scott looked straight at me. "You asked me that before. No, and I sure wish I did. I mean I ran into guys who I guessed used. I never saw them swallow pills or shoot up, but I am not friends with them."

I felt like someone let the air out of my whole body. I was sure…

"Well, thanks for your time."

"You don't believe me."

"I believe you, I'm just disappointed."

"If I hear anything…"

"Thanks."

He got out and stuck his head back in.

"What happened to your arm," he asked.

"I fell," I lied. I don't think he bought it, but he didn't press me.

"Look, what that kid did is the reason I get so mad when people ask about steroids. I compete clean only because I saw what it does to guys. I would cheat to win if I didn't think it could kill me or someone else."

"I think I would too. I am glad the opportunity never presented itself to me when I was competing," I said and smiled goodbye.

TWENTY-ONE

Monday night

I called Sam, told her what was up, and asked if she could keep Charlotte.

"Sure. Be careful," she said.

"I will. I promise. Tell Charlotte that it will all be over soon."

"That definitely doesn't sound like you are being careful."

"Not that kind of over. I think I will be safe. Really."

Sam made an unhappy noise but didn't press it.

After a quick trip to the Chinese takeout for some fried rice, I pulled into the Waffle House parking lot at 10:05 p.m. Arthur already had a cup of coffee and a half-eaten plate of waffles in front of him at a booth in the back. I slid in opposite him.

"It's an old, bad habit. I love breakfast at night," he said nodding to his food.

"Who doesn't?" I offered back.

"I imagine we both could use some comfort food. Should I…" he gestured at the waitress walking by.

I shook my head. "I have already eaten."

Arthur pushed his food around, clearly not wanting to start this way. "How is your shoulder? I am so very sorry I hurt you."

"It will be fine," I said and waited.

"Connor is having a very tough time. He is depressed and often feels hopeless. He's sick when he thinks of what happened. He blames me sometimes, and sometimes he blames the school.

But he doesn't want to fight this case, or even try to help himself. He just wants to stew in his own bitterness. He says he feels numb and angry. Or that is what he said when he would talk to me. The last time was over a month ago."

"I can't say I'd handle things any better than him."

The waitress came back by, and I asked for water. She stared at me, and I stared back. She couldn't figure out what Arthur and I were doing there together.

"Why did you want to meet me?" I asked.

"Because I am frightened."

"Of what? Or who? Kevin?"

"I wish it was just Kevin," he said.

Please God, not Haywood, I thought.

Arthur took a deep breath and hurled himself over the cliff.

"I think Connor was taking steroids since the summer before his freshman year. After his recruiting trip to Blue Ridge. It was over for him then, I realize now. We had been growing apart anyway since he was eleven or so. He doesn't like me. So, you see, long before the murders, I was worried about him. But I didn't do anything. I was busy, and figured it would somehow be okay, that getting to college he would meet good people and be part of a good team. When Kevin approached me about one of my companies, I was happy to help, happy to be part of Connor's life in some small way, even if he wouldn't know. It was the only way I had to keep a connection to him."

Arthur paused, as if to gather more fuel for the rest of the story.

"I let Kevin and some other people I wasn't introduced to into my company's lab. They were going to produce proprietary supplements with Asian ingredients that would help the team recover faster and stay sharp longer. Totally legal and safe, they said."

"Asian ingredients?"

"I know. It could have been anything. But I was blinded. You couldn't possibly understand."

"I know a little about wanting something you can't have," I said quietly.

"They came to me and bought my silence before the murders and now, if I say anything…"

"You'll go down too." I said.

"Yes."

"So, this is to save your own skin?"

"And I guess to save Connor from finding out this is all my fault."

"You know, as I understand it, confession is good for the soul."

He nodded. "I have confessed to you."

"And what can I print?"

"Nothing yet. I need some more time to extricate myself."

"Are you planning to run off to Mexico or something?"

"I don't know. I haven't thought about it. I need time to think. Can you give me that?"

"We may not have much time. The trial is almost over. If we can get the information in front of the jury that the school as engaging in systematic doping of its players, treating them like lab rats, I am sure that would help them see Connor as a victim and maybe get him a lesser sentence. Don't you want that for him?"

"I don't know."

Arthur thought about taking another bite of his cooling

waffles, but instead pushed the plate away. A passing waitress read the sign and thankfully snatched the plate.

"I need time to figure this out, and I need to save my employees at Millennium Labs from any fallout. No one else did anything wrong, and they'll get caught in the web. I don't want anyone tipped off. Will you keep this out of your stories? I'll deny it anyway," he tried to threaten.

"Sure, sure." I wanted to placate him, and I believed that he wanted to keep collateral damage to a minimum.

We parted, and I made sure he left first, just in case. Follow the money Leo had said. I thought I had followed it to Kevin and William McFarlane, but money never stops, it keeps flowing. It's a river. And you always need to find its source, not just where it ends up.

I got back to Sam's close to midnight. I could see through the window that she was up and pacing. Charlotte was watching her the same way a person would a tennis match.

"I was so worried!" Sam yelled at me as soon as I opened the door.

Charlotte barked a rebuke as well.

She smiled and clutched her heart. "The things you kids put me through. What happened?"

Charlotte nuzzled my hand until I bent down to pet her. She licked my face as I stroked her flanks.

I told Sam most of what happened with my arms full of dog.

"You're going to fix all this, aren't you?"

"I hope so," I said and held my hand out to her.

She pulled me up. "I like you. I only bandage up people that I like."

We laughed.

"Drink?" she asked?

"Definitely."

We drank Scotch until 2 a.m. sitting on the back porch swing together, not saying much. I eventually hauled myself off to the couch and fell asleep immediately.

TWENTY - TWO

Tuesday, July 19

The next morning, the judge announced that he anticipated the defense would rest today. Isaac nodded his agreement. He looked as exhausted as I felt.

I scoured the courtroom, but Arthur wasn't there. I hoped he was getting things ready so we could go forward. I was getting that tingly feeling I get when I'm getting ready to break open a story. I'm addicted to that feeling, my shrink Wilma says. She says it clouds my judgment about some choices. I tell her she has just never felt it, and we agree to disagree.

Isaac put up his final witness – a guard whose only testimony was that Connor was a model prisoner. Madison skewered him on cross, pointing out that Connor was kept in protective custody and hardly had the chance to cause any issues. When the defense rested, we were all glad. Judge Evans said closing arguments would begin after lunch.

At lunch, I saw Isaac back at our coffee shop. He came over. "Just so you know, because you deserve to know, I think it is an insult to the victims when we look too hard for excuses for the accused. A vigorous defense, yes, but too many excuses is what's wrong with the world. Don't print that."

"I won't."

Long pause.

"Look, the kid was a ticking time bomb without the steroids," he argued.

"How do you know that?" I asked.

Silence.

"This could make your career, if you get a good result," I suggested.

"And get a kid who might have killed anyway back on the street. Steroids don't make you kill people," Isaac said.

Why the change, I wondered? "Would he have killed them without steroids? Maybe. But maybe not. Isn't your obligation to fully advocate for your client regardless of your feelings? You can't control the outcome, just the process," I argued.

"Yes, but I also have an equal obligation not to waste the court's time or the community's money by presenting spurious legal defenses."

"Who's to say it wasn't his choice to take whatever he took?" Isaac added.

"Freedom of choice. Such an interesting concept. I guess we all have it, technically, but sometimes we don't feel like we do. Not when we have closed every other door and it feels like the only one left is the one in front of you. It doesn't occur to you to turn around. Or just sit down." Was I still talking about Connor, I wondered?

Isaac looked at me for a long minute and then left without saying anything.

Back at the courthouse, as is the procedure in criminal trials, the state was first to present their closing argument. Madison looked ready and even eager. It seemed like it had been an easy trial for her. She brought her yellow legal pad to the podium and set it down. She smoothed her jacket and looked at the jury.

"Ladies and gentlemen of the jury, thank you for your patience and attention during this trial. I think we are all glad to have come to its conclusion. The state has presented unimpeachable evidence of Connor Braxton's guilt. He, with malice aforethought, killed Gina Merguez and Marcus Walker. There is no other reasonable construction of the evidence."

Madison recited all the evidence from the past two weeks. She even made nods to the defense witnesses but managed to dismiss their testimony. I had to admit, it was masterful story-telling, and the jury seemed to agree.

Isaac looked confident as well. A little caffeine seemed to have erased his earlier exhaustion. He did a little head bow to Madison as she returned and then he stood up for his turn. He buttoned up his jacket as he walked to the podium. His argument followed the same pattern. He thanked the jury and said the evidence only supported "at most" a conviction of second-degree murder. Connor sat so motionless it was easy to forget he was there.

"This verdict we are asking you for is not a reflection on the value of the victims' lives. Not at all. It is simply a recognition of the facts. Would a more severe verdict bring Gina and Marcus back? No. But it would unduly punish a man—a boy—who made a mistake."

Isaac finished in about the same time it took Madison to sum up her case—25 minutes. The judge announced a short recess.

"I will instruct the jury at 3 p.m.," he added.

I opened the courtroom door, and Jill and Bennett were waiting for me looking like they just won the lottery. Jill was holding an old laptop.

"Is that what I think it is?"

"If you think this is Kevin Battier's old laptop, then yes, it is exactly what you think it is. My friend Alma who works at Computers for Kids helped us figure out where it was," Jill said.

"I'll tell my boss the *Washington Star* owes Computers

for Kids one new laptop. Come with me."

We went outside, and I called Caroline and told her what we had. "Can we come over?"

"Absolutely. Come now," she said.

When we knocked, Athena let us all in with a much more welcoming smile. Caroline appeared right behind her before the door even closed. We followed her upstairs and she plugged the device in.

"The data has been deleted," Caroline said with no trace of disappointment. In fact, she was still typing and dug out an external hard drive from her desk drawer and plugged it in.

"I'm guessing you can un-delete it?"

"I'd put money on that guess, if I were you. So long as no one used a secure deletion tool or scrubbed the hard drive. But most people can't be bothered, thank goodness," Caroline said, still typing.

We all leaned against the furniture or squatted on the floor. No one wanted to be comfortable because we knew we'd be rushing to the screen any moment.

Caroline unplugged the hard drive and plugged in her own computer. More typing.

"What are you doing?" I asked.

"It's too hard to explain and work at the same time, but I think I'm getting somewhere. I am having to try a few different things," she said.

We quieted like chastised schoolchildren for five or so minutes that felt like five hours.

"Okay," Caroline said. "I've found something. It's mostly fragments, but come look."

Photos. There were photos of handwritten notes and drug

labels. This was how he hid things, but still kept records. No one would look for photos. It was ingenuous.

Caroline got a larger screen so she could make the photos big enough that we could read the words. There were calendars with notes about when to start and stop, when to increase the dosages, and when to rest. There were more than steroids too. There was human growth hormone, which speeds recovery from injury; blood doping, which boosts an athlete's red blood cells, so the blood can carry more oxygen; everything you have ever read about, and more. There was evidence of testing done for side effects, but no notes of the results. At least that we found. Connor's name was on a calendar from January 2015, four months before the murders. He was on high doses of steroids. I wasn't even sure how it would help his play at that time.

"This is the smoking gun." I was thrilled and sickened at the same time.

"Couldn't he argue they were not his photos? That he downloaded them from somewhere else?" Bennett asked.

"I pick law school for your graduate work," I said. "Yes, you make a good point, but this is enough to run the story with an 'unidentified source' saying they saw the photos. I have got to get to work. Can I take the laptop?" I asked Caroline.

"I don't want it," she said with her eyes closed.

I squeezed her hand. "Thank you."

"No, thank you," she said. "I think I am going to lie down."

The jury was still deliberating when, at the end of the day, I had my story and headline: *Greed Kills.* Although the headline would undoubtedly be changed. Headline writers like to do their jobs and get a little fussy when you have "suggestions." I used to get fussy back, but now I let it go. Mostly.

I felt a strange kinship with the jury. We were both evaluating facts, drawing conclusions, and passing judgments. The only difference was that I had to find my own facts.

"For the past few years I've thought there was something untoward going on there," Alex said when I called her.

"Manipulating and killing college athletes is 'untoward?'"

"Well, I didn't know this was what was going on," I imagined her waving her hand over my article. "It just seemed odd to me that one, they sent any kids to the pros, and two, when they got there, within their first couple of years, they all suffered catastrophic career-ending injuries. And that suicide…"

"Billy Wilcox."

"Yeah, that was his name. Sad."

"Why didn't you tell me before you sent me into this mess?"

"I wanted you to have a chance to get un-rusty on your own," she said.

"Un-rusty?"

"There isn't another word. You know what I mean."

"I do. Thanks. But this was painful." In more ways than one I didn't say. "Sports are ugly."

"Not always," Alex countered. "Anyway, this story is going to blow everything up, and maybe even fix a few things. Maybe scare some other cheats away from the idea. I'll run it as is, if you're up for the fallout. The NCAA will have to investigate now. Are you ready? Everything's solid?"

"I've never been more ready."

It was a good thing I never told her about the shooting. She'd never run the piece.

"Fine," Alex said. "This is great work you know. We'll

246

run it Sunday."

"Thanks. I just wish…"

"Wish what?"

"Nothing."

Alex sighed. "No, you wish for everything. That is your problem. Let me know when you get back."

"I'm coming back tomorrow. I know I'll have to do some follow-up, but I figure I can do it from here." I was so ready to get out of town, I thought about leaving tonight, but I was too tired. On Sam's recommendation, I checked into a Hilton on the other side of town; its only downside was that it didn't take dogs. I left Charlotte with Sam again, and this time it was much harder. Five minutes after I hit the bed, though, I was asleep, and all my problems were behind me.

At 4 a.m., my phone rang.

"What is it?" I mumbled.

"Gale, it's Arthur. We have a problem."

I turned on a light.

"What kind of problem?"

"I don't want to explain over the phone. I need to show you some files. I think this needs to be in your story. Bring your computer so I can copy some things for you."

"Now?" I asked? "I already sent my piece in. I can do a follow up next week. Why now? And can't you just email them?"

"There is someone I need you to meet as well. He is leaving the country tonight. Today is our only chance to talk to him. He won't talk on the phone. Too nervous. It might save Connor."

"How?" I asked, rubbing my neck. "And who?"

"Just come, okay? I will send you directions."

He hung up. I tried to call back, but there was no answer. I had two choices. Go or stay. And I was too tired to think through them clearly, so I decided to go. I could always turn around and come home if the trip wasn't worth it. I would have only wasted some time. It seemed a small price to pay.

TWENTY – THREE

Wednesday, July 20

I showered just enough to wake myself up and then drove to the 7-11 to get gas for my car and a lot of coffee. A Snickers bar and a banana would have to do for breakfast. Hopefully Arthur would have something to eat at his place as a reward for hauling me out there.

I left Waynesville a little before 6 a.m. which I figured would put me there well before noon. The address he gave me was in a little town in Maryland called St. Catherine's, close to Landfall Academy, like Coach Johnson said, but also not too far from Easton; about 30 miles after crossing the Bay Bridge.

The drive was smooth. My Corvette had shaken off the effects of hitting Charlotte and my shoulder was up to the little bit of shifting I had to do. I let my mind wander and listened to jazz. As I got closer, I did try to figure out what Arthur wanted to show me, and who the mystery witness was, but I couldn't come up with anything. That should have been a warning sign.

His house was right on the shore – it was big, but not ridiculous. As I drove up, Arthur opened the front door and pointed to the garage. The door opened, and he motioned me in. I rolled down my window.

"It will be cooler in there," he said.

Couldn't argue with that, I thought. And there was plenty of room. I pulled in, put the car in park and got out. Immediately, the lights went out.

Someone very strong and quick grabbed me from behind. He clamped a wet towel over my mouth and nose. I kicked and thrashed in utter panic until I passed out.

Sometime later—I wasn't sure how long—I woke up in the bed of a pick-up truck like so much leftover lumber. Old-fashioned chloroform must have been on the rag, I figured. That's why I felt so bad. I blinked my eyes but couldn't clear the haze. I had a splitting headache. My hands and feet were tied, and I was lying on my bad shoulder. I rolled onto my back. The only thing I was grateful was that I had stopped for to pee before getting to Arthur's house.

So, this is what it feels like to be kidnapped, I thought. Stupid, stupid me. It was as bad as it looks in the movies. I couldn't feel anything other than the searing pain in my head, which was keeping me from completely freaking out.

I was bouncing around in the truck bed, so I tried to wedge my feet against the opposite wall—my head was already trapped in the front corner—so that I wouldn't be totally at the mercy of whoever was driving. And who was driving? I thought Arthur was one of the good guys, though I was no longer so sure.

I needed to figure out what to say to him, if I could reach him. The truck slowed, and I realized I could smell salt water. We couldn't have gone too far. We turned off the road we were on onto a very painful dirt road with ruts that jolted me clear off the ridged aluminum truck bed. We pulled to a stop and fear gripped my stomach. I had no plan and I could hear two people getting out of the truck. The driver was Arthur, the son of a bitch. Dammit. He lied to me. Now I was mad. The other person I did not recognize. Great, he hired some steroided thug. I needed to be able to figure out what they wanted and give it to them. My first priority was to live. I had already sent the story in anyway.

"Ms. Hightower? How was the ride?" said the one I didn't know. He walked around the back wearing a white polo shirt that stretched to accommodate his pot belly and his biceps.

Since I was gagged, I did not answer, and he didn't seem to be fazed at all by The Look. I was cartwheeling between bravado and utter terror.

"Okay, we'll assume it was fine. Arthur, will you clip this on her and untie her feet?" He gestured to something wrapped around the tree we parked next to.

Arthur attached a cable to the binding around my hands. At the other end of the cable was a cooler.

"We'd like you to be able to walk, but we'd rather you not run away. It's amateurish to be sure, but effective. I had to pay one of the locals to make it for me. The cooler is filled with cement. I said I was going to use it to train some dogs." He chuckled at the memory. "It's amazing what a person can come up with under pressure. Next time, we'll be better prepared. You caught us a bit off guard."

"Who is us?"

"I can't say I condone the use of such poor grammar by a writer, but I guess I can tell you. I am Cyrus Wade and for today's purposes, it is only relevant that I am the chair of the Presidents Council for Division III schools in the NCAA."

I remembered. "Mr. Wade on Line 1." That day in McFarlane's office. Dammit. Sloppy work on my part. I never followed up to find out who that was. If I had, maybe I wouldn't be here.

"It is a job I have waited a long time for," he continued. "One I enjoy. I have plans, and you are getting in my way. I don't much like that."

That's my way in, I realized. Ego is always a weak spot. I silently thanked him for revealing himself so early.

"So, are you ready to walk?" Cyrus asked, picking up the cooler with relative ease and placing it in my arms. "We're heading to my boat over there."

Boat my ass, I thought. He pointed about a hundred yards away to a small dock with a gleaming yacht next to it.

"Arthur, please encourage her."

Arthur, who had said nothing, pulled the same gun he used to try and kill me with—what, four days ago? —out of his pocket and said, "Walk," with all the meanness of a classic movie villain. But his eyes. His eyes said *help me*. I tried to make my eyes say, "*Help you? I'm the one who needs help here.*"

The cement cooler was heavy, and I made very slow progress, so Cyrus decided to entertain me.

"I understand you discovered our little steroid program. Quite impressive."

I played along. He had all the cards, and I couldn't figure out the rules of the game if I didn't play. "How did you know?"

"You're quite easy to spot in that yellow car of yours. I've had a tail on you from day one."

Next time, I would rent a silver Ford Fiesta and leave the Corvette at home. If there would be a next time. "I already filed my story. You can't stop that now."

"No, probably not. So, we'll have to give up on Blue Ridge University. But your story is quite incomplete, I can guarantee that. And after tonight, it will stay that way."

"I may not have that many friends, but someone will miss me. How will you hide that?"

Cyrus just smiled.

I was starting to sweat profusely and feel sick.

"You see," Cyrus said, "we have much bigger plans."

"Who is we?" I asked.

He just smiled again like the damn Cheshire Cat in Alice in Wonderland.

"Thanks to Arthur's help, we've got everything set up. And even after his personal tragedy, he has been willing to help us, because he knows it matters. You can understand, then, how important our plan is and how much support we have," Cyrus said.

"It would help if I actually understood the plan," I said, panting.

"No slowing down, now, we're halfway there. Once we're on board, I'll explain a bit."

We got to the boat and I hauled myself up the ramp and onto the deck. There Arthur tied me to the railing—a lovely polished brass—with an additional cable and locking carabiner. It dawned on me just then. *He's going to kill me and sink my body in the middle of the Chesapeake Bay.* Shit. If my heart could have beat any faster, it would have, but I think it was at maximum.

"My son was a climber. I see you noticing the hardware," Cyrus said.

"Was?"

"He died in a fall last year. The investigators said he failed to secure his anchor properly. Careless mistake."

I glanced at Arthur, who looked in physical pain.

Cyrus left to start the engine. It rumbled to life and Arthur grabbed the lines and pushed us away from the dock.

"The automatic pilot was one of the best extras I got on this baby," Cyrus said as he walked out. "So, where was I? Oh yes, our plan, which was going so well before you showed up. Well, not perfectly—sorry Arthur—but well."

"In any event, we need to shut down here for a while. But our larger goal is still intact and maybe even closer than ever, and that is to take this program to other universities and make

Division III schools the powerhouses they should be. Ticket sales to the community will increase, revenue, and therefore prestige, will increase. The playing field will be level, and we will excel. And using kids to test drugs sure makes PETA happier!" Cyrus chuckled to himself.

How exactly do drugs level the playing field, I wanted to ask. This was like East Germany in the 1980s, China in the 1990s, but with corporations doing the doping.

"Don't you think my death will be a little suspicious?"

"Aren't you already considered a little unstable?" Cyrus countered. "Our university police certainly have a few reports on you from these past two weeks."

Goddamn it. He owns the police. I should have followed up on that story, too. Now I would be the story. "Again. I already filed my story." I spit the words out.

"Yes, that is problematic for Kevin and William. But not for me, and not for Arthur. I can get a new president for Blue Ridge."

"Don't you think they will talk?" I asked.

"No, no, I don't."

"Why are you so sure I will then?"

Cyrus's head whipped around, and I could feel Arthur's body tense from five feet away.

"What are you suggesting?" Cyrus asked. I was glad he got my point. I was afraid it was a little too subtle.

"That I could be useful."

Cyrus walked over to me and looked at me for a full minute. "You're lying." He said and picked up a chair and hit me with it. I went out cold.

TWENTY - FOUR

Wednesday, later

How long had I been out? It was dark, and we weren't going very fast. They were probably trying to keep the engine quiet and not attract attention. Maybe I could escape and somehow get to shore. But with my fun little heavyweight cooler? Not a chance. I tried to move, to see lights or find a landmark, but my hands and feet were hog-tied to the railing. I was facing the water. My shoulder hurt, and I tasted blood in my mouth.

"Oh good, you're awake," Cyrus said coming up the stairs with a cocktail in hand.

God, a drink would be wonderful, I thought.

"The automatic pilot isn't working as well as I would like on this thing, but I can spare a few minutes."

"I already filed the story." I repeated.

"Fine. Then I guess we're just killing you for revenge," he replied.

"Why did you do it?"

"I like winning. So do other people. People will pay anything to help them win. I also like money. Put the two together and it's like peanut butter and chocolate." Cyrus laughed again. I hated his laugh. "Second is just never good enough."

"Yes, it is. So is ninth and thirteenth and sixtieth, you bastard. Even playing is a privilege. Are you serious? Second is awesome. What kind of people do you think these kids will become?"

"I have no control over the rest of their lives," Cyrus said.

"So screw the kids—they are just the means to an end?"

Where was Arthur, I wondered.

"They are a product. Everything—and everyone—is a product. The sooner people realize this, the sooner they can get ahead. Those who fail to realize this will be left behind. It is that simple. It is survival of the fittest."

"And let the fittest turn into murderers?"

Cyrus sighed. "Look, Connor's situation was bothersome, but it was a one in a million thing. We know to be more careful with the doses now, and to pick our players more carefully. We have started psychological testing," he declared with pride.

"I have a reputation for lying at the paper, you know. I could confess to faking the story."

"Now why would you do that?" Cyrus asked, taking a sip of his drink.

"Because I bet you'd be willing to pay me to do it. And maybe to write a couple of glowing articles." Would he buy it, I wondered? "Would you untie me, so we can at least talk about it? I have bills to pay and maybe a partnership could be useful to everyone. No one would suspect me."

"Interesting. I still think you are lying, but I am willing to consider that I may be wrong. Let me talk to Arthur and think about what I want from you. I'll be right back. I need to check our course."

Did he really almost believe me? I was playing a deadly game while my brain was operating on only two cylinders. I tried to take deep breaths, but I got a shooting pain in my left side when I did. He probably cracked a rib. Shit. Okay, shallow breaths, but regular. Force out the air. I did that until he got back, and I felt like I could think.

Five long minutes later, Cyrus walked back on deck.

"We have to agree on some matters now, don't we? First

things first, I say."

The engine coughed and slowed.

"Dammit! He said they fixed…" Cyrus went back inside, giving me time to think. What could I promise that would keep me alive? That he would believe? I tried to stretch my back a little. I could feel my body locking up, and I wanted to be ready in case I had an opportunity to fight. Luckily, I could move my back without pain. And I could flex my feet and wrists. I could manage in a fight, I decided, so long as the shoulder still worked.

"Arthur," Cyrus called, "the automatic pilot is shot. Move her inside will you? We can talk there. Don't do anything stupid, Gale."

Arthur came towards me, and I saw his gun was in the front of his pants. I thought about grabbing it as soon as he untied my hands. But then what?

"Cyrus and William came to me last night," he whispered. "They said you were becoming a problem. I said I would help. I could tell they suspected me but weren't sure. I told them when I met with you that I was just a grieving father, that I didn't give you anything. If I didn't lie, they would kill you and me. I needed to play along. When the right moment comes, I'll…"

"The right moment is now, Arthur. There will not be another chance. When you untie me, unclip the cooler too, and we can jump overboard. It's dark, Cyrus won't be able to see us. Are we close to land?"

"We're about a mile from the Bay Bridge on the Maryland side. But I can't swim very well."

"I can swim for both of us once we get away from the boat. In the first few minutes, just dog paddle for your life. Trust me. You can swim. Anyone can swim. Just don't swallow any water and don't panic. Make sure you exhale, or you'll hyperventilate."

"Hurry up Arthur! Your fumbling is tiring," Cyrus said.

"Are you sure he isn't planning to kill you too?" I asked.

Arthur did not look sure. We had about one second to decide. *Now, now, now*, my mind was screaming. He must have heard me. He started untying the ropes. Every muscle in my body was contracted, ready to spring. *Here is the race you never got*, I thought. *Go! Jump!*

I grabbed for the top railing with both hands, pushed off with my right foot and launched myself over the edge. I thought I felt Arthur in the air next to me. I flipped over in the air, and I landed hard on my back, which knocked the wind out of me. I forced myself to turn over and dove as far under as I could, dolphin kicking to get away from the boat and the shots I was sure were coming.

When I had gone as far as my lungs could stand, I surfaced, took a gulp of air and started sprinting as fast as I could. I felt more than heard the shots hit the water. Then one hit me in my right ankle. I screamed in pain and sucked in a lungful of water. I fought the survival instinct to stop and try and cough. I knew he would kill me. The only way to survive was to keep swimming.

Faster.

I needed to look for Arthur. I scanned the water with each breath. Nothing. I saw nothing. Was he under already? There was no way I could find him. I heard yelling on the boat, and then I heard the boat's engine coming toward me and felt hope sliding away. But if the autopilot was broken, and Cyrus was driving, he couldn't shoot, I realized. And that realization gave me energy to swim as hard as I could. Toward what, I didn't know.

The engine noise got closer and closer, and I realized he was trying to run me over. I dove again, and the propeller missed me by inches. It would take him a few seconds to turn that big boat around. I had to think. I couldn't see a thing, except for the headlights of the cars in the middle of the water. No, not in the middle of the water; they're on the Bay Bridge, I realized, so I headed for them. Maybe someone would see a boat going wildly in circles and call the police or the Coast Guard or something.

I swam for the lights. My right ankle was useless, and it felt like it was coming unattached. And it had to have been bleeding like crazy. I hoped there weren't any sharks in the bay. The water didn't seem salty enough. I crossed my legs at the calf, used my left ankle to support my right, and tried to grab as much water as I could with each arm stroke. It was all up to my arms now, and mostly my left arm. My right shoulder was killing me.

Cyrus brought the boat back to make another pass, and I dove again. He missed me by a lot this time. He must be panicking, and the thought gave me new hope. Until I ran smack into a concrete wall. Splayed against it like a bug on a windshield, I realized it was a bridge support, and if I swam next to those, I could make my way to the other side.

I was pretty sure I was heading west, but maybe not. Either way, if I followed the bridge, I would reach land and help. I swam like a desperate wounded seal. Then I touched bottom with my fingers, which confused the hell out of me. No, not bottom, it was some sort of submerged island. If I stayed close to it, I thought, maybe I could make the boat run aground as it chased me.

The rock island sloped off pretty quickly, enough so I could take good strokes, but Cyrus' yacht would not have enough clearance. If he followed me, he would rip open his hull. I heard him coming back around, and I had to resist the desperate urge to turn right into the open water and dive. I stayed the course and led him onto the rocks. If I was wrong, the boat would crush me. If I was right, I was free.

I kept stroking, feeling like a fox about to get ripped apart by a pack of hounds, when I heard it. It sounded like a muffled, slow motion car crash. Fiberglass being shredded by rock. It worked. I didn't look back. I swam as hard as I could. I only took a breath every six strokes. I thought my lungs would explode. Shooting pains came from my ribs. I waited for the shots, but all I heard was the engine being gunned. He was trying to get off the island, and he couldn't. I was safe, as long as I could keep swimming.

It felt like an eternity before I stopped to tread water with my one good leg and see where I was. There was some moonlight now. I tried to feel my right ankle, but just touching it made me want to scream. I was bleeding too much. I needed to take my clothes off anyway; they were just weighing me down. I used my shirt to tie around my ankle. I didn't know what to do for my shoulder. The stiches seemed to be holding, so I left it. I rolled onto my back and backstroked while looking up at the bridge, my lifeline to safety.

After a minute, I pointed myself back in the direction I had been going. I seemed to be approaching the highest part of the bridge and in an instant the current got unbelievably bad. If I really was going west, and I hoped I was, the current wanted to push me south, out to sea. I didn't want to lose the guidance of the bridge spans. They were like lane lines in a pool. If I wanted to get out of the current, I had to dolphin kick now with my good leg. I was as panicked as I was when they were shooting at me. I was nearly spent, and I couldn't see the other side.

Even swimmers can drown, I reminded myself. Well that's cheery Gale. But all I could think of was how tired I was. There was no way I could lift my arms. I rolled over on my back and considered letting the water just push me.

Then it hit me. *He can't win. I need to win.* I didn't think about how far I had to go or if I could make it. I just thought about moving one arm and then the other. Rolling my body as best I could, I was tunneling through the water, fighting the current as hard as I could. It seemed like I was swimming in place, but I had to be going forward. I just had to be.

An eternity later, I felt the current relax. Fingers of exhaustion and cold were still wrapped around me, though, taking the rest of my strength and aiming for the last of my hope.

But I could see the shore. So I just swam. I tried not to feel or think. I swam until my hand touched sand, and then I crawled out of the water.

I was so cold, probably from the shock and effort, but the sand was warm which helped. I lay down and thought about staying there, but I felt so exposed. They could find me there. Don't those big yachts have little skiffs? Cyrus could have called someone too. I couldn't stand up, so I had to crawl until I found a picnic table. It smelled awful, like cigarettes and rotten chicken, and I sliced my thigh on something sharp. It would have to do. I didn't have the strength to find another hiding place.

I curled up and passed out.

Dreams tortured me while I slept. I was swimming through dead bodies, then through mud. Then I was running. I was being shot at the whole time. Faces of everyone I ever knew were twisted with malice. They were all shooting at me.

Eventually, it got light.

"Mommy, mommy, I like this one!" a child's voice yelled.

The noise felt like a two by four slammed into my head, but the pain meant I was alive.

"Honey, that one is in the sun and too far from the grill.

How about over here?"

Yes please, I thought, over there. Not here. I was afraid of being discovered. I opened one eye and saw lots of feet.

"No, this one!" said the child.

"Okay fine, this one. You always get your way, don't you, my little man?"

"Yup!"

The child climbed on top of the table. Mom must have set something heavy next to him. Probably a cooler. Hah. How funny, I thought. God, I was so thirsty. Maybe being discovered wouldn't be so bad. I needed help, almost certainly of the hospital variety. How do I say something and not scare the living hell out of them, I wondered?

"Aaahhh-ikes!" I yelled. That probably wasn't exactly the right thing to say, but a dog was licking my shot-up ankle. The mother bent down to look under the table.

"Holy shit—are you all right?" she asked me.

"Mamma, you're not supposed to curse!"

"Ben, you are right. I am sorry. But this is kind of a unique situation." She sat on the ground next to me. The boy joined her. I lay still.

"She's naked!"

"Yes, she is. Let's get her something to wear, okay?"

The boy nodded, his head sideways under the table.

"We're going to the car. I've got my gym bag in there. Will you be all right until we get back?"

"If you leave the dog," I said and smiled. The golden fluffball had curled up next to me and was licking my face. It felt good.

"We'll be right back."

"Thank you," I said, but she didn't hear me.

The clothes didn't fit too well, but they managed to keep the bugs off, and me from scaring people. I drank a bottle of water and a juice box. The boy had a non-stop stream of questions, which I tried to answer without telling any of the horrible truth. Making up stories was easier than I thought. The mother—I never learned her name—called the police as I asked. They came quickly with sirens blazing. Two minutes after that, the ambulance showed up, and three nice men rolled me on a stretcher and lifted me in.

TWENTY – FIVE

Thursday, July 21

I didn't like waking up in a hospital for the second time in my life any more than the first. But at least this time around I knew enough to be grateful that I wasn't dead and that no one I cared about was dead.

"What day is it?" a voice asked.

Great. A test already. "I have no idea."

It tried again. "Who is the president?"

"Barack Obama. Although I think Michelle would be just as good."

That got a chuckle.

"Amen sister. Do you know where you are?" the voice asked.

"A hospital," I answered. My head hurt.

"Do you know which one?"

"Our Lady of Plastic Tubes and Flashing Red Lights?" I said sarcastically.

"Not exactly, but good enough. You are in Annapolis. Do you know why you're here?"

The persistent voice was attached to the shortest and roundest person I had ever seen. The way she held her clipboard, I could tell I had no option but to answer.

I sighed. "As far as I remember, I got beaten up and shot at by an asshole, and I swam across the Chesapeake Bay to get away."

She nodded and checked something off on that clipboard. I had passed.

"Well, you are some tough lady, and you seem to have all the faculties I would expect after enduring such an ordeal. A detective is waiting to talk to you until I say it is okay. Is it okay?"

I nodded. "No sense putting it off."

I told the detective everything I knew that happened and a few things I guessed. He stopped me a few times so his writing could catch up with me even though he also had a tape recorder. The second time he stopped me, he also radioed into the station and sent his partner out to round up the other players—Kevin, William, and Cyrus – to bring them in for questioning.

Not five minutes after he left, my nurse came back. "You know they do a race every year where you swam."

"So, can you get me a medal or a T-shirt or something? I want credit. That was hard." I couldn't believe anyone would choose to do that for fun.

"My son does the race and he's a good swimmer. He says it's the hardest thing he's ever done, and they time the race with the tides to make it as easy as possible. What you did, in the shape you were in…Well, you should enter it one year. I'm sure you'd win."

"They'd need to hire a crazy guy with a gun to chase me. I'm not sure I would do that on my own."

"I can see why you might not want to dive back in. But still, that was amazing. People who don't know that water wouldn't know. I know."

"Thank you." I said and meant it.

"Okay, well. You've got a couple of more visitors if you're up for it."

"Sure, I guess."

She opened the door and nodded.

Arthur and a policeman walked in. Arthur was in handcuffs.

"You didn't jump," I said, confused.

"You would never have made it with me. I figured in the chaos caused by your exit, I could subdue Cyrus."

"Did that work?" I pushed myself up on my one good arm. There is something embarrassing about talking to someone while you are prone.

"Sort of. It took a while. I have this policeman escort until it all gets sorted out."

"Thank you," I said to Arthur. "If you hadn't taken on Cyrus, he certainly would have killed me. Did you have to kill him?"

"Yes," Arthur said. "He was going to kill you and me."

"Self-defense and defense of others," I said. "Call Isaac. I think he can help you."

Arthur winced.

"I can't believe it got to that. It was like living a nightmare. It didn't start out that way," Arthur said.

"It never does. How is this going to affect Connor?" I wondered aloud.

"I want to get back. I'm hoping there will be a mistrial, if the jury hasn't reached a verdict yet and we can start over. Or maybe a plea deal now. Or something. At least an appeal. Something to give Connor hope, and me my son back. I want to show him I...well, not that I understand, but that I still love him."

We ran out of things to say and my ankle and shoulder were starting up a fierce competition to see who hurt the most. All the parts in between were thinking about joining. I closed my eyes.

"Ya'll need to leave," said my nurse, my savior. "Thanks for coming. Go on."

I smiled but couldn't open my eyes.

"Ma'am?" asked the policeman. "We will need to contact you again. May I have a phone number?"

I gave it to him and they left, and my sweet nurse gave me a shot of something in my IV, and I fell happily asleep.

Hours later, when it was dark, a new nurse came in.

"You have a visitor. It's after visiting hours, but he is claiming to be your brother. There's not much family resemblance, though."

She was younger and taller than my first nurse, but still funny.

It had to be Leo. I nodded, and she opened the door. It was my crazy neighbor, and I was so happy to see him, I almost cried.

Leo was crying, which made the floodgates open on my side. He tried to hug me, but it was too hard. Instead, he put the flowers he brought in my plastic water jug and blustered around the room re-arranging things.

"I'd rather not lose you, you know," Leo said, blowing his nose.

"I'd rather not be lost, I think," I admitted.

He laughed.

We turned on the television and just held hands, taking it all in. There would be plenty of time to say everything later.

The next morning, Leo was in the chair sleeping when my hospital phone rang.

It was Arthur. "Connor hanged himself."

"Oh god, no. I am so sorry," I said. And I truly was. For

a lot of reasons.

I had planned a follow-up. A full feature once all the smoke had cleared. I wanted Connor to tell his side of the story. What he felt. I wanted to see inside his mind when the steroids were out of his body. I wanted to know what kind of human was there. I wanted him to tell me what he thought his future could hold. Now I would never know. No one would ever know.

Madison Kupchak was my next and last visitor. They said they would release me in the afternoon. I just hoped it would be with a few extra of those yummy pain pills.

"Why didn't you tell me about your steroid theory? We could have protected you."

"I don't trust the state," I smiled and winced.

"Huh. You might want to re-think that next time you're in town. Did you really swim across the Chesapeake Bay with an injured shoulder and a shot up ankle?"

"I guess I did."

"Wow. I'm going to sign up for lessons. I would have drowned," she said.

"We all have different talents."

She still wanted to talk. "I feel terrible about Connor."

"Not your fault," I said.

"I know. And my job is to feel for the victims and fight for them. Still, I guess you were right in the end. He was a victim too."

"At one time or another, I think we've all been both victim and perpetrator. The only difference between us is to what degree we are each of those," I said.

268

TWENTY - SIX

Friday, July 22

I knew Leo must have rented a car to come get me, but I was surprised and pleased to see a plush Lincoln parked in the front row. As we drove, I couldn't feel a single bump in the road.

"I feel like I'm either eighty or a gangster," I said.

'Why not an eighty-year-old gangster?" Leo said. "Something to aspire to. Maybe a retirement plan?"

"All right then. I feel like an eighty-year-old gangster in this car, and it feels good." I leaned to sit further back and adjusted the hospital pillow under my shoulder.

Once we got a signal, I checked the paper's website, and the NCAA's, and the school's. The NCAA's was the only one I was really interested in. They had a doozy of a press release on their home page that was near-comical in its total avoidance of the issues:

> *We at the NCAA are saddened and horrified at the actions of one of our own and will do everything in our power to ensure such actions never happen again. The NCAA is made up of three membership classifications that are known as Divisions I, II, and III. Each division creates its own rules governing personnel, amateurism, recruiting, eligibility, benefits, financial aid, and playing and practice seasons—consistent with the overall governing principles of the Association. Every program must affiliate its core program with one of the three divisions.*
>
> *The NCAA enforcement program strives to maintain*

a level playing field for the more than 400,000 student-athletes. Commitment to fair play is a bedrock principle of the NCAA. The NCAA upholds that principle by enforcing membership-created rules that ensure equitable competition and protect the well-being of student-athletes at all member institutions.

These young men and women are different finally in participating in an environment where the overwhelming focus of athletics is the educational value and benefit provided to our student-athletes. All NCAA institutions pursue this focus, but the approach in Division III is unique. In particular, revenue generation and entertainment for broader audiences are not a priority for us.

For many fans, alumni, and former college athletes, cynicism about intercollegiate athletics is understandable. But most athletics experiences, such as those for the more than 170,000 student-athletes at the 444 colleges and universities that comprise Division III are completely aligned with the NCAA's educational mission.

The Division III experience is different from others in that the student-athletes at this level do not receive athletics scholarships. Thus, all of our student-athletes choose to play for the love of the game and are unencumbered by the significant commitments that accompany an athletics scholarship.

Division III Presidents Council members will hold an emergency meeting to determine if it is necessary to devote Division III resources to support drug-testing models other than the championships testing program already in place.

I wondered if this was the tip of the iceberg or if the fallout would be minimized by the powers that be. I wanted to talk to the person I thought Isaac was.

"Was it what you expected?" Leo asked.

"Yes and no," I said. "Or yes, it was what I should have expected, but not what I hoped for."

"That is perfectly cryptic, but you can explain it to me later. For now, the worst of the bad guys is dead, right, and the others are going to jail? You should celebrate."

"You're right. I can't change the world all at once," I grinned at Leo, and he rolled his eyes.

When Leo and I got back to Sam's, after one break for food and gas, and two stops to pee—the meds were making me thirsty—she ran out of the house with open arms to scoop us both up.

"Ow, ow, ow, ow!" I protested.

"I'm sorry, I'm sorry. Are you okay?" she asked.

"Yes, I'm okay. Where's Charlotte?" Hearing her name, my sweet dog limped around the corner with her tail wagging low and slow, unsure of all the commotion. I bent down with difficulty, and the tail speeded up. I wrapped my arms around her. She smelled like lavender.

"Did you wash her? She smells like an old lady," I said to Sam.

"It's lavender body wash, and expensive. I thought you might appreciate a clean dog, although I had to avoid all the stitches. She hated her bath, though, poor thing. Can't imagine she'll need another for a while with that short coat."

"Leo, this is Charlotte," I said with the appropriate formality. "Charlotte, this is Leo. He's like me, but better."

"Don't listen to her, Charlotte. But I am pleased to meet you." Leo bent down to her level, twisted sideways, and stuck out his hand. She sniffed it and then slid her head right under it, so he could start petting.

"She's lovely," he said, totally smitten.

"Yup," I said. "Can I pick 'em or what?"

Now everyone rolled their eyes, even Charlotte. "I picked you," those eyes seemed to say. "At great personal cost."

"Are you and Haywood going to be okay?" I asked Sam.

"I don't know. We'll see. Come visit any time. Or maybe we can have dinner, if I get him to move to Washington and give all this up."

"Good luck. Thanks for everything." I stood up and extended my hand. Sam shook it and looked at me.

"You take good care of that girl," she said.

"I will. She was definitely worth all this. I don't know how or why, but she is."

"You don't need to know," Sam said and bent down to give Charlotte a gentle full body hug.

Sam hugged me again. Leo was next and then I clipped a leash to Charlotte's collar and we limped our way back to the Lincoln. I was going to drive the Lincoln with Charlotte in the passenger seat since between my shoulder and ankle, shifting my standard transmission seemed a very bad idea. Leo led in my Corvette, and it was an easy trip, but I swear Leo spent half the time looking in the rear-view mirror to make sure I was there.

Charlotte slept almost the whole way, occasionally waking up to shift positions. We made one stop at a Sheetz for the bathrooms and some peanut M&M's.

At home, I fed Charlotte—Sam had again provided me with some kibble she had been eating. Leo made me a bed on the couch and brought me the newspaper. Then he went to the grocery store and got takeout. I would have gone with him, but someone needed to supervise the meeting of Hawk and Charlotte. Charlotte didn't notice Hawk right away, which in my mind boded well for the future of household harmony.

Hawk soon made his presence known, and he was caught in a conundrum. He was happy to see me but very startled by the new animal. He tried every squawk in his repertoire and none seemed to suit his mood, so he gave up. At the first squawk, Charlotte tried to dart for cover. But the fourth, she had located the bird and seemed content to watch him. Hawk calmed down and flew-hopped down to the coffee table. Charlotte remained seated about two feet away, which I thought was very respectful. Hawk chose not to match respect with respect. He stood on the coffee table, flapped his wings, and basically yelled at his new roommate. Charlotte still did nothing. She seemed to be letting him have his tantrum. It did wear itself out, and Hawk huffed and hopped up to my good shoulder.

"So now you love me? All I had to do was make you jealous?" I said to Hawk as I stroked his feathers. Not a bad start at all, I thought.

Leo came back and took in the scene.

"Looks like your stock has risen with Hawk," he said, "and that is one amazing dog. I got cashew chicken."

He went into the kitchen to put the groceries away and Charlotte followed him politely, but expectantly,

"Can I give her something for dessert?" he asked.

"Sure."

"What?"

273

"Dogs are omnivores, Sam said. So, anything healthy."

"You don't have much in here. Oh, a piece of cheese."

Leo walked back into the room with Charlotte trailing him and fed her the cheese tiny bit by tiny bit. She took each one very gently from his hands. Sweet, sweet dog.

We ate and watched HGTV until the rooms and houses all blurred together, and then my phone rang.

"Gale? It's Louie."

She didn't give her last name and she didn't need to. The only female Louie in the world had to be the mayor's wife, whom I pissed off royally a few months ago.

"Hi Mrs. Mattison," I replied.

"Crazy business in Waynesville," she said.

"Yes, it was," I agreed. "What can I do for you?" The call made me a little nervous.

"I'd like to help you and that dog, make sure you get good care. I know how expensive and time-consuming that can be."

"Why?"

She sighed. "Look, you did me a favor, taking the heat when I had to deny that I ever told you that my predecessor was a thief. Now I won't owe you anymore. You don't seem like someone I'd like to owe a favor to. I've made you both appointments for next week. The bills will be coming to me." She gave me the details and hung up.

TWENTY - SEVEN

Monday, July 25

Charlotte followed me into the kitchen, blinking at the bright overhead kitchen light. I grabbed a blueberry from a bowl and held it out to her. She nosed it around my palm for ages before deciding it was worth eating.

"Not a fan of berries, huh girl?"

"Just never had one," she seemed to say back, with her wagging tail.

My story *Greed Kills* was on the front page of the Sunday paper, but below the fold. Above the fold was my terrible ID badge photo from the S*tar* and a story about my "daring escape." Jerry wrote it, and it was good.

The jury was still deliberating when they got the news that Connor killed himself. I watched the foreman interviewed the next day on the Today show. He said they were 11-1 for second degree.

I decided to go to work, and I brought Charlotte. Alex said she would have a bed ready for her at my desk.

It felt like every single person who worked for the Star stopped by my desk. Charlotte wagged her tail a little bit for everyone. I remembered Sam's advice to help her get socialized and felt I was doing a pretty good job.

My inbox pinged. I saw the message was from Mrs. Merguez:

> *This is Gina's mom. I got your email address from your by-line. I am glad you are okay. While it doesn't bring back my Gina, I am also glad you helped bring the men behind all this to justice. You did a good job. Not*

that any of it makes me forgive Connor, but it does make me glad that no one else is getting away with anything. It's been a long 14 months. I still miss Gina every day. Every single day. But I guess it helps me understand a little. So thank you. Gracias.

Reporters don't get thanked very often, so I got a lump in my throat. If I gave Mrs. Merguez anything resembling a little peace, I justified my existence on this planet for a few months. I wondered about Darrell Giminsky, Marcus' uncle. Marcus got lost in all this and for that I was sorry.

I got up, leashed Charlotte, and took her out for a short walk. Alex looked up when on the way back to my desk we walked into her office uninvited. Unannounced visits are a privilege no one has unless they have been shot. It's a strange kind of worker's compensation.

"I's always been a joke that Division III is the wild west of the NCAA, but now it seems to be true," she said instead of 'hello' or 'hey, how are you doing?'

"More of a science lab, or a modern-day Tuskegee experiment," I replied.

"Some argue convincingly that the whole NCAA is corrupt," she said.

"Don't put me on that story. I need a break from sports," I said.

"Fair enough. Take some time off, heal up, then I'd like you to cover another out of town story. I think it will be right in your wheelhouse."

"I hate that term. What is a wheelhouse anyway?"

Alex shrugged. "What is anything?" she said and went back to editing. "Oh," she said, "and the assignment is not exactly for the *Star*. There is a new venture that the publisher is backing. It's a little complicated. Can we go to dinner to discuss it?"

"We've never had a meal together since I've worked here. What's going on?"

She ignored me. "Seven? At TreeTops?"

I stared at her. She was hiding something, but it seemed like something good.

"Okay," I said slowly and hoped for the best.

I got back to my desk and there was a bunch of balloons and one of those bouquets of fruit on sticks dipped in chocolate. Olivia was grinning.

"Is this from you?" I asked.

"We all chipped in. Your return deserves a little celebration."

"Aw, thank you. Oh crap, I forgot your bottle opener!"

"It's okay. I'm just glad you're back in one piece. Seriously."

"Ah, you missed me!"

Olivia just looked at me with a junior version of The Look. She had some work to do. Something about that reminded me to call Caroline, so I did. It was the last loose end. Athena and I had a nice chat before Caroline could free herself to come to the phone.

"Sorry, I was in the shower. How are you?"

"All right, considering. You?"

"Sad and horrified, but also relieved and grateful," Caroline said.

"Because it is all behind you?"

"That, and because Billy didn't take anyone else with him when he died. I think Connor lived a bigger nightmare than

277

Billy or I did."

True, I thought. And yet I still felt bad that Gina and Marcus are getting forgotten.

"Hey, I was wondering if you can de-activate whatever you put on my computer or if I need to get a new one."

"I can de-activate my bugs, but I'll also send you money for a new one. Please accept it. It's my way of saying thanks."

"How about you donate it to Computers for Kids? The paper will get me a new laptop if I need one."

I could tell she was smiling.

"I will. Thank you."

After I hung up, I sucked the chocolate off a strawberry and gave the soggy fruit to Charlotte. She gulped it down.

I reached down and scratched her chin. I wondered where we would go next.

ACKNOWLEDGEMENTS

Thanks to my husband Rob Jones for enduring endless conversations with me about the idea for this book. I am also grateful to advance readers Polly Breckenridge and Carol Grant for their support for the book and for showing me the parts in the story that didn't work. My brilliant editors – Thomas King and Foust – saved me from my bad habits and sloppy writing. Finally, I thank the real Charlotte, who was neither hit by a car nor three-legged but was a much beloved foster dog. Oh, and thank you all very much for reading.

ABOUT THE AUTHOR

Laura S. Jones is a North Carolina native currently living with her husband and animals (two awesome dogs, an elderly cat, and the occasional foster dog) in Falmouth, MA. Her previous books are *Breaking and Entering*, a collection of 13 short stories, and *Saving Sadie and Sasha*, a memoir about a cross country road trip in the middle of winter to save three dogs. Articles and essays by Jones have appeared in *The Washington Post*, *Swimmer* magazine, *Virginia / Maryland Dog Magazine* and *The Daily Progress*. She published her first piece of fiction in *Cricket* magazine when she was twelve or thirteen but can't find the clipping to prove it to you. Jones tries to maintain a blog at *Lsjwrites.blogspot.com*.

Made in the USA
Columbia, SC
05 November 2018